P9-CAL-410

Praise for the novels of
***New York Times* bestselling author**

DIANA PALMER

"Palmer's talent for character development and ability to fuse heartwarming romance with nail-biting suspense shine in *Outsider.*"
—*Booklist*

"A gentle escape mixed with real-life menace for fans of Palmer's more than 100 novels."
—*Publishers Weekly* on *Night Fever*

"The ever popular and prolific Palmer has penned another sure hit."
—*Booklist* on *Before Sunrise*

"Nobody does it better."
—*New York Times* bestselling author Linda Howard

"Palmer knows how to make the sparks fly…heartwarming."
—*Publishers Weekly* on *Renegade*

"Sensual and suspenseful."
—*Booklist* on *Lawless*

"Diana Palmer is a mesmerizing storyteller who captures the essence of what a romance should be."
—*Affaire de Coeur*

"Nobody tops Diana Palmer when it comes to delivering pure, undiluted romance. I love her stories."
—*New York Times* bestselling author Jayne Ann Krentz

Don't miss Diana's new hardcover
Dangerous
coming in June!

Also by Diana Palmer

Heartless
Fearless
Her Kind of Hero
Nora
Big Sky Winter
Man of the Hour
Trilby
Lawman
Lacy
Hard To Handle
Heart of Winter
Outsider
Night Fever
Before Sunrise
Noelle
Lawless
Diamond Spur
The Texas Ranger
Lord of the Desert
The Cowboy and the Lady
Most Wanted
Fit for a King
Paper Rose
Rage of Passion
Once in Paris
After the Music
Roomful of Roses
Champagne Girl
Passion Flower
Diamond Girl
Friends and Lovers
Cattleman's Choice
Lady Love
The Rawhide Man

DIANA PALMER

DESPERADO

HQN™

If you purchased this book without a cover you should be aware that this book is stolen property. It was reported as "unsold and destroyed" to the publisher, and neither the author nor the publisher has received any payment for this "stripped book."

HQN™

Recycling programs for this product may not exist in your area.

ISBN-13: 978-0-373-77476-0

DESPERADO

Copyright © 2002 by Diana Palmer

All rights reserved. Except for use in any review, the reproduction or utilization of this work in whole or in part in any form by any electronic, mechanical or other means, now known or hereafter invented, including xerography, photocopying and recording, or in any information storage or retrieval system, is forbidden without the written permission of the publisher, Harlequin Enterprises Limited, 225 Duncan Mill Road, Don Mills, Ontario M3B 3K9, Canada.

This is a work of fiction. Names, characters, places and incidents are either the product of the author's imagination or are used fictitiously, and any resemblance to actual persons, living or dead, business establishments, events or locales is entirely coincidental.

This edition published by arrangement with Harlequin Books S.A.

® and TM are trademarks of the publisher. Trademarks indicated with ® are registered in the United States Patent and Trademark Office, the Canadian Trade Marks Office and in other countries.

www.HQNBooks.com

Printed in U.S.A.

To the doctors and nurses of Northwestern Memorial Hospital in Chicago, Illinois, who saved my life, and to the wonderful staff, with thanks from a grateful patient.

DESPERADO

The ranch outside Houston was big and sprawling. It was surrounded by neat white fences, which concealed electrical ones, to keep in the purebred Santa Gertrudis cattle that Cord Romero owned. There was also a bull, a special bull, which had been spared from a *corrida*—a bullfight—in Spain by Cord's father, Mejias Romero, one of the most famous bullfighters in Spain just before his untimely death in America. Once Cord grew up and had money of his own, Cord had traveled to his elderly cousin's ranch in Andalusia to get the bull and have it shipped to Texas. Cord called the old bull Hijito, little boy. The creature was still all muscle, although most of it was in his huge chest. He followed Cord around the ranch like a pet dog.

As Maggie Barton exited the cab with her suitcase, the big bull snorted and tossed his head on the other side of the fence.

Maggie barely spared him a glance after she paid the driver. She'd come rushing home from Morocco in a tangle of missed planes, delays, cancellations and other obstacles that had caused her to be three days in transit. Cord, a professional mercenary and her foster brother, had been blinded. Most surprising, he'd asked for her through his friend, Eb Scott. Maggie couldn't get home fast enough. The delays had been agony.

Perhaps, finally, Cord had realized that he cared for her...!

With her heart pounding, she pressed the doorbell on the spacious front porch with its green swing and glider and rocking chairs. There were pots of ferns and flowers everywhere.

Sharp, quick footsteps sounded on the bare wooden floors in the house and Maggie frowned as she pushed the long, wavy black hair away out of her worried green eyes. Those steps didn't sound like Cord's. He had an elegance of movement in his stride that was long and effortless, masculine but gliding. This was a short, staccato step, more like a woman's. Her heart stopped. Did he have a girlfriend she didn't know about? Had she misinterpreted Eb Scott's phone call? Her confidence nosedived.

The door opened and a slight blond woman with dark eyes looked up at her. "Yes?" she asked politely.

"I came to see Cord," Maggie blurted out. Jet lag was already setting in on her. She didn't even think to give her name.

"I'm sorry, he isn't seeing people just yet. He's been in an accident."

"I know that," Maggie said impatiently. She softened the words with a smile. "Tell him it's Maggie. Please."

The other woman, who must have been all of nineteen, grimaced. "He'll kill me if I let you in! He said he didn't want to see anybody. I'm really sorry..."

Jet lag and irritability combined to break the bonds of Maggie's temper. "Listen, I've just come over three thousand miles—oh, the hell with it! Cord?" she yelled past the girl, who grimaced again. "Cord!"

There was a pause, then a cold, short, "Let her in, June!"

June stepped aside at once. Maggie was made uneasy by the harsh note in Cord's deep voice. She left her suitcase on the porch. June gave it a curious glance before she closed the door.

Cord was standing at the fireplace in the spacious living room. Just the sight of him fed Maggie's heart. He was tall and lean, powerfully built for all his slimness, a tiger of a man who feared nothing in this world. He made his living as a professional soldier, and he had few peers. He was handsome, with light olive skin and jet-black hair that had a slight wave. His eyes were large, deep-set, dark brown. His eyebrows were drawn into a scowl as Maggie walked in, and except for the red wounds around his eyes and cheeks, he actually looked normal. He looked as if he could see her. Ridiculous, of course. A bomb he'd tried to defuse had gone off right in his face. Eb said he was blind.

She stared at him. This man was the love of her life. There had never been anyone but him in her heart. She was amazed that he'd never noticed, in the eighteen years their lives had been connected. Even his brief, tragic marriage hadn't altered those feelings. Like him, she was widowed—but she didn't grieve for her husband the way he'd grieved for Patricia.

Her gaze fell helplessly to his wide, chiseled mouth. She remembered, oh, so well, the feel of it on hers in the darkness. It had been heaven to be held by him, kissed by him, after years of anguished longing. But very quickly, the pleasure had become pain. Cord hadn't known she was innocent, and he was too drunk to notice at the time. It was just after his wife committed suicide, the night their foster mother had died...

"How are you?" Maggie blurted out, hesitating just beyond the doorway, suddenly tongue-tied.

His square jaw seemed to tighten, but he smiled coldly. "A bomb exploded in my face four days ago. How the hell do you think I am?" he drawled sarcastically.

He was anything but welcoming. So much for fantasies. He didn't need her. He didn't want her around. It was just like old times. And she'd come running. What a joke.

"It amazes me that even a bomb could faze you," she remarked with her old self-possession. She even smiled. "Mr. Cold Steel repels bullets, bombs, and especially, me!"

He didn't react. "Nice of you to stop by. And so promptly," he added.

She didn't understand the remark. He seemed to feel she'd procrastinated about visiting. "Eb Scott phoned and said you'd been hurt. He said..." She hesitated, uncertain whether or not to tell him everything Eb had said to her. She went for broke, but she laughed to camouflage her raw emotions. "He said you wanted me to come nurse you. Funny, huh?"

He didn't laugh. "Hilarious."

She felt the familiar whip of his sarcasm with pain she didn't try to hide. After all, he couldn't see it. "That's our Eb," she agreed. "A real kidder. I guess you have—what was her name?—June to take care of you?" she added with forced lightness.

"That's right. I have June. She's been here since I got home." He emphasized the pronoun, for reasons of his own. He smiled deliberately. "June is all I need. She's sweet and kindhearted, and she really cares about me."

She forced a smile. "She's pretty, too."

He nodded. "Isn't she, though? Pretty, smart, and a good cook. And she's blond," he added in a cold, soft voice that made chills run down her spine.

She didn't have to puzzle out the remark. He was partial to blondes. His late wife, Patricia, had been a blonde. He'd loved Patricia...

She rubbed her fingers over the strap of her shoulder bag and realized with a start how tired she was. Airport after airport, dragging her suitcase, agonizing over Cord's true state of health for three long days, just trying to get home to him—and he acted as if she'd pushed her way in. Perhaps she had. Eb should have told her the truth, that Cord still didn't want her in his life, even when he was injured.

She gave him a long, anguished look and moved one shoulder restlessly. "Well, that puts me in my place," she said pleasantly. "I'm sure not blond. Nice to see you're still on your feet. But I'm sorry about your eyes," she added.

"What about my eyes?" he asked curtly, scowling fiercely.

"Eb said you were blinded," she replied.

"Temporarily blinded," he corrected. "It's not a permanent condition. I can see fairly well now, and the ophthalmologist expects a complete recovery."

Her heart jumped. He could see? She realized then that he was watching her, not just staring into a void. It came as a shock. She hadn't been guarding her expressions. She felt uncomfortable, knowing he'd been able to glimpse the misery and worry on her face.

"No kidding? That's great news!" she said, and forced a convincing smile. She was getting the hang of this. Her face would be permanently gleeful, like a piece of fired sculpture. She could hire it out for celebrations. This wasn't one.

"Isn't it?" he agreed, but his returned smile wasn't pleasant at all.

She shifted the strap of her bag again, feeling weak at the knees and embarrassed by her headlong rush to his side. She'd given up her new job and come running home to take care of Cord. But he didn't need her, or want her here. Now she had no job, no place to live, and only her savings to get her through the time until she could find employment. She never learned.

He was barely courteous, and his expression was hostile. "Thanks for coming. I'm sorry you have to leave so soon," he added. "I'll be glad to walk you to the door."

She lifted an eyebrow, and gave him a sardonic look. "No need to give me the bum's rush," she said. "I got the message, loud and clear. I'm not welcome. Fine. I'll leave skid marks going out the door. You can have June scrub them off later."

"Everything's a joke with you," he accused coldly.

"It beats crying," she replied pleasantly. "I need my head read for coming out here in the first place. I don't know why I bothered!"

"Neither do I," he agreed with soft venom. "A day late and a dollar short, at that."

That was enigmatic, but she was too angry to question his phrasing. "You don't have to belabor the point. I'm going," she assured him. "In fact, it's just a matter of another few interviews and I can arrange things so that you'll never have to see me again."

"That would be a real pleasure," he said with a bite in his deep voice. He was still glaring at her. "I'll give a party."

He was laying it on thick. It was as if he were furious with her, for some reason. Perhaps just her presence was enough to set him off. That was nothing new.

She only laughed. She'd had years to perfect her emotional camouflage. It was dangerous to give Cord an opening. He had no compunction about sticking the knife in. They were old adversaries.

"I won't expect an invitation," she told him complacently. "Ever thought of taking early retirement, while you still have a head that can be blown off?" she added.

He didn't answer.

She shrugged and sighed. "I must be in demand somewhere," she told the room at large. "I'll have myself paged at the airport and find out."

She gave him one long, last look, certain that it would be the last time her eyes would see that handsome face. There was some old saying about divine punishment in the form of showing paradise to a victim and then tossing him back into reality. It was like that with Maggie, having known the utter delight of Cord's lovemaking only once. Despite the pain and embarrassment, and his fury afterward, she'd never been able to forget the wonder of his mouth on her body for the first time. The rejection she felt now was almost palpable, and she had to hide it. It wasn't easy.

"Thanks for the caring concern," he drawled.

"Oh, anytime," she replied merrily. "But you can phone me yourself next time you stick your face in a bomb and want tending. And just for the record, you can tell Eb his sense of humor stinks!"

"Tell him yourself," he shot back. "You were engaged to him, weren't you?"

Only because I couldn't have you, she thought, *and your marriage was killing me.* But she didn't say another word. She smiled carelessly, dragged her eyes away from him, turned neatly on her heel and started back out the door.

She'd just gone through the doorway when he called to her suddenly, reluctantly, in a husky tone, "Maggie!"

She didn't hesitate for a second. She was angry now, too, angry that she'd come three thousand miles, that she'd been stupid enough to care about a man who'd never returned her feelings, that she'd believed Eb Scott when he said Cord had asked for her.

June was in the hall, frowning. The frown deepened when she saw Maggie's face, saw the hurt the woman was trying valiantly to hide.

"Are you all right?" she asked in a quick whisper.

Maggie couldn't manage many words at that point. June was Cord's new love interest. Maggie couldn't bear to look at her. She just nodded, a curt jerk of her head. "Thanks," she bit off, and kept walking.

She went out the front door and closed it behind her. Despite that faint call, Cord hadn't pursued her. Maybe he felt momentarily guilty for being so unwelcoming. His sense of hospitality was probably outraged, but she knew from the past that he didn't dwell on his conscience. Meanwhile, she wanted nothing more than to get her long fingernails into Eb Scott. He was happily married now, and she knew he hadn't phoned her to be malicious, but he'd caused her untold misery by upsetting her about Cord's condition. Why?

She stood on the front porch for a moment, trying to get herself together again. Houston was about twenty minutes miles away, and she'd sent the cab off, expecting to stay with Cord and take care of him. She laughed out loud.

She looked toward the highway. Oh, well. As they said,

walking was great exercise. She was glad that she'd worn sneakers instead of high heels with her nice gray pantsuit. She could spend the time it took walking to Houston thinking about her stupidity. She noticed that Cord didn't strain his sense of hospitality offering her a ride, either.

She tugged her wheeled suitcase along with her down the steps and started down the driveway with growing amusement at the absurdity of her predicament. She glanced down at the suitcase with a whimsical smile. "I don't even have a horse to ride off into the sunset on. Well, it's just you and me, old paint," she said, reaching down to pat the suitcase. "Let's mosey!"

Back in the living room, Cord Romero was standing where Maggie had left him, frozen with anger by the fireplace.

June looked in, worried. "She seemed concerned about you," she began.

"Sure," he said on a cold laugh. "It's twenty minutes from Houston and she couldn't drive out here any sooner than this. Some concern!"

"But she had a—!" she began, about to tell him about the suitcase Maggie had left on the porch.

He held up a big, lean hand. "Not another word," he said firmly. "I don't want to hear one more thing about her. Bring me a cup of coffee, would you? Then send Red Davis in here."

"Yes, sir," she said.

"And tell your father I want to see him when he's through

overseeing the loading of those cattle we've culled," he added, because her father was the livestock foreman.

"Yes, sir," she said again, and left.

Cord cursed under his breath. He hadn't seen Maggie in weeks. It was as if she'd vanished off the face of the earth. He'd actually gone by her apartment once, although she'd refused to answer the doorbell, even after he'd spent five minutes ringing it. She wouldn't answer her damned telephone, either. He didn't want to admit that he'd missed her, or that it hurt like hell that she'd waited four days to come and see about him.

Their lives had been entwined since he was sixteen and she was eight when they'd been taken in by Mrs. Amy Barton, a socialite whose sister was an employee at the juvenile detention center. Cord's parents had died in a fire while they were all visiting Houston on a rare vacation. Maggie had been abandoned by her family about the same time, and both were held at the juvenile center. Mrs. Barton, childless and lonely, had impulsively decided to be a foster parent to the two children. Eventually she'd adopted Maggie.

Cord had been in trouble with the law at eighteen, and Maggie had been his mainstay. At the age of ten, she was so mature with her advice and loyalty for him that Mrs. Barton had laughed even through her agony at his predicament. Maggie was fiercely protective of her older foster brother. He remembered her holding his hand so tightly when his case was called before the judge, her whispered assurances that everything would be all right. Maggie had always taken care of him.

When his wife, Patricia, had killed herself, Maggie had stayed right with him through the inquest and the funeral. When Mrs. Barton had died, Maggie had given him loving comfort, and he'd repaid her with pain…

He couldn't bear to think about that night. It was one of the worst memories of his life. He stared blankly out the window at the pasture where his big bull Hijito roamed, and grimaced as he recalled Maggie's face only minutes before. Her life had been no bed of roses, either. He knew nothing of her childhood, or why she'd been taken away from her stepfather. Mrs. Barton had refused to discuss it, and Maggie had avoided the question ever since he'd known her.

Maggie had inexplicably married, less than a month after Mrs. Barton's death, and to a man she'd only known briefly. It hadn't been a happy relationship. The man she married, a wealthy banker, was twenty years older than she was and divorced. Cord recalled hearing that she'd had some sort of accident at home, and that her husband had been killed in a car crash while she was still in the hospital.

Cord had come home from Africa when he'd heard, just to see about her. She'd been at home when he came, too sick even to go to her husband's funeral for reasons nobody told him. She hadn't wanted Cord there. She'd refused to talk to him, even to look at him. It had hurt, because he knew why. The night Mrs. Barton had died, he'd taken Maggie to bed. He'd been drinking, one of only two times in his life he'd ever had too much to drink, and he'd hurt her. Incredibly she'd been a virgin. He didn't remember much of what had happened, only her tears and harsh sobs, and his shocked realization that she wasn't the experienced woman he'd imagined her. His anger at himself had translated itself into harsh accusations at her for what had happened. Even through the haze of time, he could still see her anguished tears, her shivering body wrapped in a sheet, her eyes avoiding the sight of his powerful body without clothing as he stood over her and raged.

They'd seen each other very few times since then, and Maggie's discomfort in his presence had been obvious. After she was widowed, she'd taken back her maiden name, thrown herself into her work as vice president of an investment firm and avoided Cord totally. It should have pleased him. He'd avoided her for years before Amy Barton's death. She didn't know that he'd married Patricia in a vain effort to head off his inexplicable obsession with Maggie. He'd spent so many years trying not to let her get close to him. He'd loved his pretty little American mother, worshiped his Spanish father. Their tragic deaths, in a fire that had spared him, had warped his emotions at an early age. He knew the danger of loving that led to the agony of loss. Patricia's suicide had compounded his misery. When Mrs. Barton died, it was the last straw. Everything he loved, everyone he loved, was taken from him. It was easier, much easier, to stop feeling deeply.

His stint in the Houston Police Department, interrupted by service with the army in Operation Desert Storm, had given him a taste for danger that had led him into the FBI.

After Patricia's suicide, for which he felt guilt because of reasons he'd never shared with another living soul, he'd gone into work as a professional mercenary. His specialty was demolition, and he was good at it. Or he had been, until he'd let himself be lured into a trap by an old adversary in Miami. His instincts had saved him from certain death, only to learn that the whole thing had been a setup. Maggie didn't know that, and he had no reason to tell her. She was obviously unconcerned with his health, showing up so late after the fact. He knew that his adversary was going to come after him again. But he wasn't going to let himself be surprised a second time.

He turned away from the window with a sigh and regretted, deeply, his treatment of Maggie. He was responsible for her distaste for him, for the indifference that had brought her to his side four days after the accident instead of hours afterward. If she'd still cared for him at all, she wouldn't have waited. She'd have been frantic to see him. He laughed at his own idiocy. He'd hurt her, been icy cold to her, pushed her out of his life at every turn for years, and now he was resentful because she didn't care very much that he'd been injured. He was only reaping the harvest of his abuse. It wasn't Maggie's fault.

For one vulnerable moment, he'd called her name and tried to find the words for an apology. But his pride had stopped him from following her when she ignored him. She'd go away and probably never come back. And he deserved it.

* * *

Maggie was halfway down the long, paved driveway between neat white fences when the sound of a pickup truck coming up fast from behind made her step off the pavement.

But instead of passing her, the truck stopped and the passenger door was pushed open.

Red Davis, one of Cord's ranch foremen, leaned forward, his wide-brimmed straw hat pulled down over his red hair and blue eyes. He smiled. "It's too hot to walk a suitcase to Houston. Get in," he said. "I'll drive you."

She chuckled, even as she was touched by an act of kindness she hadn't expected. She hesitated for just a minute. "Cord didn't send you, did he?" she asked abruptly. If he had, she wasn't taking one step into that double-cabbed, six-wheeled truck!

"No, ma'am, he didn't," he replied. "He didn't know you brought the suitcase. And I wouldn't tell him even if he tortured me," he swore with a hand over his heart and a twinkle in his eyes.

She laughed. "Okay, then. Thanks!" She slid her suitcase into the backseat and jumped up into the cab beside Davis, closing the door and fastening her seat belt.

He started up the engine again and roared down the driveway. "I guess you didn't come from town?" he probed.

"Leave it alone, Red," she said. "It doesn't matter."

"You brought a suitcase," he persisted. "Why?"

"You're a pest, Davis!"

"And I don't respond to insecticide, either," he grinned. "Come on, Maggie. Tell Uncle Red why you turned up with that trunk on wheels."

"All right, I came from Morocco," she replied finally when he just grinned at her scowl. "Straight from Morocco, at that, despite delays and layovers and flight cancellations. I haven't slept in thirty-six hours. I expected to find him blind and helpless." She laughed. "I should have known better. He laid into me the minute I walked into the house and booted me out the door." She shook her head. "Just like old times. Nothing ever changes. Just the sight of me rubs him the wrong way."

"What were you doing in Morocco?" he asked, startled.

"Having a vacation before I took up my new job in Qawi," she confessed. "My best friend is taking it instead. So here I am with everything I own in a suitcase, no place to live, no job, no nothing." She shot him a half-amused glance. "If I weren't such a tough nut, I'd bawl my head off."

"Cord didn't offer you a room?" he exclaimed, horrified.

"Cord doesn't know I came from Morocco," she said stiffly. "He doesn't even know I was in Morocco in the first place. I didn't tell him I was leaving Houston. Not that he would have cared, even if he'd noticed." She leaned her head back against the leather headrest with a sigh and closed her eyes. "You'd think I'd stop bashing my head against stone walls, wouldn't you?"

The thinly veiled reference to her feelings for her foster brother wasn't lost on the man beside her. He wasn't close to

Cord Romero, but he recognized unrequited love when he saw it. He was sorry for this pretty, strong woman who looked as if she was at the end of her rope. He wondered why his boss couldn't see how much she cared about him. He was supremely indifferent to her, and had been ever since Davis had come to work for him.

"Besides," she added in a voice that betrayed more than she realized, "he's got June to take care of him, now, hasn't he?"

He shot her an odd glance. "Not in the way you're thinking," he volunteered.

She was suddenly interested. "Excuse me?"

"June is Darren Travis's daughter," he explained. "He's Cord's cattle foreman, looks after the purebred Santa Gertrudis herd. June's taken over the housekeeping and cooking just temporarily, because Cord's regular woman remarried and left. But June's sweet on a Houston police officer, and vice versa. She's scared of Cord. Most people are. He isn't the easiest boss in the world, and he has moods."

She was really confused now. "But he said...! I mean—" she lowered her voice "—he insinuated that he and June were involved."

He chuckled. "She has to be forced to go to him with problems. She usually tells her father and has him relay any requests. She thinks Cord's a holy terror. She told me once she couldn't imagine a woman brave enough to take him on. It really amazed her that he'd been married at all."

"It amazed all of us, at the time," Maggie recalled reluctantly.

His marriage had hurt her terribly. It was a whirlwind courtship at that. Maggie had wanted to die when he walked in the front door with Patricia. Their foster mother, Amy Barton, had been equally shocked. Cord didn't strike anyone as a marrying man.

"He hasn't had women around in years," Davis said thoughtfully. "He goes out occasionally, but he never brings anybody home, and he's never out late. Funny, that. He's a good-looking man, only in his thirties, in a dangerous profession and rich. You'd think he'd have pretty women tripping over him. He's something of a recluse."

She glanced at him. "That dangerous profession is probably why. He knows every assignment could be his last. I don't imagine he'd want to wish that on a woman."

"Danger draws women, though, doesn't it?"

She laughed. "Not this woman," she confessed, stifling a yawn and lying through her teeth. "I'd rather marry a guy who worked the drive-in window at a fast-food joint than a professional demolition expert. Not much risk of being blown up handling hamburgers and fries," she added drolly, and was rewarded by a chuckle.

Maggie had been briefly engaged to Eb Scott just after Cord married Patricia. Now, she could admit that it had only been an engagement of friends, one of so many futile attempts to get over Cord. She and Eb had never been really attracted to each other physically. Cord had assumed that they were sleeping together, which explained his stark horror at Maggie's innocence years later, on the night Mrs. Barton died. But

Maggie had never been able to think of any man except Cord intimately—at least, until they were intimate. Now her older, more frightening memories of things sexual were intermixed with new ones of discomfort and embarrassment. Why, oh, why, couldn't she get him out of her heart, her mind?

"You've known Cord a long time, haven't you?" Red mused.

"Since I was eight and he was sixteen," she murmured, getting drowsy, lulled by the soft motion of the truck on the smooth pavement of the highway that led into Houston. "That old saying that brothers and sisters fight like cats and dogs isn't so far off, you know," she murmured. "Even foster ones."

"Really?" he said, almost to himself.

"Really." She yawned and his next comment fell on deaf ears. She drifted off into a brief oblivion.

It wasn't a long drive, but it felt as if they'd just left the ranch when Maggie was brought awake by a tap from Davis's hand. She opened her eyes and noticed that they'd already reached the city limits of Houston.

"Sorry to wake you, but we're in town now. Do you have any idea where you want me to take you?" Davis asked gently.

"To a nice, comfortable, cheap hotel," she murmured dryly. "I'm living on my savings until I get another job, and they don't amount to much."

He grimaced. "You should have told him."

"Oh, no!" she disagreed. She smoothed her pink-tipped

fingernails over her white purse. "I'm not his responsibility. I only wanted to take care of him. Funny, isn't it? He doesn't need anybody. He never has." She turned her eyes out the window. She wasn't a weepy sort of person. She was strong and spirited and independent. The hard knocks of her life had made her strong. But she was tired and sleepy and she felt Cord's cold rejection deeply. She was momentarily weak and she didn't want Davis to see it.

Davis mumbled something under his breath. It sounded like "damned idiot," but Maggie wasn't rising to the bait.

"It isn't right," he said angrily. "Letting you out the door without even knowing if you had a way back to town."

"Don't you dare tell him about the suitcase or the trip," she said impatiently when she saw the look on his face. "Don't you dare, Red!"

"I won't tell him about the suitcase," he agreed, mentally crossing his fingers. "There's a good hotel downtown, not expensive, where my mother stays when she comes to see me," he added quickly. "You'll like it."

She nodded. "Okay. That'll do. I think I could sleep for a week."

"I don't doubt it."

"Tomorrow, I'll get a newspaper and find a job." She yawned again. "Things will look bright tomorrow."

"I'm sorry you had such a rough day," he told her as he pulled up in front of a nice, but nondescript hotel downtown.

"They're all rough days, lately," she murmured with a smile.

"Life is trial by fire, didn't you know? It's an obstacle course. If you survive it, you get to wear wings and float around feeling sorry for the living!"

"Think so?" he teased.

"Of course, when I think about Cord, I want to come back as a stump and trip him twice a day," she commented dryly. She turned toward him. "Thanks for the ride, Red. Thanks a lot. It would have been a long walk."

"No problem."

He went around and got her suitcase out for her. She walked into the hotel dragging it behind her. Davis thought he'd never seen such poise, and the thought "grace under fire" came unwillingly to his mind. And Cord Romero could turn his back on a woman like that! The man had to be nuts.

Maggie checked in, went up to her room, locked the door, took off her pantsuit and fell into the bed. She put Cord's handsome face out of her mind firmly and closed her eyes. She was asleep seconds later.

Back at the ranch, Cord was sipping coffee and going over ledgers on his computer. He'd spent a lot of time away in recent months, and it was tough catching up on business.

He wondered sometimes why he didn't just sell the ranch and move into an apartment. He was all on his own, and he never planned to marry again. Life would be less complicated if he lived out of a suitcase, as he'd done most of his adult life except during his brief marriage. But he loved his cattle, and the pair of Andalusian horses he'd purchased on his last visit to his cousin in Andalusia, in the south of Spain not too long a drive from the Rock of Gibraltar.

He leaned back and stared blankly at the black type on the computer screen. He couldn't get Maggie's eyes out of his thoughts. When she'd first seen him, before he spoke, those green eyes had been alive with concern, with pleasure, with tentative affection, with joy. So soon, they'd faded to dullness and the joy in them had eclipsed into a sadness that was painful to recall, although she'd quickly hidden it.

It didn't take good eyesight to recognize her unrequited love for him. At some level, he'd known about it for years. He simply ignored it. She'd grown up, become engaged to his best friend, but married someone else, been widowed—her life had been more of thorns than roses. He'd offered her pain in return for those years of fierce loyalty and affection.

When she'd gone out of his life, he'd expected to have peace, finally. But the loneliness had worn him down until he became careless. In the past, it would have taken far more than a simple electronic bomb to damage him.

In past weeks, for reasons he didn't really understand, she'd avoided him completely. That had hurt. He'd taken a case in Florida, wounded because Maggie didn't want to see him. He'd let down his guard and had almost been killed, by an old enemy whose livelihood had been threatened by Cord's investigation of an employment agency with which he was somehow connected. He'd planted a bomb and Cord had walked into a trap because his mind had been on Maggie instead of the job.

At least she'd finally come to see about him! He'd known that Eb was going to get in touch with her. But he'd stopped just short of telling the man to ask her to come and see about him. He'd expected—no, he'd hoped—that she cared enough to come running the minute he got home. But she hadn't. It had shaken him.

He'd become accustomed to Maggie on the fringes of his life, always laughing, making him laugh, making him feel safe. She was always there, always waiting for him to...

He cursed under his breath and ran an angry hand through his thick, dark hair. Maggie had finally given up on him. She'd decided that he was never going to turn to her with anything more than sarcasm or indifference. She'd removed herself from the periphery of his life and cut him out of hers. That was what had hurt the most. Having her wait days to acknowledge his injury had only added fuel to the fire.

Well, he'd chased her away for the last time and he wasn't going to sit around counting his regrets. He couldn't blame her for not caring, when her place in his life had always been a reluctant one, a remote one, barely tolerated, and totally unappreciated. He couldn't remember a single time when he'd admitted how much it mattered that she was concerned for him. He'd never told her the comfort it gave him when Patricia died, when he was wounded, when he was in trouble, to have her hold his big hand in her small one so tightly and never let go.

She was a rock in hard times. He hadn't realized how much he counted on her presence for comfort, for security. Now that comfort was removed, perhaps forever, and her absence was like a hole inside him that nothing could ever fill again. He forced his attention back to the computer screen, grateful that he still had his vision, even if he lost everything else. Not that he was going to advertise his recovery. Not yet.

Impulsively he closed down the spreadsheet and logged on to the Internet. He wanted to know where his nemesis was and what illegal activities might have prompted the attack on Cord in Miami. With a smile of pure arrogance, he walked into the back door of a government agency and right into the protected files on one Raoul Gruber, who had connections in the Cote d'Ivoire of Africa, in Madrid, and in Amsterdam....

2

After a mostly sleepless night, Cord sat down to breakfast. He'd gone over the latest herd records with June's father the day before, and he was satisfied with the breeding program and the sales figures. He'd called down to the bunkhouse for Red Davis last night to discuss a problem with some irrigation equipment, since Red had charge of ranch equipment and supplies, but the cowboy who answered the phone said Davis was off on a date, as usual. Cord wondered how a man with such a cocky attitude and such a big mouth could draw so many women. His own social life was stagnant by comparison. But that suited him, he told himself. He had no time for women.

The back door opened just as he finished his last bite of egg and biscuit, and Davis walked in yawning. His hat was pushed far back over his red hair and he was neat as a pin, in blue jeans and a short-sleeved checked shirt. He was twenty-seven, years younger than Cord, but he seemed even younger at times. Cord mused that he'd lived through more than Davis probably ever would. It wasn't the age, didn't they say, but the mileage that made people old. If he were a used car, he thought, he'd be in a junkyard.

"I heard you were looking for me last night, boss," Davis said at once, pulling out a chair to straddle. "Sorry, I had a date."

"You always have a date," Cord muttered, sipping coffee.

Davis grinned wickedly. "Have to make hay while the sun shines. One day, I'll be ancient and decrepit like you."

Cord's mouth drew down sardonically. "And I'd just decided to give you a raise!"

"I'd rather have girls hanging out of my truck," Davis said, but he grinned again.

"Never mind. We've got problems with that irrigation system again," he added. "I want you to get that serviceman out there and tell him I want it fixed this time, repaired with new parts, not held together with duct tape and baling wire."

"I told him that last time."

"Then call the customer service people and tell them to send somebody else. The equipment's still under warranty," he added. "If they can't fix it, they shouldn't sell it. I want it up and running by tomorrow. Okay?"

"Okay, boss, I'll give it my best. But you probably should have a lawyer talk to them about their customer service department. I think they employ robots."

Cord stifled a grin. "You took computer courses. Reprogram them."

"I'll get right on it," Davis said, chuckling. But he didn't get up. He stared at his boss, hesitating.

"Something bothering you?" Cord asked bluntly.

Davis traced a pattern on the back of the wooden chair he was straddling. "Yeah. Something. I promised I wouldn't tell, but I think you should know."

"Know what?" Cord asked absently as he finished his coffee.

"Miss Barton had a suitcase with her," he said, noting the sudden attention the older man gave him. "She came straight here from the airport. She was in Morocco. She said it took her three days just to get home. She was dead on her feet."

Remembering his cold treatment of her, Cord was shocked. "She was in Morocco? What in hell for?" he burst out.

"She said she'd just taken a job overseas. She was having a holiday with a girlfriend on the way. She came rushing back to see about you." The younger man's eyes became accusing. "She was walking back to Houston with her suitcase when I drove up beside her. I drove her to town."

Cord felt the sickness in the pit of his stomach like acid. The expression that washed over his handsome features knocked the outrage right out of Davis's eyes.

"Where did you take her?" Cord asked in a subdued tone and without meeting the other man's gaze.

"The Lone Star Hotel downtown," he replied.

Cord made an awkward movement. “Thanks, Davis,” he said curtly.

“You bet. I’ll get on that irrigation system,” Davis added as he rose.

“Do that.” Cord didn’t even see him go. He was reliving that painful few minutes with Maggie. He hadn’t told her that he was hurt because he’d thought she’d waited to come and see about him. He’d assumed that she’d been in town and reluctant to come around him. But she’d come halfway around the world as fast as she could, just to take care of him. He’d misread the whole situation and sent her packing. Now she’d be wounded and angry, and she’d go away again; maybe somewhere that he couldn’t even find her. That hurt.

He put his head in his hands with a groan. The most painful realization was that she’d taken a job far away. He remembered calling her and going by her apartment without getting an answer in the past two weeks. Now he knew why. She’d left the country. She’d given up trying to get his attention, and he hadn’t even noticed her departure. That must have hurt her. Maggie was proud. She wouldn’t beg for his interest. After all the years of being pushed away by him, she’d decided to cut her losses. If he hadn’t been injured, and Eb Scott hadn’t tracked her down in Morocco and told her about it, he wouldn’t even have known where she was. She’d have been gone for good.

Now that he knew the truth, it didn’t solve the problem. It only complicated things. He wondered if it wouldn’t be kinder to just let her go, let her think he didn't care about her, let her think that he was involved with June. But he was oddly reluctant to do that. It made him ashamed to think how much she cared, to come all that way, to sacrifice so much, because she was concerned for him.

There was only one thing to do. He had to go and find her, and tell her how badly he'd misjudged her. Then, if she left, at least they wouldn't part with a sword between them.

He had one of his ranch hands drive him into town, wearing dark glasses to maintain the fiction about his lack of sight. He got Maggie's room number from the hotel desk, on the pretext of phoning her later. Then he ducked into the elevator, went up to her room, and easily let himself in with skills learned in a dozen covert operations around the world.

She was asleep in a huge double bed, moving restlessly. It was warm in the room, but she was huddled under the covers as if it were winter. He'd never known her to sleep with the sheet off, even in the hottest summer night when the air-conditioning in Mrs. Barton's house was on the blink. Odd, that he'd never noticed that before...

She looked younger when she slept. He remembered the first time he'd ever seen her, when she was eight. She was clutching a ragged toy bear and she looked as if she'd seen hell and lived to tell about it. She didn't smile. She hid behind Mrs. Barton's ample girth and looked at Cord as if he were responsible for the seven deadly sins.

It had taken weeks for her to come near him. She loved Mrs. Barton, but she was uneasy around boys or men. He attributed that to her age. But as she grew older, she began to cling to Cord. He was her source of stability. She anchored herself to him and hid from any sort of social activity. Despite the age difference, she became possessive of him. When he got in trouble at the age of eighteen and was faced with the possibility of going to jail, it was Maggie who sat beside him and held his hand while Mrs. Barton had hysterics and became the voice of doom. Maggie, in her quiet, gentle way, gave him the comfort and strength he needed to face his problems and overcome them.

She'd only been ten years old, but she had a maturity even then that was surprising. She was an introvert by nature, but she seemed to sense that Cord needed someone bright and happy to bring out the best in him. So she developed a sense of humor and picked at Cord and teased him and made him play. Maggie had taught him how to laugh.

He studied her wan, drawn face on the white pillowcase and wondered why he'd always treated her as an outsider. He was alternately hostile and sarcastic, never kind or welcoming. Maggie had done more for him than anyone in his life except their foster parent. Maybe, he pondered, it was because she knew him so well. Despite his spiny outward appearance, Maggie knew him right inside, where he lived. She knew that he had nightmares about the night his parents had died in a hotel fire. She knew that he was haunted by Patricia's suicide.

She knew that when he was being his most sarcastic, he was hiding wounds. He couldn't hide anything from Maggie.

But she hid her whole life from him. He knew next to nothing about her, really. She'd been a sad, frightened, jumpy child with odd moods and terrors. She'd avoided relationships like the devil, yet she'd married a man she hardly knew, a much-older man, and been married and widowed in weeks. She never spoke of her husband. She was job-oriented and somber as a judge usually. Even a brief engagement to his friend Eb Scott hadn't really softened her much, long before her marriage to Evans. He'd wondered at the outward distance she seemed to keep from Eb. It hadn't made sense, until later, when he understood the magnitude of his misconceptions about her.

She looked so fragile, so vulnerable, lying there. Even in sleep, she looked tormented. She looked tired. No wonder. Flying all the way from Morocco without a pause, and then out to his ranch only to be turned away practically at the door. He hadn't even asked if she had a way back to town. That was harsh. Even for him.

He hesitated for an instant before he reached out and touched her arm through the cotton fabric that concealed it.

Maggie was dreaming. She was walking through a field of wildflowers in the sun. In the distance, a man was laughing, holding out his arms to her—a tall, dark-haired man. She ran toward him, ran as fast as she could, but she never closed the distance. He watched her from afar, like a cat toying with a desperate mouse. *Cord,* she thought. *It was Cord, and he was taunting her as he always had.* She could hear his voice, hear it as clearly as if it were in the room with her...

A hand was shaking her, hard. She moaned in protest. She didn't want to wake up. If she woke up, Cord wouldn't be there anymore.

"Maggie!" came the deep, insistent voice.

She gasped and opened her eyes. She wasn't dreaming. Cord was sitting on the edge of her bed, one lean hand beside her head on the pillow supporting his leaning posture.

He studied her face, devoid of makeup, framed by long, wavy dark hair in soft tangles. She was wearing pajamas, a jacket and pants that covered her up completely. It used to puzzle him that Maggie dressed in a luxurious but conventional style to go to work, and she slept in the most unisex clothing she could find. She never wore sexy clothes, even when she'd been a teenager, and she never walked around in her nightclothes, even when she was little and they were living with Mrs. Barton. He wondered why he'd never noticed that before.

She focused on him and her face clenched. "What are you doing here?"

He grimaced. "Field-dressing crow. I'm sure it'll taste terrible, too."

Her eyebrows shot up. "Excuse me?"

He shrugged one powerful shoulder. He didn't like admitting his faults, but he owed her. "I didn't know you were in Morocco. I thought you were right here in Houston, and that you'd waited four days to drive out to see about me."

Her heart ran wild. Cord had never explained anything to her. Over the years, she'd become accustomed to his barbed remarks, his hostility, his sarcasm. He'd never apologized or shown any signs of caring what she thought about him.

Her eyes drank in his strong, handsome face. "Maybe I'm still asleep," she murmured.

"Pity," he said, studying her drowsy face with a faint smile. "I don't apologize very often."

She watched him. "You didn't tell Eb you wanted me to come at all, did you?"

He hated to admit that. She looked as cynical as he usually did. But he wasn't accustomed to lies. "No," he replied honestly.

She laughed ruefully. "I should have known that."

"Why were you going to work in Qawi?" he asked abruptly.

"I was in a rut," she said simply. "I needed a change. I wanted adventure."

"You lost your job because of me," he persisted, frowning.

"Big deal! There are jobs everywhere, and I have a good background in investments. I'll find something. Preferably," she added teasingly, "in a multinational corporation, so that I can work overseas and never get in your hair again."

"Why do you want to leave the country?" he asked irritably.

"What is there for me here?" she countered simply. "I'm twenty-six, Cord. If I don't do something, I'll dry up and blow away. I don't want to spend the best years of my life commuting to downtown Houston to play with numbers. I'm not a baby anymore. If I have to work, at least I can choose something in an exotic location. Preferably something adventurous, and exciting," she said as an afterthought.

He frowned. "Why do you have to work?" he asked suddenly. "Amy left us both a little money. Besides, Bart Evans had an extensive stock portfolio and you were his widow."

Her face hardened. "I didn't take one penny of his money. Not property, not stocks, not savings. Nothing!"

That was surprising. "Why not?"

She lowered her eyes to the coverlet and closed them briefly under a wave of pain she didn't want him to see. "He cost me the most precious thing in my life," she said in a husky, throbbing tone.

That was an enigmatic statement. He didn't understand it. "Nobody forced you to marry him," he pointed out, and with more bitterness than he realized.

That's what you think, she thought to herself, but she didn't say it aloud. She crumpled the coverlet under her bright pink fingernails and looked up at him bravely. "I had his estate divided between his two ex-wives."

He laughed shortly in surprise. "You did what?"

"You heard me," she remarked with a shrug. She let go of her grip on the bedspread. "I thought they deserved the money more than I did. They lived with him longer than I did. He had no living relatives."

His dark eyes narrowed. He'd been curious about her marriage for a long time. He'd never mentioned it to her, because she closed up like a clam when her husband's name came up. She never discussed it. But it had left scars on her emotions that were obvious to anyone with a grain of sensitivity.

"Not a happy marriage, Maggie?" he asked quietly.

"No." She met his eyes evenly. "And that's the only thing I'll ever say about it," she added firmly. "Digging up the past solves nothing."

He studied her wan face. "I used to think that way, too. But the past shapes the future. I never got over Patricia's death."

"I know."

She said it in an odd sort of way. "What do you mean?" he asked.

"You aren't exactly Don Juan these days," she pointed out.

He bristled with stung pride. It was true that he didn't have affairs, or spend a lot of time living the life of a playboy, but he didn't like her knowing it. His dark eyes flashed. "You know nothing about that side of my life," he said coldly. "And you never will."

There was a brief, incredulous look on her face, and he could have bitten his tongue. They'd slept together, once, even if it wasn't a memory she liked. She knew him in a way few women ever had. It was a thoughtless remark.

"On second thought," he began abruptly.

She held up a hand. "You said it yourself, digging up the past doesn't solve anything."

He drew in a long, slow breath. "I hurt you."

Her face flamed. She wasn't going to get trapped into that conversation. "Let it go, Cord. It all happened a long time ago. Now I have to get up and start job-hunting. If you don't mind going out of here so I can get dressed...?"

But he wouldn't leave it alone. "You're twenty-six and a widow," he said shortly, irritated by her embarrassment. "And I know every inch of you. So stop acting coy."

Her teeth clenched so hard she thought she might chip them. Her eyes were furious. "You have no idea how much I hate the memory of that night," she said spitefully.

The words stung, as she meant them to. He got to his feet abruptly and noticed how she dragged the covers up to her chin, as if she couldn't bear him to look at her body at all.

"You must have noticed that I was drunk," he said curtly. "If I hadn't been, I'd never have touched you!"

"I drank too much myself," she shot back. "Or I'd never have let you touch me!"

"Having made ourselves clear on that point," he added, turning away from her. "I'm sorry about what happened."

He sounded as if he was about to choke on the words. She noticed that his face was clenched as tightly as her fingers.

"Two apologies in one day," she said with mock surprise. "Do you have something fatal and you're trying to win points with God while there's still time?"

He laughed faintly. "You could be forgiven for thinking so, I suppose." He turned and looked at her for a long time, as if he needed to reconcile his memory of her with the reality. "You were eight when we came to live with Mrs. Barton. That means you've been part of my life for eighteen years." His eyes grew contemplative. "I've given you nothing but hostility, all that time. But the minute I get in trouble or get hurt, you come running. Why?"

"Habit," she said at once. "And a monstrous appetite for verbal abuse," she added with a faintly wicked smile.

He burst out laughing, and this time it was genuine. It changed him. It made his eyes sparkle, his face so handsome that it hurt her to see it. He'd been this way with Patricia, his wife, she supposed. Maybe he'd been happy with other women, too, over the years. But he only smiled at Maggie if she teased him. So, through the years, she'd tried to do that. It was one way of getting attention from him, even if the only way.

"You didn't need to come here and apologize," she added. "I'm used to having you snarl at me."

He frowned as he considered that. She spoke as if she expected nothing else. There was so much about her past that he didn't know, couldn't know. She volunteered nothing. It was a reminder that she knew far more about him than he knew about her.

"You can come and stay out at the ranch while you look for work," he said out of the blue.

Her heart skipped, but she wouldn't meet his eyes. "No, thanks. I like it where I am."

He hadn't expected the refusal. "What's the matter, scared I'll lose my temper and throw you out in your nightgown one rainy night?"

She sighed. "It would be in character," she said with resignation. "You'd make sure it was on a main street, too."

He grimaced. "I was kidding!"

She looked up. "I wasn't."

His jaw clenched. "You don't know me, Maggie."

She laughed shortly. She sat up, pushing back the thick waves of her long hair before she leaned forward with her head in her hands, her elbows resting on her drawn-up knees. "My head hurts. I'm not used to traveling so far at one time."

"You're jet-lagged," he said. He knew a lot about overseas travel. He'd done more than his share. "You probably went to sleep the minute you got here. You should have tried to wait until bedtime."

She gave him a speaking glance. "I had a trying day."

He sighed and stuck his hands in the pockets of his khaki slacks. "So you did."

Her eyes lifted to his face, tracing the new cuts and stitches. "It's a miracle that you didn't lose your sight," she said softly.

"It was. And I'm not going to make it public that I haven't. Note the dark glasses," he added, indicating them hanging out of one pocket by an earpiece. "I even had one of my boys drive me into town and bring me up on the elevator, just to keep the fiction going." He didn't say why. He jingled his car keys in his pocket restlessly. "Watch your back while you're in town," he added suddenly. "I'm pretty sure that an old enemy of mine set me up. If I'm right, he's going to be on my trail pretty soon, to make sure I don't put him out of business. He wouldn't stop at attacking anybody close to me."

"Well, that certainly puts me out of danger," she said pertly.

He glared at her. "You're family. If he doesn't know it, he'll find it out. You could be in danger. I think he's involved with people here in Houston."

"You've had plenty of enemies over the years. None of them considered me family, even if you do."

His gaze was narrow and contemplative. "I don't know how I think of you," he said absently. "I've never taken time to do an inventory."

"You could do it between sips of coffee." She laughed.

"Don't sell yourself short," he said unexpectedly.

She met his eyes, and her whole life was suddenly stark and painful in her face. She couldn't bear the memories sometimes. He knew nothing about her past. She hoped he would never have to know. She couldn't imagine why he was being so nice to her. He must have a guilty conscience.

"No need for flattery, Cord," she said with a faint smile. "I know what you think of me."

He moved back to the bed and sat down beside her. One lean hand went to her cheek and he turned her face up so that he could see it. He felt the tension in her, the choked breath, the wild heartbeat. Her eyes reflected the helpless response that her body betrayed. That, at least, never changed.

She might hate the memory of what he'd done to her—no less than he hated it himself—but she was as hopelessly attracted to him as she'd always been. It comforted him on some level to know that.

"Don't play with me anymore," she said tautly, her eyes telling him that she hated the hopeless attraction he could see. It was almost physically painful to have him so near, to see the chiseled line of his wide mouth and remember the feel of it, to know the warm strength of that powerful body so very close.

He read those reactions with textbook accuracy. His proud head lifted. His eyes narrowed. His lean hand spread against her cheek and his thumb suddenly swept hard over her soft lips, dragging a gasp from them.

His other hand caught in her thick hair and he pulled her, lifted her, until she was lying across his body with her head in the crook of his arm.

Her breasts were flattened against his broad, hair-roughened chest over the thin cotton shirt he wore. She looked up at him with helpless desire. He gently smoothed his hand up and down her throat, caressing, tantalizing, while his head bent and his hard lips hovered maddeningly just above her mouth.

"What makes you think I'm playing?" he murmured roughly.

Her nails dug into his shoulder as she hung there, vulnerable, aching for him to bend those scant inches and crush his mouth down hard on her parted lips. She could smell the coffee he'd had for breakfast on his breath. She could smell the clean, spicy scent of his skin. Where his sports shirt was open at the throat, she could see the thick press of curling dark hair that covered his broad, muscular chest. She remembered unwillingly the way it had felt against her bare breasts that one time in their lives when she'd thought he really wanted her. Even the memory of pain and embarrassed shame that came afterward didn't diminish her reactions to him. They were eternal. He touched her and she melted into him. She belonged to him, just as she had at the age of eight. And he knew it. He'd always known.

Involuntarily her cold fingers went trembling to his cheek, up into the thick darkness of his hair at his temple, where that slight wave gave it definition. He always felt clean to the touch. He always smelled good. She felt safe when she was with him, despite his hostility. He was the first male thing in her young life that had ever given her a feeling of security. He was the only man she'd ever trusted.

He caught her hand and held it tightly while he looked into her wide eyes. Abruptly he dragged her palm to his mouth and kissed it with something like desperation, burying his mouth in it. His eyes closed as he savored the softness of it.

She felt the fever in him, but didn't understand it. He didn't want her, not really. He never had. But he looked...tormented, somehow.

He drew her hand back to her cheek and looked at her with

passion. "I hurt you every time I touch you," he whispered harshly. "Don't you think I know it?"

She couldn't drag her eyes away from his. "You have nothing to give me. I know. I've always known." She laughed painfully. "It doesn't seem to matter."

He drew her close and held her, his arms strong around her, his mouth against her hair. He took a deep breath and felt all the anger and misery of the past few years drain out of him. He laid his cheek against her dark, soft hair and closed his eyes. It was like coming home.

She held him, too, drinking in the clean, spicy scent of his muscular body as she tried valiantly to ignore the fever of passion his touch kindled. It gave her comfort, as it did him. He wasn't an emotional person. He kept his deepest feelings hidden carefully inside. Maggie knew all about that, because she did the same thing. If people could get close to you, they could hurt you. It was a lesson Maggie and Cord had learned early in their lives. It had made them cautious about involvement.

His hand brushed the length of her hair and he smiled lazily. "I love long hair," he murmured.

She didn't answer. She didn't have to. He knew she kept it long because of him.

"We're poison to each other. Maybe," he began slowly, "it would be for the best if you did start over somewhere else, somewhere...far away."

"Better for me, certainly," she murmured huskily. Her fingers caressed his hair at the temple. "But who would take care of you if I did?" she added, her voice teasing to disguise her hunger for him.

His indrawn breath was audible, and his arms loosened, freeing her abruptly. "I don't need taking care of!" he said shortly.

The truce was over. Just that quickly. She smiled sadly as she watched him get to his feet and move away from the bed. "Don't pop any blood vessels over a figure of speech," she chided. She searched his hard face quietly, savoring its nooks and crannies. Soon, she thought, it would be out of her sight forever.

"I'm through with what passes for love," he said with cold sarcasm. "Just in case you start seeing me as a long-range project."

"Does June know?" she asked wickedly.

He glared at her. "June is none of your business!"

Her eyebrows arched. "Excuse me! We can just forget that I barged into your hotel room and started making passionate advances toward you!" she added facetiously.

His eyes were smoldering now. "I'm leaving."

"I noticed," she agreed.

He got as far as the bedroom door, and then he remembered Gruber. He'd almost lost his eyes, if not his life, to the man's vengeance. Maggie was alone and vulnerable, and Gruber had contacts here.

"I still want you out at the ranch," he said curtly.

"Save your breath," she said pleasantly. "I'm not going."

"If anything should happen to you..." he began tightly, and was amazed at the fear that clenched his heart. If anything happened to her, he'd be alone in the world. He'd have no one at all.

"My, my, wouldn't that uncomplicate your life?" she inserted pertly.

"That isn't true," he snapped.

"Yes, it is," she replied. "You just don't like admitting it. I can call the police anytime I need help, they said so on television just last night. Meanwhile, I'll find a job as quickly as I can and light a fire out of Houston." She smiled deliberately. "Won't that give you a whole new lease on life? I won't even ask you to send me a Christmas card!"

He started to speak, and he couldn't. He just glared.

She struck a seductive pose, knowing it would infuriate him. There was no danger in enticing Cord, he was impervious. She tugged the pajama top lightly away from her long neck. "Want to ravish me before you go?" she offered with mischievous eyes. "I can call room service and get them to send up an emergency condom," she added, wiggling her eyebrows suggestively.

"Damn you!" he bit off furiously. He turned abruptly and slammed out of the door without a backward glance.

Maggie watched him go with sparkling eyes. She could always throw him off balance like that, from their earliest acquaintance. It made her proud, because even his precious Patricia had never been able to do that. It was the one weapon in her arsenal, and a great pride-saver. It was all bluff, of course. She tingled from head to toe just thinking about how it might have been if he'd taken her up on it.

3

Cord's visit unsettled Maggie. It was several minutes before she could get herself together enough to shower and dress and go downstairs for breakfast. She had a light meal and looked up the addresses of several employment agencies in the phone book. Then she started making the rounds.

She'd just come out of the third office on her list, with no results, when she walked straight into a tall brunette she hadn't noticed rounding a nearby corner.

"Oh, I'm sorry!" Maggie exclaimed, steadying the taller woman. "I wasn't even looking where I was..." She hesitated. The other woman was familiar. "You're Kit Deverell!" she exclaimed, smiling broadly. "I met you and your husband at an investment seminar year before last. We've seen each other at several seminars since. I'm Maggie Barton."

Kit Deverell's eyes lit up with recognition. "Of course! You're Cord's foster sister."

Maggie's face closed up at once, defensively.

Kit grimaced. "Sorry. I shouldn't have blurted that out. You see, my boss is Dane Lassiter, who founded the Lassiter Detective Agency here in town. He met Cord some years ago after he started the detective agency—one of his operatives was a rookie when Cord was, and knew him!"

"Yes. I've...heard Cord mention him once or twice, at odd times when we were speaking to each other," she added with a grin.

"You don't get along well, do you?" Kit asked sympathetically. "I shouldn't have mentioned Cord. What are you doing at an employment agency, for heaven's sake?" she added. "You're vice president at Kemp's Investment Agency, aren't you?"

Maggie nodded. "I was. I gave it up to take a job in Qawi. But it didn't pan out," she summarized, avoiding the reason. "Now I'm out of work."

"But Logan's got an opening in his investment firm," Kit continued, chuckling. "Isn't that fate at work? Really, his partner quit and went to work over in Victoria. He's pulling out his hair trying to manage all the accounts by himself. *Please* come and interview," she added, tugging at Maggie's arm. "He's got me doing stock research in my spare time, and I hate it! I work for Lassiter as a skip tracer, you see. I had to fight Logan, but it's not dangerous work and we have a really good babysitter for our son, Bryce. Logan's brother's wife, Della, is pregnant and unable to work because of complications. You'd be saving my life if you could take some of the strain off. Would you? Please?"

Maggie laughed with pure delight. "If there's a job going, I'd love to interview. Actually I sort of had in mind a position that would get me out of the country. But perhaps I can take the job temporarily, while your husband looks for someone permanent and I look for something international..."

"That would work," Kit said with a grin. "Come on!"

Maggie went to interview. Logan Deverell was a huge man with dark hair, not overweight, but tall and muscular. He obviously doted on his wife, and vice versa.

"You're the answer to a prayer," he said after they shook hands and the three of them were seated in Logan's spacious office, his long oak desk covered with photos of Kit and a mischievous-looking little boy of about two years of age. "Tom Walker and I were partners, until he moved to Jacobsville. Then I took on another partner. He married several months ago, but he just quit and moved to Victoria, where his wife has family. She's expecting their first child. So here I am, empty-handed and up to my neck in clients."

Maggie chuckled. "I'm glad I happened along, then. I gave up a lucrative position to rush back here, because I heard that Cord was blinded." She sighed and smiled self-consciously. "I had hoped to find something permanent overseas."

"We'll keep our ears open," Logan promised, "if you're serious. But meantime, how about signing on with me? You can even have your own office," he added with a chuckle. "We acquired the suite next door. Lassiter and his people have the whole third floor. We went in together and bought the building. What we don't use ourselves, we rent out. It pays for itself."

"And," Maggie pointed out, "it's a good investment."

He laughed out loud. "So it is."

He outlined her duties, and her salary, and she was delighted to take the job on a temporary basis. She still wanted to get out of Houston. Living near Cord was painful now that she'd decided to burn her bridges. She'd spent enough of her life aching for a man who didn't care about her.

Although, just for a few seconds in her hotel bedroom, his eyes had burned with desire. He'd wanted her. But that had never been enough for Maggie. She wanted his love. Just as she knew that she'd never have it. She could close her eyes and taste his breath on her mouth, feel the strength of his arms warm and comforting around her. If only she could have that, just for herself, for the rest of her life. It would have been worth more than the most luxurious lifestyle imaginable.

Presumably Cord wanted to live and die alone. Maggie didn't. Perhaps she might even meet a man she could settle for. She might actually get over Cord. Anything was possible. Even with her past.

* * *

She started work at Deverell's the next morning. It was complicated business, but she liked his spin on stocks and bonds, and she liked the mutual funds he recommended. He had a state-of-the-art computer system and an expert who did nothing but scan the Internet for stock prices and update information. Logan was honest, straightforward, and he didn't pretend that he knew everything. He had a built-in sense of diplomacy that Kit told her privately was a hoot—Logan had a temper and he wasn't shy about showing it. He was only diplomatic when it suited him.

Her fifth day on the job, she and Kit went out to lunch together with Dane Lassiter's wife, Tess. Dane and Tess had a little boy and a little girl, and Tess seemed to regard both children as miracles. Later, Kit told her that Dane had been convinced that he couldn't have a child. Tess had loved him helplessly, obsessively, for years. It had taken an unexpected pregnancy and a near-tragedy to convince Dane that love was worth taking a chance on. Despite their stormy beginnings, the Lassiters were quite an item around town. It was rare to see one without the other, and they usually traveled as a family unit off the job.

Maggie got to meet Dane Lassiter that same day. The former Texas Ranger was tall and dark, not really a handsome man, but with an authority and self-confidence that were striking. There was just enough arrogance with it to make him attractive. He'd started out with the Houston Police, where he still had contacts and from which he'd garnered his first operatives when he opened the detective agency. One of his men and Cord had been police officers together in Houston.

When they got back to Logan's offices, Kit told Maggie that the Lassiters were working on a very hot and dangerous assignment—trying to shut down an international agency that was really a smuggler of human cargo. They didn't stop with illegal immigrants in the United States, either. The agency dealt in child slave labor in west Africa and South America, procuring young children to work in mines and on huge farms and ranches. They even dabbled in child pornography, with a branch office in Amsterdam. They literally sold children to a shady global corporation through the agency. Rumor had it that Raoul Gruber was the chief executive officer of the corporation—but it had been impossible to link him to it.

"Children being bought and sold like animals? You have got to be kidding!" Maggie exclaimed. "This is the twenty-first century!"

"I know," Kit said sadly. "But some horrible things happen in the world. While the news media harps on the latest political sex scandal, little children no older than six and seven are being peddled like raw meat. They're forced to work down mine shafts, in agricultural fields, on cattle ranches, doing dangerous work sometimes twelve and fourteen hours a day. There are no child labor laws in these rural places, and the children are considered expendable."

Maggie felt homicidal. "It's barbaric," she said with husky fury.

"I agree. That's why I'm so glad Dane took the case. He's coordinating with a whole shipload of federal agencies, including the INS, the NEA, Customs, the State Department and Interpol. The case has ties everywhere in the country, with a corporate network of field offices in several states." She hesitated. "One of them is in Miami," she added. "And Dane said that Cord's accident wasn't an accident at all. The man who's involved with the slave trafficking is an old enemy of Cord's who's newly linked to this labor operation. Cord knows things about him that he doesn't want uncovered."

Maggie's heart jumped. "Cord mentioned that I should watch my back," she said slowly. "He said an old enemy might even target me, but I didn't think much about it at the time."

"You'd better," Kit said. "You might tell Cord what we're investigating," she added. "Dane and his operatives will help keep an eye on you, just as they're watching me. If we can get enough evidence on this rat, we can put him away forever. But it's going to take time and patience. And a lot of caution."

"I won't see Cord to tell him anything," she replied in a subdued tone. "We aren't speaking right now."

"I'm sorry."

"Is there anything I can do to help you with the case?" Maggie asked. "My life is so dull and boring that even surveillance would be exciting right now."

The other woman laughed. "You wouldn't think so, if you'd ever had to do it. But I'll keep you in mind." She checked her watch. "Oops. Got to run or I'll be late for work. If I don't see you before you get off, have a nice weekend. Logan's very pleased with you. I guess you know that, though."

Maggie smiled. "I'm glad to hear it. I like my job a lot. I'm sorry I won't be permanent."

"That makes three of us," Kit said, and meant it.

When Maggie got to her hotel, there was a message waiting for her to phone Cord. She hesitated about doing it. She wasn't up to any more angry encounters with him. But she was still worried about him, now more than ever, since he'd told her about his old enemy deliberately targeting him. He could be in great danger. She couldn't bear the thought of anything happening to him. She was nervous about returning his phone call but she couldn't really resist it. He must have gotten over his anger at her.

She phoned the ranch. A man answered and a couple of minutes later, Cord came on the line.

"You left me a message to call you," she said formally.

He hesitated uncharacteristically. "Come out here for supper tonight," he replied.

The eyes he couldn't see, twinkled. She was surprised at his words. "Is that an invitation, or a royal command?"

He chuckled. "It's an invitation. We're having cherry pie for dessert," he added.

She sighed. "Hit me in my weak spot, why don't you?"

"I just did. Can't resist it, can you?"

She was tired and hungry but she did want to see him, so badly. "Okay. I'll get a cab out..."

"The hell you will. I'll drive in and get you. Fifteen minutes."

He hung up before she could argue any further.

She got out of her business suit and put on jeans and a neat short-sleeved red-and-white-striped shirt with a gray vest. It wasn't couture, but it looked good on her, outlining her slender body in a nice way.

She left her hair long, for Cord, and picked up a light sweater in case it got cool later in the evening. There was a cold front on the way and Texas could be cool in the evenings, even in spring.

While she waited for Cord, she thought about what Kit had told her, about Gruber and his interests, especially the remark about child pornography. She hated the very thought of children being exploited sexually. She hated people who would use innocence in such a way, only for profit. It made her furious out of all proportion.

Cord knocked on her door exactly fifteen minutes later. She went out to meet him and locked the door behind her.

He was in beige slacks and a sports shirt with a beige-and-brown patterned sports coat. He looked trendy and very handsome.

"I'm glad you didn't dress up," he said as they entered the elevator. He pushed the ground floor button and turned to study her in the deserted elevator. "We're just having chili and Mexican corn bread."

"And cherry pie." She wanted to make sure he didn't forget.

He held her eyes and smiled slowly. "Amy always made one

for your birthday, from scratch," he recalled. "It was one of the few times you really smiled. Amy said she didn't think you'd ever had a real birthday party in your whole young life."

"I hadn't." She clutched her purse and sweater close to her chest, and her eyes reflected the old sadness. "When my father died, all the laughter went out of my life. Then Mama let pneumonia take her out only two years later."

He scowled. This was news. "When you were eight," he guessed.

She lifted her face. "Why...no. When I was six."

"Then where did you go until Amy fostered you? Did you have grandparents?"

She shivered. "A stepfather." Her voice was low and soft and full of pain.

He started to ask another question when the elevator stopped. She got off ahead of him and headed toward the front, where the car was parked. He knew he wasn't being tailed, so he wasn't being cautious.

He followed along behind her. A stepfather. She'd apparently lived with him for two years before she'd come to Amy Barton's house. He was full of questions, but she'd closed up like a flower. It didn't take a mind reader to know that she wasn't going to answer any more questions right now. Her sharp glance told him so.

"How's the job hunt going?" he asked as they reached the expensive black sports car he drove.

"I'm working already," she said. "Logan Deverell hired me

to work for his investment firm, just temporarily. His wife, Kit, works for the Lassiter Detective Agency, in the same building. They say you know Dane."

"I do," he replied abruptly. He opened her door and helped her inside, before he went around and climbed in under the wheel.

But he didn't start the car immediately. He put an arm across the back of her seat and looked at her. "Lassiter deals in dangerous cases," he pointed out. "I don't like the idea of your working so close to him."

"You don't imagine that I care what you like?" she replied with a pleasant smile.

His jaw tautened as he stared at her, his thick eyebrows drawn together at the bridge of his nose. "I'm serious. Lassiter and his wife were involved in a shoot-out not too many years ago, right in his office. It's well-known that he takes on cases other detectives won't touch."

"I'm going to be in the same building with him, not in his office," she pointed out. "I do investment counseling, not detective work. Although, a change of careers is pretty tempting right now," she added to irritate him.

He was overreacting. He knew it, but he couldn't seem to help himself. Maggie's abrupt departure from the country had shaken him more than he'd realized at first. The thought of never seeing her again was unsettling. Involuntarily he reached out a lean hand and caught a strand of her long, dark hair between his fingers, testing its silkiness.

"Just being in Houston right now is dangerous for you," he said quietly. "You're walking into something I can't even tell you about."

Which she knew already, thanks to Kit. She didn't let on.

"I'm twenty-six," she pointed out, trying not to react to the feel of those sensuous fingers in her hair.

His eyes flashed up to meet hers. They were stormy, intimidating, full of secrets. "In some ways, you're unbelievably naive," he countered. "The world is a bad place. You've never seen how dark it can be."

She laughed without humor. "Do you think so?" she murmured with a strange look in her eyes.

He didn't understand her response to the statement. Maggie kept secrets. He wondered just how terrible they were. The two of them had never been confidants, because he wouldn't let her near him emotionally. He'd pushed her away, kept her at bay, all the long, lonely years. For the first time, he regretted it. Maggie had been the one person in the world who really cared about him. Because he was afraid of loss, he resisted close contact. But soon she could be half a world away, and there would never be another human being who shared his memories, his pain, his loneliness.

"You look sad," she remarked involuntarily.

He grimaced. "You're the only other person alive who remembers our time with Amy," he said slowly, "my brush with the law, Patricia's suicide, Amy's illness and death."

"All the bad memories," she remarked.

"No!" He met her eyes. "There were other things. Picnics.

Birthday parties. The time she brought home a model train set for Christmas—one we knew she had to have made sacrifices to buy because she didn't have much of her fortune left by then—and the shock on her face when you loved it as much as I did. We spent hours lying on the rug in the dark, watching the lighted train go around."

She smiled with memory. "Yes. And I helped you make the little scale buildings that went with it. You were out of school and in college then, just before you dropped out and went with the Houston Police. Amy was devastated. So was I," she added, dropping her eyes.

"You both thought I'd end up in a coffin after my first week," he scoffed.

"We should have known better. You were always thorough and methodical."

His eyes narrowed. "Except once. The night Amy died."

She jerked back away from him, her scalp stinging as he was forced to let go of her hair or risk hurting her more. She massaged the hurt place with her fingers, avoiding his eyes. "That was a long time ago."

"Did you ever sleep with your husband?" he asked unexpectedly.

She actually gasped. The question was so blunt that she couldn't believe what he'd just asked.

He studied her shocked face, rigid with distaste, for a long moment. "I didn't think so," he said after a minute. "His second wife in the divorce decree accused him of being impotent and abusive. He pretended to be an invalid, but there wasn't anything much wrong with him. Except extreme alcoholism, and a violent temper."

Maggie knew her face was white. "How...?"

"I went down to the courthouse and researched him," he said. His expression grew hard. "He had a history of arrests for drunkenness and at least two for domestic abuse. Did you know that when you married him?"

Her jaw clenched, but her lips were trembling. She averted her gaze to the windshield. Memories flooded her mind, sickening memories. "Please, don't," she choked.

"Did he hit you, Maggie?" he demanded.

Her hand reached for the door handle automatically. She was halfway out when he pulled her gently back inside and closed the door again. The position he was in, his body close to hers, his chest at an angle above her, made her tremble.

He looked down into her wide eyes at such proximity that she could see the black rims around his very dark brown corneas. She could see the thick, straight, short lashes on his eyelids. She could smell the coffee on his breath and the clean scent of his body and clothes.

"I never understood why you married him," he continued, his eyes narrowing as they searched hers. "You had nothing in common and he was twenty years your senior. It was quick, too—less than a month after Amy's death, and one of your coworkers said you barely knew him. Everybody thought it was for his money. He was rich."

"I can't...I won't...talk about him," she choked. "Cord, please...!"

He felt her hand pushing against his chest, but he ignored it. "You said he cost you something precious. What?"

Her gaze fell to his wide, hard mouth, to the chiseled look of it with perfect white teeth barely visible in its parting. She remembered the feel of it on hers. Even the memory of pain and embarrassment didn't ease the hunger for it. She wondered if he knew?

He did. He felt the quick rush of her breath at his mouth. He could see the hammer of her pulse at the collar of her shirt. He could feel the coldness of her perfectly manicured fingers through his shirt. She wanted him. That, at least, had never ebbed.

His fingers went to her chin and traced the skin next to her lips. "And here we are again," he whispered. He bent, his mouth poised above her parted lips. He hung there, his fingers maddening on the corner of her mouth, on her lower lip, where they touched in sensuous little tracings.

She moaned helplessly. She bit the sound off almost as it exited her throat, but she knew he heard it.

His nose brushed against hers as he felt the softness of her lips under his fingertips. She was still perfect to him, the most perfect woman he'd ever known, physically, mentally, emotionally. He couldn't get within two feet of her without having her draw him like a magnet. He was helpless. He hated it.

"Cord," she groaned, stretching up toward him, enticing his mouth. Her fingers went into the thick hair above his ears and dug into his scalp, pleading for more than the sensual torture he was offering her. The clean, spicy scent of him was in her nostrils, the soft warm whip of his breath teasing her parted lips. She ached to have that hard mouth crush down on hers and drive her mad with pleasure!

He moved closer. His chest pressed down against hers involuntarily. He could feel her full breasts against him, feel the hard tips biting into his chest even through two layers of fabric. Her mouth taunted his, followed it, lifted to tempt it into coming closer. He drank in the fragrance of roses that clung to her and felt himself caving in. He needed to hold her. He needed to kiss her. He couldn't help it. He had to...!

The sudden opening of car doors close by jerked him back from Maggie. He saw three men getting out of a sedan a few parking spaces away, giving them amused looks.

He got back under the steering wheel without looking at her again. He started the car and put it into gear, ignoring the glances of the three men on their way toward the hotel.

Maggie's hands were shaking. She wanted to scream and throw things. This was the second time she'd let him torment her physically. And had she fought, protested, dragged herself away, dared him to touch her? Of course not. She'd melted into him the minute he touched her. Great self-control, girl, she told herself with silent contempt. Really great!

He didn't look at her until they were out of town on the road that led to his ranch. She was more composed now, but she still looked devastated. He couldn't blame her. He felt the same way. He didn't want to be attracted to her, but he was. He always had been. But the older he got, the more uncontrollable it was.

"Don't beat yourself to death over it," he said carelessly. "Maybe we've both spent too much time alone lately."

"June will be shocked to hear that!"

He chuckled at the sting in her tone. He gave her a wry glance. "She's dating a corporal with the police department," he drawled. "Her father likes him, but he thinks she's too young to marry. She doesn't agree."

She raised both eyebrows. She didn't say a word.

He grimaced. "I was furious because you waited four days to come and see me, to see if the blindness was permanent," he said.

It wasn't much of an explanation, but she understood. June was a cutting tool he'd used on her heart. He wasn't certain that she was jealous of him, but he thought she'd be hurt if he threw another woman in her face. She was. It was chilling that he knew her that well. On the other hand, he'd admitted that she could hurt him, as well. It was a milestone in their stormy relationship.

He glanced at her as he turned down the long driveway with painted white fences on both sides.

"Amazing, isn't it?" he mused. "I never have to explain anything to you."

"That works both ways." She turned her eyes toward the old fighting bull in the pasture on her side of the car. "Maybe it's some sort of mental shorthand."

"Maybe it's ESP," he murmured dryly.

"Someday we'll have to find out if it works across oceans," she replied smartly.

That stung. She probably knew it. "Why do you have to leave the country?" he asked quietly.

"I told you. I'm twenty-six. I want to do something adventurous while I can do it without leaning on a cane."

"Adventure isn't what it's cut out to be," he told her.

"Davy Crockett wouldn't agree with you," she informed him. "Neither would Jim Bowie, or George Custer, or Crazy Horse or Pancho Villa or Genghis Khan."

He pursed his lips. "You certainly covered all walks of life with that group."

She chuckled.

"Why don't you move out here with me?" he asked out of the blue. "You can learn the cattle business. We could play with the train sets in our spare time. I've got a whole room dedicated to them, complete with buildings and tunnels, mountains and even running water for trestles to go over."

She turned her purse in her hands and hated the invitation. He was inviting his foster sister to move in. Nothing more.

He pulled up in the driveway that circled at the front door and cut off the engine. He turned to her with narrowed eyes. "You want me," he said bluntly. "I know it. I want you. You know that, too. But nothing will ever come of it unless you want it to. I made a vicious mistake with you once because I was out of my mind with grief and alcohol. I never make the same mistake twice. You'll be safe here."

"That's an interesting choice of words," she replied slowly. "Safe from your old enemy, you mean."

His chin lifted. "From him, and from me, Maggie," he replied. "I won't make you afraid of me. Not in any way."

She laughed mirthlessly. "I've been afraid of you for years, in between attacks of helpless attraction," she said matter-of-factly. "There has to be a cure somewhere. If I go far enough, maybe I can find it."

It was a confession, of sorts. He rested one arm over the steering wheel and studied her sadly. "All we have left," he said softly, "is each other."

Her eyes flew to his. She was pale, confused, uneasy. She frowned. "Don't do that," she said irritably. "Don't make it sound like you need me. You never have and you never will. I'm a memory adjunct. That's all I'll ever be."

"Our lives are intertwined. You can't break an eighteen-year bond just like that," he pointed out. "Some marriages don't last a fraction that long."

The word froze her. She averted her face.

"It wasn't an insult," he said at once, misunderstanding her reaction. "Your husband wasn't good to you. You had every reason not to want to remember him."

"I have more reason than you'll ever know," she said without meeting his speculative gaze. "Happy marriages are a fairy tale."

"Dane Lassiter wouldn't agree with you," he mused. "Neither would your friend Kit."

She shrugged. "They got lucky."

"You don't think you could?"

She rubbed at a spot on her purse. "I don't ever want to marry again."

He hesitated. "Maggie, don't you want children someday?"

The question sent her gaze flying up to meet his. The pain, the anguish, the haunted look in them shocked him.

She opened the door and got out.

He followed, determined to find out why she looked that way, when Red Davis sped up the driveway and stopped even with Cord.

"The irrigation equipment's up and running like a track star, boss," he called with a grin. "And they promised to replace any part that misfires again!"

"Good work."

"Thanks! How are you doing, Maggie?" he called to her with a big grin.

Cord's eyes flashed. "I don't pay you to flirt with my foster sister," he shot at the younger man, and he wasn't teasing.

Davis saw that. He cut his losses, waved and shot off again down the ranch road.

Cord's attitude puzzled Maggie. It was oddly like jealousy. But that was an outlandish assumption. It would take a miracle to get Cord jealous of her.

He led the way through the living room, where she left her purse, and into the dining room. Four places were set at the table, and an older white-haired man was occupying one of them while June put dishes of food on it.

"Hi!" she called to Maggie. "I hope you like chili and Mexican corn bread."

"Love them. And there's supposed to be a cherry pie?" she added hopefully.

June grinned, with a glance at Cord. "Oh, I heard somebody had a passion for it. I'm famous for my cherry pie. You can even have vanilla ice cream on it, if you like. It's homemade, too," she added.

Maggie smiled at her. "I think I've died and gone to heaven!"

The meal was pleasant. Maggie liked June's father, who was a veteran cowboy. He was good company, and he had a hatful of funny stories about places he'd worked. One involved his breaking a mustang on a West Texas ranch. The wild critter had jumped the corral fence, with him hanging on, just as the boss's wife drove up in her brand-new blue Cadillac convertible. Seconds later, the horse was sitting in the backseat.

Maggie almost fell over. "What did you do?" she exclaimed.

"Picked myself up off the ground and ran for my life. I jumped in my old truck and took off, without even asking for my week's wages." He shook his head. "The awful thing was that I met the man again a few years back, when I was working at a ranch outside San Antonio. It turns out he and his wife were already having problems, but when she pitched that fit, he divorced her. He said he'd laughed about me and that mustang for years."

"Serves you right for running away," June quipped.

He chuckled. "It surely did. I haven't run from anything much since then. But I was eighteen years old and new to cowboying at the time. Sort of like Red Davis is now."

Cord's eyes glittered. "Davis is a pain in the neck. If he wasn't so good with equipment and inventory, he'd already be a memory."

Darren Travis chuckled. "Well, he's pretty good with horses, too. And don't forget that he talked that newspaper reporter out of doing a story on your stint with the FBI."

"I could have talked him out of it," Cord said curtly.

"Yes," Travis said, clearing his throat. "But Red did it without using his fists."

"Asset or not, he'd better watch his step."

Maggie ate her chili quietly, listening to the byplay with amusement but without commenting. She noticed June giving her curious looks, followed by curious looks at Cord. Maggie wondered what June had noticed that she hadn't.

Cord could have told her, although he wouldn't. Davis had paid just a little too much attention to Maggie. Cord didn't like it. Until now, Davis had been one of his favorite employees.

"Cord said you were a widow," Travis said suddenly, smiling at Maggie over his chili spoon. "Wasn't your husband Bart Evans from Houston?"

Maggie stiffened. "Yes."

"Dad..." June said abruptly, trying to ward off trouble.

Her father waved a hand at her. "I'm not being nosy, but I knew him, is why I mentioned it. That was when he was living with his second wife," he recalled, totally oblivious to the discomfort he was causing Maggie. He sighed, fingering his spoon. "Her name was Dana," he added with a faint smile. "She was pretty and sweet, never hurt a living soul." His face hardened. "He put her in the hospital."

Cord actually flinched. He knew Maggie had gone rigid. He scowled at Travis. "He did what?"

Travis winced when he saw the turmoil he was responsible for in his dinner companions. "Gosh, I'm sorry! I didn't think..."

"He put his wife in the hospital?" Cord was relentless. "How?"

Travis sent an apologetic glance at Maggie, who was white and totally without appetite now. "He beat her senseless because she burned the bacon," he continued. "It wasn't the first time, but it was when she finally confessed it. I made her tell a police officer, and her husband was arrested and charged with domestic abuse. He denied it, of course, and then he apologized to Dana and tried to get her to come back to him," he added angrily. "But I wasn't having that. Men who abuse women don't stop. I took her to a good lawyer and we convinced her to file for divorce. She wouldn't even take a settlement. She was such a good person." He put down his chili spoon with painful deliberation. "She had a stroke two months later that left her paralyzed on one side and unable to function alone ever again. They said it was probably from the beating she took, but nobody could prove it. He had a great lawyer."

Cord felt sick to his stomach. He'd suspected Evans might have hit his second wife. He'd never suspected that sort of violence. And what had Maggie gone through? He stared at her with muted anger. She'd never told him anything about this, and she certainly knew about it.

"I'm sorry," Maggie told Travis unexpectedly. "I know that she's still in the nursing home."

Travis's intake of breath was audible. "You do?"

She nodded. "When my husband...died—" she almost choked on the word "—I had his estate split between his two ex-wives. There was more than enough to keep Dana in comfort for the rest of her life—even enough to hire the best specialists in stroke management. I don't guess you know that she can speak now, and she's relearning other skills as well—reading and writing, too. I don't know that she'd remember you, but I imagine she'd enjoy company. She has no family."

Cord was shocked. He'd not only just learned what Maggie had done with her wealthy late husband's fortune, but even more surprising news.

"You go to see her?" Cord asked.

She nodded. "Frequently. From what was left of his estate, after I split it between his ex-wives, I funded an outreach program for abused wives that helps them with money to finish their education or learn a technical trade."

"Good out of evil," Travis said, and his eyes warmed as he looked at Maggie. "You're a winner, Miss Barton. A real winner."

"It was a way of making amends for him. Maybe he wasn't

a bad person when he started out in life," she said. "Some people just snap, in different ways. He had a drinking problem that he wouldn't admit." She shrugged. "Later it turned to a drug problem he wouldn't admit. He was self-destructive."

"He was a potential murderer," Cord said coldly, without knowing how close to the truth he really was.

Maggie didn't look at him. She couldn't afford to let him see how accurate that guess was.

"He was," Travis agreed surprisingly. "Dana told me that his first wife had a hip injury from a beating that left her crippled, as well. She moved out of state to get away from him."

Maggie smiled. "I found her in Florida. She was working in a home for elderly women and coaching a volunteer baseball team at the facility. It was a real hit. She can't run, but she can still bat." She glanced shyly at Cord. "She's using her share of the money to found a baseball camp of her own for retired people. I hear she's got an ex-vice-president and two ex-governors on one team."

Everybody laughed. But Cord was looking at her with different eyes. This was a facet of Maggie that she'd never let him see. She did her good works without telling anybody. He'd always assumed that she lived on her inheritance from her late husband. It had come as a surprise to find her having to work for a living at all. Amy had left them a little money, but she'd lost the bulk of her fortune to bad investments long before she'd died. He'd often wondered if that wasn't why Maggie chose investment as a career.

Now he could see how caring a person she really was. Bart Evans had left an estate worth a fortune. He couldn't imagine a woman who would willingly give up that kind of money out of the goodness of her heart. Until now.

"She went through enough, like poor Dana did, to deserve something good in her life," Travis said, watching Maggie. "But you kept nothing for yourself. Why?"

Maggie lifted her coffee cup in numb hands and sipped at the cooling liquid. "I wanted nothing of his."

Travis's eyes narrowed. "Your memories must be pretty bad, too."

She didn't answer. She didn't look at him. But her fingers trembled as she put her cup down. Something exploded inside Cord.

He tossed his napkin down impatiently, got to his feet and pulled Maggie to hers. "You can have your cherry pie later. I want to talk to you," he said, nodding to the others as he took her hand and led her away to his office.

He closed the door behind them, glaring at her. "Why do I constantly have to learn things about you from strangers?" he demanded. "You couldn't tell me that the rat was abusing you? I'd have mopped the floor with him!"

"From Africa?" she asked deliberately. "From the Middle East? From Central America? And exactly how would I have found you to tell you? And why would you have listened? You hated me!"

It was a painful question. His conscience had driven him

clear of the States after Amy's funeral. He couldn't even face Maggie, remembering what had happened between them.

He turned, with his hands rammed deep into his slacks' pockets. "Eb could have found me," he said dully.

"I can handle my own problems, Cord, whether you think so or not," she replied. She perched herself on the thick arm of a leather chair. "I'd already started divorce proceedings when Bart...crashed his car. I did them from the hospital..." She stopped at once, but it was too late.

His eyes flashed at her from the window. "The hospital?"

She bit her lower lip, hard. "All right. I was his third victim. But it was only the one time," she added firmly. "And he knew as soon as he'd done it that I'd go after him with everything I had. I told him so, even before the ambulance came!" Her face looked odd, full of hatred and outrage. "I called my attorney and the police, in that order, and I had a call in to Eb," she confessed, averting her eyes.

That irritated him. "Why to Eb and not me?"

Because Eb would have known where to find Cord, and she'd wanted him at that moment, wanted someone to share her pain and grief and anger. But it had taken Eb a while to phone back. By then, she'd come to her senses. She told him only that she'd had an accident and didn't want him to find out and contact Cord, because it was a minor one. She'd lied her head off, then and now. She was tired of lies, but afraid to let Cord know the truth. It would serve no purpose now, except to hurt him. She couldn't do that.

"He was afraid of you," she recalled quietly. "I think that was why he ran."

He moved close to her, staring down into her eyes intently. "Keep going," he coaxed when she stopped.

She shrugged. "He got in his car and took off as soon as the ambulance picked me up. He was drinking heavily. He ran his car into a telephone pole doing ninety. It was instantly fatal."

"And no great loss," he replied tersely. "All this time, and you never said a word!"

"The past is the past, Cord," she told him, her eyes searching over his face like loving hands. "You've had tragedies enough of your own, without adding my problems to them. I'm an adult. I have to be responsible for myself."

His face clenched. "Is that what you think? That I'm too wrapped up in myself to care what happens to you?"

"I'm just a stray kid that Amy Barton picked up," she replied. "No relation to you. None at all."

That hurt. It really hurt. He was picturing Maggie being beaten to her knees, badly enough to send her to the hospital, by a drunken man, and no one to protect her. He hated the thought of Bart Evans. He wanted, so badly, to go back in time and be less selfish. If he'd stayed in Houston, instead of running off to lick his wounds, Maggie could have been spared that anguish. He'd failed her. And it wasn't the first time.

"He'd never have touched you if I'd been in town," he said coldly.

She lowered her eyes to her lap. If he'd been in town, and learned the truth, he'd have killed Bart Evans. It was better that he never knew.

"It cured me of wanting to get married, at least," she said whimsically.

"What a waste," he said without thinking.

She looked up, surprised.

He wasn't smiling. He looked sad. "What a hell of a life you've had," he murmured. "And I have a feeling that I don't know the half of it."

Her flush of color told him that he'd guessed accurately. He wondered just how many terrible secrets she was keeping.

"You don't trust me with secrets, do you?" he asked, frowning.

She closed up. "You have enough of your own. I don't share mine." She stood up. "I want my cherry pie."

He caught her by the waist as she started past him. "Not yet. Evans must have had a reason for hitting you, no matter how drunk he was. What was it?"

Her heart ran away. She could still picture his furious face when he realized that Cord was responsible for her condition. He was outraged, infuriated, ready to kill her.

Her eyes were shadowed, full of pain. Bart had told her what he was going to do to her, and that she'd never disgrace him. He was going to eliminate this problem! And he'd hit her, and hit her, finally knocking her violently down over the stair railing and into a marble table. She'd fought back, for all the good it did her. But when she hit the table, breaking it, and felt the agonizing, twisting pain in her belly, she knew what he'd done. She'd screamed at him, threatened him with what was going to happen when Cord knew. He wasn't so drunk that he didn't remember who Cord was, and what he did for a living. He'd managed to dial the emergency number and waited only until a weeping, moaning Maggie was carried off to the hospital until he'd packed a bag and gotten into his luxury car for a rushed trip out of town. It had ended in his own death. Maggie had her own grief to face.

"You look as if the memories are killing you," Cord remarked, bringing her back to the present. He drew her closer. "Talk to me. Tell me."

Her sad eyes met his and she shook her head. "It's all over."

His thumbs moved lazily against her rib cage while he watched her reaction to his touch. "You like me to touch you," he murmured quietly. "I don't know how I went so many years without noticing. Or maybe I just didn't want to notice."

She pulled against his hands, to no avail. "I'm leaving the country very soon," she pointed out, hating the breathless sound of her voice. "You won't ever have to notice anything again."

"I'll be completely alone," he said solemnly. "So will you."

Her face tautened. "I've always been alone," she said in a husky tone. "Let me go."

He caught the hands that pressed into his chest and guided them up around his neck. She shivered and tried to pull away. His arms encircled her and captured her there, against him.

"No you don't," he said softly. "It's time we both came to terms with this."

She was panicking. It was in her eyes. "I don't want to come to terms with anything! I just want to go!"

He scowled, all too aware that he was aroused and she knew it, and that her hips were straining violently away from his.

"You're afraid of me," he whispered, shattered.

She bit her lower lip hard. "I'm afraid of any man, this close, especially you!" she blurted out, visible tears stinging her eyes. "Oh, please, let me go!"

He allowed her to move back to what she considered a decent proximity, but he wouldn't let go completely. "It couldn't have been that one night with me that made you this way," he said, thinking aloud. "Because you've always worn clothes that showed nothing of your body. You dress like an old woman to go to bed. You don't even flirt—except one time when we went out to dinner together and ran into Eb Scott. And you only did that to irritate me."

"I never understood why you asked me out at all. You'd only just gotten back into the country."

He reached out and slid his hand against her cheek, caressing it. "It was an impulse," he said softly. "I wanted to see if marriage had changed you. It had, but not in the way I expected. You were even more tense and nervous than before. Now I understand why."

She met his gaze. "No, you don't," she said abruptly.

He bent unexpectedly and put his mouth against her eyelids,

closing them. She shivered, once, and then she relaxed, letting him draw her close. He kissed her eyebrows, running his tongue softly along them, and then he kissed her cheeks, working his way up her nose and over to her eyes again. It was the most tender caress she'd felt in her whole life. It shocked her into submission, when submission had been the very last thing on her mind.

His hands slid up her back and into the thick wealth of her long hair. "I love long hair," he breathed against her temple. "You know it."

Her hands curled into the thick hair behind his head, short and cool in her fingers. Her body was on fire with unsatisfied hungers that she hadn't felt in years, not since the night Amy had died and, at first, she'd vibrated with delicious unknown sensations when he started touching her.

The memory made her uncertain and she stiffened again.

He lifted his head to look down into her frightened eyes. "I was drunk," he said very gently, because he knew what she was remembering. "No man should ever touch a woman in that condition. I wasn't brutal to you, but I hurt you, just the same, because I was out of control."

Her eyes were wide and uncertain and strangely curious.

"You don't understand," he murmured, reading it in her face. "A man has to control his desire long enough to arouse the woman he's with, Maggie," he said gently. "It takes longer for a woman to feel the things a man does, especially when it's her first time."

She flushed a little, but she didn't look away.

"Your body didn't reject me, but you were tense and embarrassed and I went too fast," he said with a frown. "I remember thinking how odd it was that your body didn't feel virginal even if your reactions were those of an innocent."

She closed her eyes and hated her past. She hadn't known that a man could tell that.

He stared at her with growing suspicion. A woman who had been abused as a child...

She tugged at his arms, breaking his train of thought.

"No," he said softly, pulling her back. He tilted her face up to his. His eyes were smoldering, intent on her mouth. "I should have done this years ago," he murmured as he bent. "I kissed you when we were younger, but I barely brushed your mouth with mine. This time," he whispered huskily, "I'm going to do a hell of a lot more...!"

She waited, breathless, for him to suddenly change his mind, for car doors to slam, for something to interrupt the sensual haze he'd caressed her into.

Nothing did. His fingers cupped her chin and his hard mouth settled slowly, gently, firmly, on her parted lips.

It was like no time before. She felt the very texture of his lips as they moved softly over her mouth, teasing, tasting, lifting. It was as if he were sketching her mouth with a fine sable brush. She went very still as he seduced her mouth with slow, skillful caresses.

She felt his thumb working at the corner of her mouth,

testing its softness as he kissed it, enjoying its texture, its slow response.

He nibbled her lower lip with his teeth, smiling when she lifted toward him for the first time.

"That's it," he whispered. His lips worked their way between hers and he hesitated, his breath coming quickly at her moist lips. "Open it, little one," he whispered. "Open it. Let me inside..."

The words, unfamiliar, deep and sensual, did something unexpected to her body. She felt heat shoot through her. She felt all her defenses fall. She arched up toward him, opening her lips.

She felt his arms slowly lift, riveting her to his hips. She felt his excitement, but she didn't protest the intimacy. It was drugging, to feel him wanting her, to taste the heat and power of his hard mouth as it explored hers deeply.

Even that terrible night, at first, there hadn't been this slow, drugging intimacy that made her want to feel his mouth on her body, his hands on her bare skin. The depth of her hunger shocked her. She'd never known desire, except for brief, infrequent tastes when she was with Cord. This was an adventure in the world of the senses, a slow banquet of tasting and touching.

She wasn't even aware that her fingers were on the hem of his knit shirt, or that he was lifting away to coax them under it. She moved her hands quickly up to the thick pelt of hair that covered his warm muscular chest. She felt him gasp against her mouth when she buried her fingers in it.

She drew back, uncertain.

His face was hard, his cheekbones flushed, his mouth swollen from the long, intimate contact with hers. "I like it," he said in a husky tone. "Wait." He dragged the shirt over his head and threw it aside. He didn't even look to see where it landed before he pulled her hands back to his body and guided them against it. His whole body throbbed, vibrated, from this almost innocent love play.

"Don't be afraid," he whispered, as he bent back to her mouth. "I'd cut off my arm before I'd hurt you again!"

She felt that, in the tenderness of his touch, in the exquisite caress of his mouth on her lips.

She gave in to the moment, refusing to think of the past or the future. Even if it was all she could ever have, she could have this. She reached up to him and lifted her body against his until they were riveted together at the hips. He groaned harshly and bent quickly to lift her.

She felt him moving, felt the shock of his steps against her body as he carried her to the chaise longue and draped her over it. He slid alongside her, his mouth under her shirt as his fingers worked at buttons and catches. She felt him shiver faintly as his lips moved onto the soft skin of her breast.

But just as he pushed the bra out of his way, she felt a skirl of fear, and she caught it to her breast, refusing to let go.

He wasn't angry. He only smiled. He bent again and his lips opened, smoothing over the soft skin above the bra's edge. She caught her breath when she felt his tongue there, too.

There was something she was supposed to do. She couldn't remember what it was. His lips trespassed farther and farther and she arched up, pulling the fabric out of the way of his mouth. It felt, oh, so good! She wanted it lower. She wanted his mouth to cover that tiny hardness that ached, that throbbed, that hurt, for his touch. She wanted him to kiss it...

She felt his laughter ripple against her breast. She didn't realize that she was speaking aloud, or that her sudden weakness increased his strength, his virility.

"You make me feel ten feet tall," he whispered against her skin. His hand slid along her rib cage, feeling the undulating motion of her body that was trying so hard to coax his mouth lower.

She moaned with pure frustration, out of her senses with the single-minded pursuit of pleasure. She couldn't believe what she was feeling with him. It was unimaginable, with her past.

He lifted his head and looked right down into her wide, frustrated eyes. "Do you want me to suckle you?" he whispered sensuously.

"Yes!" she moaned, beyond pride, beyond embarrassment. Her body twisted up toward him. "Oh, Cord, please, please...!"

He touched her mouth gently, his heart bursting with her headlong response, with her hunger for him, despite the past when he'd hurt her.

"I would do," he whispered huskily, "anything for you. Anything!"

He bent to her body, tugging the bra out of her nerveless

hands to dash it and the shirt and vest onto the floor beside them. His face was intent with pleasure, with need. He touched her firm, pretty breast with its rosy little crown as if it fascinated him. Then he bent with a faint groan, and covered it tenderly with his lips.

He heard her helpless cry of pleasure as he began to suckle her, his tongue working hard against the nipple, the rough pressure dragging a shocked little sound from her throat.

She lifted to his mouth, arched her body to hold him, tempt him there.

"Is it good?" he whispered huskily.

"Yes...!" Her voice broke on the words. "Yes...!" She pressed her mouth deeply into his throat, opening it, tasting his skin in a throbbing hot silence. "Please...don't... stop!"

He laughed hoarsely. "I don't know if I could," he whispered roughly as he bent to her body again.

When his mouth finally lifted and moved to cover hers, she met it hungrily, her arms dragging him down to her.

He was lost. He pressed roughly between her long legs in the jeans, his body throbbing, aching, as he moved against her in a helpless parody of intimacy. She shivered and sobbed and clung as he kissed her. Just a little longer, just a little longer, just a little...!

He felt her body thrusting up at his and he realized almost too late what was happening. He groaned out loud and suddenly dragged his body away from hers. He flung his legs off the divan and bent forward, with his elbows propped on his knees and his head in his hands. He shuddered again and again with fierce pain.

Maggie sat up, too, her bare breasts pressing to his bare back. "Cord," she whispered dazedly.

"Don't touch me!" he exploded, thrusting her away while he still could.

He dragged himself to his feet, still shivering as he went to the liquor cabinet behind his desk and poured whiskey into a glass with shaking hands.

Maggie was scrambling back into her clothes, horrified and sickened at her behavior. She could hear voices from her past, accusing voices, whispered voices, disgusted voices. She was no better than a streetwalker. She'd heard them say that. She'd heard them whisper that. And at her age…!

She got to her feet, wide-eyed, shaking. She ran for the door and went through it while Cord was still trying to recover from what had happened.

She'd forgotten her purse, but it didn't matter, she wasn't going back for it. She went out the door and sat down on the porch, hoping nobody had seen or heard what was going on in that room. How could she ever face Cord again? She was devastated!

Even as she was thinking it, the front door opened, and he came out onto the porch. He stopped as he saw her sitting on the swing with her arms tightly around herself.

She saw his long, powerful legs in front of her, and the

shiny polish of his black tooled leather boots. She didn't look up. She couldn't. She was too ashamed. Now he had a good reason to hate her.

5

But the disgust, the anger, that Maggie had expected didn't come. Cord sat down beside her and slid an arm behind her. He stared at her until she lifted her shamed face and met his eyes. They weren't angry, or disgusted. They were quiet, curious. They were kind.

"We need to have a long talk about the dangers of heavy petting," he said with a faint smile.

She colored furiously and averted her face again.

"Maggie, you didn't commit a cardinal sin," he said gently. "Will you please stop looking like a whipped child?"

She felt the tears falling down her cheeks without realizing it until she heard his shocked breath and felt his arms catching her up, lifting her onto his lap. He held her gently, smoothing her hair, until the sobs lessened.

"I don't have a handkerchief," he remarked ruefully, using his fingers to loosen the last stray tears from her eyelashes.

"Neither do I." She fumbled in her pocket and found a paper towel she'd stuck there that morning after using it to dry her hands. Amazing foresight, she thought miserably as she mopped herself up.

He rocked the swing into motion, watching her lie exhausted in his arms. "I feel like a teenager," he murmured.

She glared up at him from red eyes. "Don't you ever do that again!" she raged from hurt embarrassment.

He touched her soft mouth. "Spoilsport," he murmured softly, and he smiled.

She flushed, lowering her eyes to his chest. That reminded her of how they'd been, just at the last, and she moved her gaze beyond him to the pastures.

He held her down and kept swinging. He shook his head, staring out at the grazing red-coated cattle in his pasture. "I don't know why I ever thought you were experienced," he said.

"My private life is none of your business!" she muttered.

"Then why did you let me take off your bra?" he asked reasonably.

She hit his chest with a tight little fist. He caught it, chuckling, and unfolded it, pressing it into his knit shirt. He stretched and exhaled, his face more relaxed than she ever remembered seeing it.

"I have to go back to town," she said tautly.

"We haven't had dessert," he returned. "You can have cherry pie and homemade vanilla ice cream and coffee when your eyes look normal again."

She knew what he meant, they were probably swollen and fiery red, as they always became when she cried.

Cord was getting a picture of her that bore no resemblance to the woman he thought he knew. There was something sexual in her past, but not a pleasant memory, and long ago, maybe in childhood. If she'd spent two years with a stepfather, God knew what she might have endured as a little girl. It made him sick to remember his own treatment of her during their one intimacy.

"Do you still ride?" he asked lazily.

"I haven't, in years."

He smoothed his fingers over her long, pink fingernails. "You've toned the polish down, haven't you?" he murmured absently. "You used to wear red on your nails all the time."

"Pink lasts longer," she replied.

"You can come back tomorrow," he continued. "We can go riding in the morning."

She wondered if she wouldn't do better to join the Peace Corps in the morning! It was easier when he hated her. Now she was faced with the choice of running again or being seduced into a sexual relationship with him. She wasn't ready for that. She might never be.

He noticed her lack of response to the suggestion, and her worried look. He tipped her face up to his. "I won't seduce you," he said at once. "That's a promise."

Her lower lip trembled. She dragged her eyes down to his collar.

His chest rose and fell against her. He smoothed down her long hair worriedly. She was fragile like this. She was vulnerable in a way he'd never dreamed she could be. It was a shock to see a strong, independent, fiery woman like Maggie reduced to absolute submission in a man's arms. Especially, he thought, in his arms.

He drew her close, resting his cheek against the hair at her temple while the swing rocked back and forth, its chains making a rhythmic metallic sound. Cattle lowed in the distance, and he heard dogs bark—probably his nearest neighbors'. They barked at most everything. The sound was oddly comforting in the early evening. It was growing dark. He heard crickets and birds humming around them, while the scent of honeysuckle and jasmine settled on the heavy, humid night air.

"You've got fireflies everywhere," she murmured, watching the insects emit brief green flashes as they flew among the flowers and the trees near the porch.

"Remember when you used to catch them in a mason jar with holes in the lid?" he mused.

She laughed softly. "And Amy made me let them go. She couldn't bear to see anything shut up, even an insect. But they were pretty."

"They're prettier flying around," he chided.

She curled her fingers into the soft fabric of his shirt. She was helpless when he held her. She should resent it, she told herself, but all she could manage was delighted happiness.

His fingers curled into hers. His cheek moved against her soft, cool hair. "I don't think I ever sat and held you like this, did I?"

"When I was nine," she recalled. "The neighbor's cat, the one they had declawed, bit my arm. I squalled and cried, and you picked me up and rocked me until Amy got home."

"I'd forgotten."

"Of course," she said without rancor. "It wasn't important."

But it was to her, because she remembered. He wondered how often he'd hurt her with his indifference over the years. It was beginning to dawn on him how deeply her feelings went, especially after what had just happened in his study.

"We could go riding tomorrow," he repeated.

She hesitated. "I have a lot of paperwork to get through," she said finally. "But thanks anyway."

He lifted his head and looked down into her face. "You're going to take a long step back and refuse any invitation I make from now on," he guessed accurately. "Then you're going to get out of the country as fast as you can, so that you don't suffer another lapse of willpower with me. Does that about cover it?"

"In a nutshell," she confessed, because it was useless to lie now.

He traced her small shell-like ear. "Running away isn't the answer."

"I won't be your mistress," she said curtly. "Just in case the idea had occurred to you."

"It hadn't," he replied with equal bluntness. His face was solemn, thoughtful. "Something happened to you, something traumatic," he continued. "You can't even talk about it. I should have been more perceptive. And I should never have touched you when I'd been drinking. It makes me sick to think of the damage I did to you that night."

Her eyebrows arched. She hadn't expected regrets—not from him. He'd never acted as if he were sorry. In fact, he'd blamed her for the whole sordid mess.

"Yes, I know," he mused, as if he read the thoughts right in her mind. "I blamed it on you. I hated myself. I couldn't even bear to think of what I'd done, and to someone who'd always given me comfort and affection."

"You never said that."

He shrugged. "How could I? Pride is an obstacle to most apologies. I had more than my share. It was tough being a Spanish kid in an American city. I didn't fit in anywhere at first."

"I didn't remember that," she said suddenly.

"You didn't even notice that I was foreign," he returned. "You appropriated me the first day we were together. You were fluent in Spanish, even at the age of eight. You never said where you learned it."

"From my mother," she replied. "Her mother was from Sonora, in Mexico." She smiled. "And her mother's mother was one of the women who traveled with the revolutionaries under Pancho Villa during the Mexican revolution! Mama had a picture of her grandmother, wrapped in ammunition belts and carrying a carbine!"

He was pleasantly surprised. "One of my father's great-uncles fought with Villa," he recalled. "His son still breeds fighting bulls. He lives north of Málaga, in Andalusia. He's my cousin."

"I never thought how hard it must have been for you here, at first," she recalled. "You always seemed mature beyond your years, and you were never afraid of anything."

He smiled. "Neither were you. Well, maybe of biting cats," he added, teasing.

She laughed. "And snakes," she said.

He traced her thin eyebrows lazily. "You were an odd child," he recalled. "At times, you seemed five years older than your actual age. And you never seemed to like boys." He pursed his lips. "Except me," he added tauntingly.

"You were close to hand, and you always protected me," she pointed out.

"You protected me, as well," he said, and he didn't smile. "I didn't like it very much at the time, but it was hard to miss. Sometimes I felt like a possession."

She studied an undone button at his collar. "You were the only security I had. In fact, you were the only security I'd ever known. I felt so safe with you, as if nobody could ever hurt me again as long as you were near."

"Then I married Patricia and you got involved with that wild-eyed artist," he said, scowling.

"He was gay," she blurted out. "Mannie was one of the best friends I ever had. He taught me to take life at face value and never run from trouble." She frowned sadly. "He got AIDs and nobody would touch him. I used to visit him at the nursing home, just so I could hug him. You can't catch it that way, you know, and sick people miss human contact the most of everything. But most people are scared to get close." She smiled. "I remember newsreels of Mother Teresa handing an AIDs infected child to a businessman and how terrified he looked. She wasn't afraid at all."

His fingers contracted on her back. "You make me ashamed."

"Of what?"

He smoothed her hair. "You give so much, Maggie," he replied. "I don't have that generosity of spirit. I've had to fight for everything I ever got, even when I was a kid in Spain. My father was a bullfighter, you know," he added when she looked puzzled. "Even in Spain, bullfighting is under fire."

"I didn't realize...!"

"I was sorry I hadn't died with my parents in that fire," he recalled. "I had nobody back home who could be responsible for me and since my mother was an American citizen, they couldn't deport me. I ended up where you did, in juvenile hall. I was buried in grief and anger at fate, at God, at everybody." He searched her face. "Then Amy took me home, and there was this quiet little tomboy who sat with me on the porch and spoke the most beautiful Spanish to me when I refused to respond in English." He smiled. "You made me feel at home, wherever you were. When I got in trouble with drugs, you sat beside me and held my hand, so tight, and promised me that everything was going to be all right. I got teased about that a lot. A big, strong, tough guy like me at eighteen being comforted by a ten-year-old."

"I was old for my age," she said.

"You still are." He caught her hand in his and held it tight. "You and I share a bond. I've always known it, even when I resented it and tried to ignore it." He looked down into her eyes. "It isn't possible to ignore it anymore. Not after what just happened between us."

She scrambled away from him and stood up, breathless. "Please. I don't want to...I can't...do that."

He moved in front of her. The sunset beyond the porch was spectacular, all reds and golds and oranges, but she wasn't looking. "I'm not asking you for one single thing," he said gently.

She looked up at him with emotional scars that were briefly visible. "I'm afraid of sex," she whispered, as if it were some terrible secret. "It's sordid and nasty, and..."

He put his fingers over her lips, shocked. "Maggie, lovemaking is a beautiful expression of what a man and a woman feel for each other," he said earnestly. "It's not sordid and nasty. If I made you feel that way about it, God forgive me!"

He looked wounded. She drew back from the contact of his fingers. "You didn't," she said. "What happened that night was...unfortunate. I was drinking, too, and I guess I did something that made you think I wanted it. I'm sorry, too. I could never want...that...to happen if I was sober. I've hated it my whole life."

He was really shocked now. She looked somber, but completely honest. "Why?" he asked softly.

She winced. "It's so horrible," she whispered, her eyes vacant. "So horrible!"

The look on her face disarmed him. He couldn't imagine what had happened to make her feel that way about physical intimacy. She said it wasn't her experience with him. What, then? He promised himself, he was going to find out.

Meanwhile, he was going to start over with her. That brief interlude had assured him that they had something powerful together, something that needed exploring. He, who shunned intimacy, was suddenly hungry for it.

"If you won't go riding tomorrow, how about a movie next week?" he asked abruptly.

"Cord, it's not a good idea," she said quickly. "We can just forget today. It was a flash in the pan. It didn't mean anything!"

"You're afraid," he said gently. "I know that, and I'm not going to back you into a corner. We can be friends, if that's all you want. I meant what I said inside," he added in a deep, husky tone. His dark eyes almost glowed with emotion. "I'd give you anything you wanted, Maggie. Anything in the world!"

She felt her body tingle as she remembered when he'd said it. Even now, his voice was so tender that it made her ache. But she didn't trust him. It was too soon. She turned away from him, toward the front door. "I want my cherry pie."

"Just a minute." He drew her into the light of the window and checked her eyes. He smiled and touched her mouth gently. "You'll do. I wouldn't want the Travises to think I made you cry, even if I did."

She looked up at him quietly. "I thought you were disgusted at the way I acted, when you pushed me away," she stammered. "I felt...dirty."

His eyes closed and he cursed silently. "Never!" he said harshly, opening his eyes on a wave of regret. "I was trying to spare you another trauma," he said honestly. "It's too soon for that sort of physical involvement, for both of us. We're different people now. I was shocked when I knew about your marriage, and ashamed of the way I'd treated you. I never meant things to get so physical." He shrugged. "I kissed you and I couldn't stop." His cheekbones went ruddy and he looked away, almost as if he were embarrassed to admit that. "I pushed you away before I made another stupid mistake that I couldn't undo."

"Oh," she said. "That was why?"

He met her eyes. "That was why, Maggie. Disgust?" He laughed shortly. "What a joke. I thought I'd die trying to let you go. I've never..." He stopped and turned away.

She touched his arm, very lightly. "You've never...?" she prompted.

His head lifted, but he wouldn't look at her. "I've never wanted a woman so much."

She let go of him, but the words echoed in her mind. Not disgust. Desire. Violent desire. She'd felt it, too.

"Is it normal?" she whispered aloud, without realizing she had spoken.

He turned back. "Is what normal?"

"To want somebody, like that," she said shyly.

"Haven't you ever wanted a man so much that it was like torture to pull away?"

She stuck her hands in her jeans pockets. She looked at his chest. "Only you."

He was quiet so long that she thought she'd insulted him. Then she noticed his chest rising and falling at a fast, hard rate. She looked up, surprised to see a hot, almost violent look in his dark eyes.

She grimaced. "There I go again, eating my foot. Sorry. I really do want my cherry pie."

She opened the door and he stopped her, his hand going past her ear.

"I'm sorry, too, sorry to ask so blatant a question, but I need to know. Maggie, have you ever had a man—besides me?"

She swallowed hard. They were far beyond lies. "Not that way, no," she said with quiet dignity, and without realizing her exact phrasing.

Cord's arm was removed, as if her answer had shocked him. Which it had.

She went through the door and back to the kitchen. After a minute, he followed her, quiet and subdued.

They were polite and pleasant to each other until the pie and coffee were consumed, but both had withdrawn from their former intensity. They avoided any personal conversation. They smiled and talked and then Cord drove Maggie back to her hotel.

Despite her protests, he walked her to her door.

"It's too late for you to be roaming the halls of any hotel alone," he said when they reached her room. "It may be a few years late, but I'm going to take better care of you."

She glanced at him curiously. "Don't get into any new habits," she told him. "I'm only in town until I find the job I'm looking for."

His face hardened. "And then it's goodbye forever?"

She couldn't look at him and agree. "The farther apart we are, the better off we'll be," she said. "I'd only poison your life. Neither of us is looking for anything permanent, and I can't even look at something temporary. I'm not meant for brief, intense affairs."

He laughed huskily. "That's a joke. You, having an affair with anyone, even me."

She looked up, curious, with her key card inserted into the slot. "Why?"

"You've got more hang-ups than you realize," he said softly. He shook his head. "It will take a patient man to get through all of them."

"Something nobody would ever accuse *you* of being," she replied sweetly.

He pursed his lips. "Oh, I don't know, I thought I was doing pretty good for a while today."

She got his meaning and glared at him. He was grinning, the beast!

For the first time in memory, he gave her slender figure a speaking, sensual scrutiny. "You have a beautiful body," he remarked. "You're slender, but your breasts are just right..."

"You stop talking about my breasts!" she exclaimed, folding her arms over them defensively.

"It's better than doing what I'm thinking," he replied with a long, meaningful glance at them with pursed lips.

She felt the heat go through her like a jolt of lightning. It showed, too.

He smiled slowly. "I see you know what I'm talking about," he chided.

"I do not!"

His gaze fell to her mouth. "I'd love to kiss you good-night, Maggie," he said in a tone that curled her toes. "But I don't think I'd ever get out the door if I did."

She couldn't manage a snappy reply. He disabled all her defensive skills when he spoke in that low, velvety tone.

He knew it. His eyes met hers, and the smile faded. "You just went on the endangered list," he said abruptly. "I won't come at your blind side, and I won't pressure you. But I want you."

"I've told you...!"

"It's reciprocal. You can have me whenever you want me," he continued, as if she hadn't spoken, his voice deep and soft and slow. His gaze was relentless, sensual. "Wherever you want me. On a bed, on the floor, standing against a wall, I don't care. But it will be your decision, and on your terms. From now on, I won't even touch you unless you tell me you want me to," he added quietly.

"I…don't understand," she stammered.

He reached out and touched her cheek, his eyes narrow and quiet. "I spent a good part of my life in law enforcement. I know an abused child when I see one," he said bluntly. "Even if it took me years to realize it."

She winced.

"Don't do that," he said roughly. "It's nothing to be ashamed of! A child can't help what happens to her or him!"

Tears welled up in her eyes. She felt dizzy. The hall started spinning around as sickening memories flooded into her mind, crippling her, terrifying her. "Cord," she whispered, and fainted at his feet.

When she came to, she was lying on the coverlet of her bed. Cord was sitting beside her with a glass of water in his hand, his other hand behind her head, coaxing her lips to it. His face was white under its tan.

She managed a sip and choked. He put the glass down and helped her to sit up. He smoothed her hair while she fought for breath and sanity again.

"I'm sorry," he said. "I should have kept my mouth shut."

She swallowed and swallowed again. He had no idea what sort of memories he'd resurrected. They weren't as simple or direct as his assumption of what had happened to her as a child.

"Are you going to be all right?" he persisted.

She forced a smile. It wasn't his fault. He didn't know about her past. He made assumptions. So many people did, without a clue as to the depravity to which some men could stoop in their pursuit of the good life, the fast buck.

"It's all right, Cord," she said in a wan voice. "I've had a hard week. Maybe it just caught up with me. Delayed jet lag."

His eyes were worried. He wasn't buying it. "Don't you want to come back to the ranch with me?" he asked. "June could stay with you."

She shook her head. "You don't understand. It was all a long time ago. I've come to grips with it. Really."

He nodded and gave her an impatient stare. "Of course you have, sweetheart. That's why you fainted."

Her eyelids flashed at the endearment. She'd known Cord for eighteen years. He'd never called her by a pet name.

He seemed to realize why she was shocked. He chuckled softly. "Is that a weak spot? I'll have to exploit it."

"It won't work twice," she said firmly.

"Right. Honey," he drawled softly.

She flushed.

His eyes sparkled with delight. "I'll think up a few more before I come back next week. I'm free Wednesday or Thursday. You can pick the movie and the restaurant."

She was worried. "Cord...?"

"I won't touch you," he repeated. "Dinner and a movie. Period."

"But, I'm going away," she continued. "It will just make things worse..."

"Worse for who, you or me?" he asked.

"All right, for me," she said, hating the fact that he knew how she felt about him. "Don't torment me."

He hesitated. She did look tormented. He took one of her hands in his and held it tight. His thumb smoothed over her neat fingernails. "You've got every right to feel the way you do. I don't blame you. But don't push me completely out of your life, Maggie," he added, lifting dark eyes to hers. "I can even settle for friendship, if that's all you have to offer."

The remark was surprising. She didn't really trust it, either, because she'd felt his hunger for her. How ironic, that she loved him but couldn't imagine making love to him, and he wanted her but without loving her.

"We could go back to being foster children," she said.

"Foster brother and sister?" he asked, and he didn't smile.

She nodded.

He let go of her hand and got to his feet. "If that's what you really want, okay," he said with cold pride. "But be sure, Maggie. Be very sure. There are plenty of women in the world, some of whom wouldn't consider it an ordeal to be my lover."

That hurt, as it was meant to. She picked up the glass of water and sipped it. She didn't speak. Words would choke her. She knew he was giving her an ultimatum. It was the old game, all over again, strike out before you were hit. But she wasn't going to play anymore.

"No reply?" he taunted.

She sipped the water again.

He swore roundly, turned on his heel, went out the door

and slammed it. A second later, he opened it again. "Keep this damned thing locked," he said shortly, dark eyes blazing. "I told you before, I have an enemy, and he may try to target you. Don't take chances."

"Okay."

He waited with visible impatience until she got up and started toward the door. He glared at her. His body ached just looking at her, and she was closing doors before he even got the key in the lock.

"Don't worry, you made your point. Bodies are cheap," she said as she met his eyes. "You can find one anywhere."

His jaw clenched. "That was a low remark," he replied.

She shrugged. "You've already told me I'm not in the running unless I'm willing to jump into bed with you. There are women lined up, waiting. I get the point." She smiled. "Lucky you!"

He looked as if he wanted to bite off part of the wall. "That wasn't the point!"

"Good night, Cord."

He stepped out into the hall, but he turned almost at once. She'd fainted because he mentioned her past. She had hidden terrors because of it. And here he was, pressuring her, when he'd promised not to. It was frustration talking, not his heart.

He stared down at her with regret eating at him. "I tell lies," he muttered. "I make promises I don't keep." He shrugged. "I wouldn't want to go out with me, either, after the way I've behaved tonight. But keep your door locked, okay?"

"Okay."

He shrugged and started down the hall, both hands in his pockets.

She stared after him. When he got to the elevator, she was still there, her eyes on him. He got in and started to push the button when he saw her. He hesitated, frowning, his stare intent. He moved, just a fraction, as if he thought about getting off the elevator and coming back, rushing back, to her.

That thought was frightening. She wasn't ready for it. She couldn't bear another passionate embrace tonight, not after the things he'd already said.

She moved back into her room and closed the door, hard, leaning back against it with her heart pounding.

6

Maggie slept fitfully for the rest of the weekend and was bleary-eyed and drowsy when she got into the office on Monday morning. She'd showered, and been embarrassed all over again when she looked in the mirror and saw a vivid red mark on her breast where it had been suckled. There were other faint marks, too, all evidence of a torrid interlude.

Nobody could see the marks, of course. But the memory had kept her awake half the night with burning recollections of Cord in her arms, his kisses on her mouth. After years of futile dreams, the reality was such a shock that she could barely believe it. Above all, he'd been cold sober, and he certainly hadn't hurt her. He'd been so tender that her body rippled all over just thinking about it. Even days before, despite her feelings for him, she couldn't have imagined him like that. Her memories of his lovemaking were painful. But perhaps the new memories would be even worse. Cord was a wonderful lover. Now she knew what she was missing, and what she stood to lose if she really took a job out of the country.

But what good would it do her to stay? Cord had been furious with her because she wanted to distance herself from him. It had been in self-defense. She had nothing to look forward to with him, despite his new attitude. He didn't want to get married. She did. She'd lied about it to spare her pride, but she'd have loved being married to Cord, bearing his children. *His children.* The pain went through her like a knife. She finished getting dressed and refused to think any more about it.

She had sessions with two clients, and fortunately, she was astute enough to convince them that she was alert and on-the-job.

Kit invited her out to lunch, packing a camera.

"What's that for?" she asked.

Kit grinned. "We're having lunch at a restaurant right next door to the agency where this guy we're investigating works," she said. "I'm hoping to catch him with somebody, anybody, we can photograph. We still don't know what his exact connections are, or to whom. It would give us a foot up if we could get a good photo of him with one or two of his cronies."

"What a great idea! Does your husband know what you're up to?" Maggie added quickly.

"No," she said, and scowled. "And don't you dare tell him. Logan is a battering ram with big feet and ears. He is not liberated. But this is my job and I'm doing it. What he doesn't know won't hurt him."

"I can see us now, with your husband racing down the street, chasing us with a computer mouse." She grinned. "But won't it be fun?"

"Fun, and beneficial, too," Kit said smugly. "This guy needs to be stopped. Imagine little kids being bought and sold on the international job market. If anyone did that to Bryce, I'd turn him every which way but loose!"

Maggie understood how the other woman felt.

They ate at a steak restaurant next to an employment agency with a very nice storefront.

"Are you sure that's the one?" Maggie asked under her breath when they were past it. "Gosh, it's elegant!"

"Of course it is. That's their cover. And not only in Texas. They have agencies in Florida and New York, as well," Kit replied. "But Lassiter says the other agencies are legitimate, and just a front for this one. This JobFair is connected with a global corporation that deals in stolen children that they use for free labor to make profits, and Gruber's controlling it somehow."

"What a sick world we live in," Maggie remarked.

They placed their orders and sipped coffee while they waited for it to be prepared.

"Look, there they are!" Kit groaned, looking out the

window. "They'll get away before I can even get my camera out...!"

"No, they won't." Maggie got up, weaving through the tables, and rushed outside. "Follow me with the camera, and hurry!"

Two men, one short and balding, the other tall and dark-headed and tough-looking, were talking on the sidewalk in a language that sounded like Spanish.

"Jake!" Maggie exclaimed, moving quickly toward the taller man with a huge smile. "How nice to see you again! I thought I recognized you..." She trailed off deliberately and assumed an embarrassed look. "Oh, I'm so sorry! I thought you were a business associate. Please, excuse me!"

She turned and walked away quickly, hoping against hope that Kit had been quick. She went back into the restaurant, resisting the urge to turn around and see the mens' reaction.

Kit was grinning when Maggie got back to their table. "I got it! You brainy lady!" she exclaimed. "Lunch is on me!"

"That was exhilarating," Maggie replied breathlessly. "I think I may be a natural born detective. Do you know who they were?"

"The short man is the one we're investigating. His name is Alvarez Adams. But I think the tall one is the associate we've been trying to connect him with, the man who's in charge of the African child trade—a man called Raoul Gruber. He works mainly out of Madrid, but he has close connections with JobFair, and we think he and Adams are joint partners with the global enterprise. It's so chilling to think about. We've got contacts—well, Mr. Lassiter has contacts—in all the government agencies that deal with this sort of thing, and we're feeding whatever we get right to them."

"I hope they can shut down the operation."

"So do we," Kit said glumly. "But unless this man is Gruber, we don't have much of a chance. Adams is so slippery that we don't have a single thing on him. On the other hand, if he's working with Gruber, there's the connection and we've got a foundation to build on."

"Did they pay me much attention when I came back in?" Maggie asked, because something was niggling in the back of her mind about the man.

"The tall one watched you all the way." Kit confirmed her worst suspicions. "It was almost as if he recognized you. Isn't that wild?"

Maggie's heart jumped. What if the man was the one who had tried to kill Cord? Hadn't Cord said something about an employment agency connection? She had to know if it could be this one.

But she didn't say anything to Kit. There was no reason to make her boss's wife feel bad, because Kit hadn't asked her to do anything. It had been her own idea. Even now, she didn't regret it. She felt as if she were doing something important, something worthwhile. Besides, she'd had a taste of the famous adrenaline rush. No wonder Cord wouldn't quit what he did!

* * *

She went through the rest of the day in a daze, certain that she didn't want to spend the rest of her life advising people on stocks. Maybe Mr. Lassiter could use another employee?

But her foolhardy action weighed on her mind. She began to realize how dangerous Gruber might really be. If he knew who she was, and suspected that she was spying on him, things could get dangerous. So when she got back to her hotel, she phoned the ranch. Cord wasn't there, but she left word for him to call her, and went into her small sitting room in her shorts and T-shirt, barefoot, to work on the latest account figures on her laptop computer.

Two hours passed before she even realized it. The insistent buzz of the doorbell caught her attention. As she went to answer it, she realized that she hadn't even thought about supper. She looked through the peephole, and there was Cord, in designer jeans and boots, a Western-cut shirt and bolo tie, with a Stetson slanted across his eyes.

Surprised, because she'd only asked him to phone, she opened the door. He gave her a long, appreciative look before he walked in and let her close the door behind him.

"I wanted to tell you..." she began.

He bent, lifting her clear of the floor in his arms in mid-sentence, and kissed her hungrily.

She forgot everything she was going to say. She let him kiss her, entranced by the soft delight of his lips on hers. He wasn't demanding, insistent, even pushy. He was slow and delicately sensuous without anything blatant. She melted.

He lifted his head and looked into her eyes with one eyebrow raised. "Yes? You wanted to tell me...?"

She couldn't get her breath, much less make her brain work. "You're wearing a cowboy hat," she pointed out.

"I'm a cowboy. What did you want to tell me?"

She laughed softly, embarrassed. "I can't think."

"I'm flattered." He pursed his lips. "Want me to do it again?"

She swallowed. "Not right now."

He put her down gently. "That's promising, at least," he remarked. "What are you doing?"

"Inputting data." She gestured toward the computer, shaken by his actions. "I forgot the time."

"Obviously. Let's dress you in something nice and go out to eat at this steak place I know," he murmured, watching her.

"We're not dressing me," she informed him.

He sighed. "There goes dessert." He frowned. "Not that I mind, but why did you call me?"

She wiped her hair back with a nervous hand. "I was going to tell you about the man we saw at lunch, walking with Alvarez Adams," she began.

All the humor went out of him. He was suddenly deadly serious, and she had an unwelcome glimpse of the man he became when he worked as a mercenary. "How do you know Adams and where did you see him?"

"Kit recognized him. Lassiter's investigating him. We ate at a restaurant next to where he works, that JobFair employment place," she continued, curious about the expression on Cord's hard face. "There was a man with him, a tall and dark man with a scar across his mouth..."

"Gruber!" he exclaimed. "He's in Houston already? My God!"

She paused without another word. The name was very familiar now.

"Did he see you?" he persisted.

"Well, I was trying to tell you, Kit wanted a photo of the men and they were about to leave, so I went outside and pretended to know the tall one, then admitted that I didn't so Kit could get their picture. They didn't know she got it," she added quickly, because Cord looked frightening.

"You little fool," he said under his breath. "Raoul Gruber is the man who planted the bomb I found. He tried to kill me. He's not stupid. He'll know by now who you are and who you were with, which means you and your lunatic friend are both in danger!"

"I should call Kit," she began worriedly.

"You should pack," he said firmly. "You're not staying here alone, not when Gruber knows who you are. By now he'll know where you are, as well. Go and get your things together. Do it right now, Maggie. I'm not leaving without you. Kit is Logan Deverell's wife, isn't she?"

"Yes, but..."

"I'll phone him when we get to the ranch," he said. "Get packed. You're checking out, right now."

She hesitated. She was being railroaded. She was a modern

woman. She shouldn't knuckle under like this. There were dozens of books written about men like Cord. She should have read one.

"What are you waiting for, a bullet through the window?" he burst out when she stood where she was. "I'm not making conversation! This man stands to lose millions if he's exposed. He's killed children, for God's sake! He won't hesitate at one stubborn woman!"

She put her hands on her hips and glared at him. "Now you just listen here a minute...!"

He was too worried and exasperated for courtesy. He picked her up, threw her over one broad shoulder and went out the door. He closed it behind him while she raged at his back. He carried her down the hall to the amused looks of guests, and right into the elevator.

"Cord!" she squealed, embarrassed to be in her shorts and in such a position. He shifted her into his arms.

"There, there, darlin'," he said gently, exchanging a warm look with an elderly couple that was riding down to the lobby with them. "She's in the family way," he confided, to Maggie's horror. "I worry if she even walks."

"I know just how you feel," the elderly man said, while Maggie glared and the elderly woman looked amused. "She—" he indicated his wife "—was working at a drugstore when she went into labor, and she wouldn't go to the hospital because they were doing inventory and she was needed. She had the baby right on the floor in Health and Beauty Aids!"

The elderly woman scoffed. "It was a baby, not a life-threatening event! Don't you let him coddle you too much, dear," she told Maggie gently. "Exercise is the best thing!"

Maggie wanted to say something, but she didn't get the chance. They were heading through the lobby as he called goodbye to their companions. A minute later, bare feet and all, she was sitting in the passenger seat of Cord's truck.

"I'll go back for your clothes and your laptop," he told her smugly.

"You don't have the key!" she muttered.

He looked amused, despite the gravity of the situation. "How do you think I got into your room the morning after you came by the ranch?"

"You lock-picker!"

"Count on it," he mused. "I'm a professional mercenary. I have all sorts of skills you don't know about. Sit tight. I won't be a minute."

She threw up her hands. Arguing got her nowhere. Now she was going to arrive at the ranch in shorts and no shoes, and everybody would stare. Well, let him explain her state of dishevel, she thought furiously! She hoped everybody stared!

Minutes later, with her suitcase and other carryalls packed and thrown into the backseat, they were back at the ranch. Maggie, still self-conscious about her appearance, walked into a pretty bedroom behind Cord, who was carrying her luggage and her laptop. Fortunately, neither June nor anyone else was in sight.

The room was done in pinks and blues, and had a canopied bed. "Wow," she murmured. "Whoever decorated this cornered the lace market, huh?"

He turned. "I decorated it," he said.

She was wondering for whom, because he'd bought the ranch after Patricia died.

"Who likes French Provençal furniture and Priscilla curtains?" he asked with long-suffering patience.

Her heart jumped. "I do," she blurted out. "But...why would you decorate a room for me?"

"Temporary insanity," he muttered. "I'm having myself psychoanalyzed Friday."

She couldn't stop looking at him. "You really did this—for me?" she stammered in helpless disbelief.

He moved closer, taking her gently by the shoulders. "Why are you so surprised? I told you before, you're an integral part of my life. I always assumed that you'd come here and spend the night eventually, even if it was only for the occasional weekend."

"You never said that," she replied sadly. "You never even hinted at it."

His fingers tightened and released on her shoulders. "It's hard for me to let people close," he confessed reluctantly, and he wouldn't meet her eyes. "I lost both parents, my wife, Amy... I don't have a good track record with...affection."

He was going to say *love,* but he couldn't get the word past his lips. She could understand. She'd been betrayed herself, by the people who should have put her welfare first. Trust didn't come easily to either of them.

She searched his eyes slowly, seeing the deep lines between his elegant eyebrows, the lines of stress between his nose and his mouth, the hard set of his lean face with its olive complexion.

"I know how that feels," she said slowly. "Except that people have left you because of circumstances they couldn't control, even Patricia. In my life, the people who were closest to me have betrayed me."

"Who betrayed you?" he asked softly, discerning that she wanted to talk.

"Just about everybody," she said after a long moment. She winced, remembering Bart's horrible act and its ultimate cost. Her eyes closed and opened. "I'll never trust a man again."

"Can't you tell me what happened?" he persisted, tilting her face up.

She searched his eyes slowly. "It would be cruel," she said absently, and then regretted the slip of the tongue when she saw his intelligent eyes flicker.

The unexpected answer made him curious. "Cruel to me? Why? How?"

She pulled away and moved to her suitcase. "I'm going to put on something else."

"What's wrong with shorts?" he asked, diverted. "You're home."

She shrugged. "I don't ever wear shorts except when I'm alone."

He was watching her, alert, assessing. "Who molested you, Maggie?"

She dropped the pair of jeans she was holding.

He went to the door, closed it, and came back to her, turning her to face him. He forced her eyes up to his. "It was your stepfather, wasn't it?"

She winced.

"Did you have therapy?" he asked.

She shook her head. "I could never talk about it, to a total stranger."

His thumbs rubbed gently against her cheeks as he framed her face. "I know a woman. She's a merc, but she has a degree in psychology. She's tough and honest. I think you'd like her. She's the sort of person you could talk to, and she could help you."

"Do you think so?"

He bent so that she had to meet his eyes. "Do you want to go through life alone, without a family or children?"

"I don't know if I can have children anymore," she said huskily and in pain.

His hands stilled on her face. "Why?"

"The beating I took when Bart hit me...was...devastating," she confessed hesitantly. "I fell into a marble coffee table and it shattered. I damaged one of my ovaries. The other one works...but the doctors told me that it might be difficult to get pregnant."

He immediately thought of ways and means to get her that way, and it shocked him. Children, family life, had never been a priority. He was in a line of work that predisposed him to bachelor status.

But she looked torn, wounded, helpless. Inadequate. He thought about the long, lonely years ahead when she would substitute work for love and companionship and the family she could have had. It was a terrible waste.

He scowled as he looked down into her wan face. "Difficult, but not impossible," he said huskily, and his whole body went taut. He laughed at the unexpected arousal.

"What's so funny?"

He pursed his lips. "I thought about kids and got aroused. That's a first."

She flushed, pulling away from him.

With a long sigh, he pushed his itching hands into his slacks pockets to keep from grabbing her. "Well, it's a challenge, isn't it? I love a challenge."

Her hands were shaking. She folded them at her waist. "I really should change."

"I really would love to watch," he said softly, and he didn't smile. "Your skin has a delicate sheen, like that on a pearl. You feel like the most delicate rose petal, silky and delicious, and the smell of roses clings to you like an aura." He searched over her hair, her face, her body, hungrily. "I've had women all my adult life, not in droves, but in sufficient numbers to appreciate them. You surpass every one of them, in every way. If I had an ideal of womanhood, you'd be it."

She didn't know how to take such sweeping comments. They embarrassed her, even as they flattered her. But this was Cord passing them out, Cord, who had been her most persistent enemy for years.

"Are you...feeling sorry for me," she queried, "and that's why you say those things?"

He scowled. "Why would I pity you?"

Because she knew pity. She had an intimate knowledge of it. People were sorry for you, they tried to spoil you to make up for the trauma. They wanted to help, and when words were all they had to use, they flattered. But the words meant nothing.

"So many secrets, Maggie," he murmured as he watched her ponder his remarks. "You don't trust me, either, do you?"

"It's not personal," she said in a stark whisper while her eyes mirrored troubling memories.

"If I'm slow, and careful, and I don't pressure you," he said gently, "can I win your trust?"

"What would you expect in return?" she asked with helpless suspicion.

That was when he realized what a long, slow road it was going to be. And it wouldn't be an overnight victory.

His lips parted as he looked at her and hungered for her. He frowned, because he hadn't thought much about the end result, only the path that led to it. He cocked his head. "I'm thirty-four," he said slowly. "I've lived fast and hard. I've done things I'm not proud of, and I've done a lot of them for nothing more noble than money. But this Gruber thing has changed me. Now, I want to stop him and his cronies, and it isn't for money." He hesitated, choosing his words. "If I had a child, of eight or nine, and had to see it become nothing more than a slave in a cocoa field, or a mine, or a sweatshop—and I could do nothing to save it because I had no money at all..." He drew in a sharp breath.

"Cocoa field?" She moved closer to him, curious. "Little children?"

He nodded. "Little children. Some are sold for as little as eleven or twelve dollars, because their parents can't provide for them and hope they'll find a better life working for some multinational corporation in another country. But what happens is the children are taken away, worked up to eighteen hours a day and beaten when they don't work. And they're never given a dime for their labors."

She gasped. "Good Lord! How can things like that happen in a civilized world?"

"Civilization isn't all that far-reaching," he told him. "Especially in developing nations, which need economic assistance just to keep their people from starving. Many of them look the other way when their own citizens become slave dealers. But Gruber is setting a precedent—he's organizing a global labor pool to sell to those corporations which will deal with him, to cut their production costs in a tightening retail market that lowers their profits."

"That's dirty," she said icily.

"Dirty. Cowardly. Merciless. Yes, it is. And very few of the nations outside the industrial ones can, or will, crack down on the labor exploitation. Some of it has been exposed on television news programs, but it was mostly the use of child labor to produce retail merchandise for resale in this country and others. And it was a sanitized version. They don't show the scarred little bodies, or the malnutrition, or the squalor in which these children live." His face hardened. "Gruber also has a nice little prostitution racket going, with the same source, which exploits young girls as sexual slaves. Imagine a twelve-year-old girl who's never known a man, in a brothel where she's worked like a mule."

She could. She lowered her eyes, sickened. "He should be stopped."

"I agree. But—" he added, cupping her face in his hands "—you don't need to be involved in this. By sticking your nose into it with Kit, you've put yourself square on the firing line. I can't let you get hurt. I'll go see Lassiter tomorrow and we'll make plans. I know more about Gruber than he does, and I have access to information even he can't get. I'll share."

Her eyes widened with fear. "But you could be hurt, too...!"

"Oh, I like that," he said in a husky tone. "I like having you afraid for me. You always have been. Why didn't I see it?"

"You didn't want to," she said abruptly. "You've given up seeing things that make you feel."

He nodded slowly. "Yes. And so have you."

She couldn't deny it. "People can hurt you if you let them get too close," she murmured absently, lost in his dark, warm eyes.

His thumb smoothed gently over her parted lips. "As I hurt you," he said quietly. "You can't imagine how much I regret what I did to you, that night," he added with genuine sorrow. "For years I dreamed how it would be, to make love to you slowly and gently, to bring soft little moans out of your throat and make you fly into the sun with delight. And when the opportunity finally presented itself," he said on a heavy, harsh sigh, "I damaged you, in every way possible."

She deliberated on what to say, on how to answer him. It was surprising that he'd thought about it before it happened. "I didn't know...that it would hurt so much." She couldn't tell him that she had all too much knowledge of what happened between men and women, or that her past had convinced her that sex would be easy for her if she could stomach it.

"You weren't ready for me," he said simply. "I didn't arouse you."

She searched his hard face with curious eyes. "Is that what happened, in your study the other night?" she asked in a small voice. "Is that...how it would have been if you'd been sober?"

"Yes," he replied. He traced her mouth with his forefinger. "I would have done that, and more."

"And it wouldn't...have hurt?"

"Maybe a little," he said honestly. He caught both her hands in his and held them. "A virgin's body is tight inside," he said. "It can be uncomfortable for a woman if she's not aroused properly first. The rush, plus the alcohol, is what made it so painful for you."

"Oh."

His fingers entwined with hers, liking their warm softness in his grasp. "At least, there wasn't a physical barrier to get out of the way."

She couldn't meet his eyes. She couldn't bear the memory. She couldn't even talk about it.

He seemed to understand. He bent and kissed her eyelids. "I'm not making accusations. I know you were a virgin, Maggie."

"How?" she blurted out.

"Because everything I did shocked you," he said flatly. "And because you were obviously uncomfortable just at the last."

She colored, keeping her face down. Her hands, in his, were nerveless. "I was afraid of it."

"Of the pain," he agreed.

"No. Of the..." She swallowed. "It kept feeling better and better, and I thought I was going to burst wide open. I was afraid of the pleasure, it was going to be too much..."

He jerked her into his arms and held her hard, bruisingly hard. She could hear his heartbeat, strong and fast against her breasts. He groaned once, harshly, and held her even closer.

"What's wrong?" she asked.

His cheek rubbed against hers. "At least you had something," he muttered.

Her fingers worried the pocket of his shirt. "If I'd given in, if I hadn't fought against it, what...would have happened?"

"Have you ever had a climax?" he whispered.

She jerked in his arms. She knew what he meant, even if she hadn't experienced it.

"No," she said after a minute.

His mouth touched her face lightly, his lips hot and hungry as they moved onto her mouth and kissed it with growing insistence.

"Suppose," he whispered roughly, "you let me give you one."

Her heart jumped. His hands had moved down to her hips and were pulling them rhythmically into his, in the same way he had in the study, on the chaise lounge. Her body began to tauten, to burn with curiosity and growing pleasure.

Her nails dug into his chest, but she didn't protest. She was curious. She was alive. She was hungry.

He moved, so that one long, lean leg slid in between both of hers and began to move in a slow, deadly rhythm. Her body followed its darting motion, lifting toward it, hungry for the closeness of him.

"I can give you heaven," he murmured against her parted lips. "Let me."

She opened her mouth to his hot, deep kiss, moaning when it sparked off even more drugging sensations of pleasure.

"Yes?" he whispered into her mouth. "Maggie, yes?"

She wanted to say the word. She shouldn't. It was wrong. He would despise her. He would taunt her with it, as he had before. He would...oh, if only he would never stop!

She moaned and her mouth tugged away from his just a breath, just enough to get that one word out that would open the gates to paradise, that would make her his woman, truly his woman...!

The knock on the door was hard, loud and cruel. He jerked back from her like a man in a daze, shivering with reaction, with frustrated desire, with shocked wonder at her headlong response.

"Yes?" he called harshly.

"Sorry to disturb you, Mr. Romero, but there's a Dane Lassiter on the phone, asking for you!" came June's hesitant voice.

Cord was still unsteady on his feet when he picked up the telephone receiver in the living room.

"Romero," he said in a voice that sounded strangled. No wonder. He'd almost seduced Maggie right there, when he'd promised not to.

"Dane Lassiter," came the reply in a deep, slow voice. "I just had a call from Logan Deverell about a photograph his wife and Maggie Barton conspired to get at lunchtime. Has Maggie told you?"

"Yes," he replied curtly.

"Do you know who the man in the photo with Adams is?"

"I know all right. The photo Kit Deverell took was of Alvarez Adams and a man named Raoul Gruber. Gruber traffics in child labor and he's opening up new areas of exploitation in West Africa and Central America, more children to make money for the multinational corporation he heads. Gruber planted the bomb that almost blinded me. Maggie put her life on the line when she met up with him. I made her come out to the ranch with me, so that I can protect her."

There was a brief silence. "I see."

"You didn't know?"

"I knew Adams. I've been working on him for four months, trying to find enough evidence to force his arrest for importing and exploiting illegal aliens. I knew that he had a colleague named Gruber, and my information was that JobFair had links to him. I didn't know that the man in Kit's photo was Gruber. I phoned you because I thought you might be able to identify him."

"I can identify him, all right. Gruber's a killer," he added. "He doesn't stop at men. He's killed children. I know him from years past. He suckered my group into a coup attempt in Africa that cost us several men. We ended up fighting kids with automatic weapons. We went after Gruber, but he ducked out of the country and we couldn't trace him."

There was another pause. "It's like peeling an onion," Lassiter said deeply. "Just when you get to what you think is the last layer, a new one presents itself."

"I want to talk to you in person," Cord said. "I have access to sources of information that you don't. I can give you Gruber and probably Alvarez."

"I don't want them," came the suddenly amused reply, "but

I'd love to give them to a government agency that does. My client isn't that generous. His family would like Adams served up cold."

"His family?"

"I can't divulge much," Lassiter said. "But I can tell you that Adams was involved in the abduction and murder of two of their sons. They were accidentally taken in a raid on a small Central American village, and when the authorities got too close, Gruber simply had them all eliminated. The parents have a rich cousin who came to me in an attempt to provide evidence of it. I was investigating Adams, but then the trail led to Gruber. Adams has no record for violent crime. Gruber does. I think my clients fingered the wrong man."

"They have, if my information is accurate," Cord said. "And I think it is, because I got it from a member of the U.S. Senate, who wants Gruber shut down as badly as I do."

"You have nice connections," Lassiter mused.

"Oh, I've got some even better than that," Cord chuckled, "including a foreign head of state. I'll give you as much help as I can."

"I understand that Logan Deverell and his wife have had a hell of a mixer about her actions today," Lassiter remarked. "I don't think she'll be taking any more photographs for me, even if I'm allowed to keep her in the agency. Logan didn't know about Gruber, but he did know that Adams is dangerous. He was pretty mad."

"Maggie's impulsive," Cord said quietly. "She doesn't always think things through before she acts. I gather that Kit is much the same."

"The difference is that Kit has a two-year-old son. She can't afford to put herself at risk. I'm in all morning tomorrow. How does eight-thirty suit you?"

"Suits me fine," Cord said. "I can drop Maggie off at her office on the way." He hesitated. "Listen, I don't like the idea of letting her go back to work at all, but I don't fancy another confrontation—I had to pick her up and carry her out of the hotel to get her to the ranch."

"I've got operatives with no pending cases," Lassiter said immediately. "Maggie will be safe in this building. I give you my word."

"Don't underestimate Gruber," came the terse reply. "I did, and it almost cost me my life."

"We learn from mistakes, if they don't kill us. I've made my share of them, too. I'll see you at eight-thirty."

"Fine."

Cord hung up and traced a line down the receiver while he thought about Maggie's situation. He wouldn't be overprotective, but he didn't want her anyplace where Gruber might be able to abduct her. Gruber wouldn't hesitate at killing her. She didn't seem to understand how dangerous the man was. Cord would have to keep a close eye on her without appearing to. She was fiercely independent.

By the time June had a late supper on the table, Maggie was back in her jeans and short-sleeved knit sweater, with her hair in a ponytail and no makeup. She looked young and oddly carefree.

Cord watched her covertly while she talked to June about a new fabric that had turned up in clothing lines, soft and nice-looking. The two women seemed to get along very well. Cord was glad about it, and sorry that he'd tried to give Maggie a wrong impression of his relationship with the younger woman. It could have had disastrous consequences.

He noticed that Maggie was reluctant to meet his eyes, but he caught her glancing at him once, and it made him feel lighter than air.

Neither of the Travises knew why Maggie had come to the ranch, but Cord had to tell them. When he wasn't around, for any reason, he had to have someone aware of the danger.

"I want you to tell Davis, too," Cord told Travis when he'd summarized the problem. "If I'm not here, the two of you have to make sure the ranch is secure. Gruber will hesitate to rush in if he knows I'm here, but I'm not sure how many contacts he has, or what they know."

"I'm glad you agreed to come out here, where Cord can look out for you," June told Maggie with genuine concern.

Maggie looked uncomfortable.

Cord pursed his lips. "Oh, she didn't come voluntarily," he told them. "I carried her out of the hotel over my shoulder, kicking and screaming."

"In front of God and the whole world!" she exploded, flushing. "And what you told that elderly couple...!"

He chuckled. "Well, it kept you diverted so that you didn't rush back upstairs, didn't it?"

She sighed angrily. “Honest to God, if Amy could see you now.” She shook her head.

“She’d probably be laughing her head off in the hereafter,” he finished for her, his dark eyes twinkling.

June glanced from one to the other and smiled. She’d never heard Cord Romero laugh until Maggie came back into his life. When she and her father had first come to work for him, he was a little intimidating, and he never seemed to smile. He was all business, and there were some wary, tough-looking men going in and out of the house at odd hours. June had been nervous around him most of the time. But now, with Maggie, he was like a different person. She got a glimpse of the man he had been, perhaps, before his line of work made him hard and cold. She wondered if he realized how much Maggie had changed him already.

“Barefoot and in shorts,” Maggie scoffed, sipping coffee. “If any of my clients had seen me...!”

“You’d be doing more business than you could handle,” Cord mused. “I know—” he held up his hand “—that was a sexist remark. But, honey, you do look enchanting in a pair of shorts and with your hair down.”

Maggie looked flustered. She couldn’t even come up with a snappy reply. She finished her coffee instead.

Later, they went into the living room to watch television, but Maggie was uneasy.

“You don’t really think Gruber will come after both of us, do you?” she asked.

Cord smiled. "Of course he will," he replied. "I'm going to see Lassiter in the morning and we're going to talk about strategies. I'll drop you off at your office on the way. I'll come with Davis to pick you up after work, too."

She started to protest. Her mouth was open. But all at once, she closed it. This was his business. He made his living anticipating dark threats, danger, violence. If the man did have evil in mind, there wasn't anybody better than Cord to deal with it.

"What? No protests?" Cord exclaimed.

She shifted on the sofa. "You're very good at what you do," she replied softly. Her eyes touched his face. "I know you can deal with anything that comes up."

He was pleasantly surprised at the remark. He smiled. "Thank you," said softly.

"I'm not flattering you," she returned. "I mean it."

His eyes searched hers. "You feel safe with me."

"Oh, I wouldn't go that far," she proclaimed with a gleam in her eyes.

He chuckled. "Now, that really is flattery," he told her. He switched channels. "Remember this?" he asked, turning to a TV station that aired episodes of classic TV shows. They were running a police drama that Cord and Maggie shared a love for many years back.

"Yes!" she exclaimed. "I used to sit and watch it with you, on the rare occasions when you came home for weekends."

"I still watch it."

She smiled shyly. "So do I."

"At least," he said, almost to himself, "some of the memories are good ones."

Maggie slept soundly for the first time in years, cocooned in the soft bed in the room that Cord had decorated just for her. She still could hardly believe that he'd gone to that much trouble. Especially with the difficulties they'd had being civil to each other in the recent past.

But it was different, now. There was a tenderness between them that delighted her, surprised her. She felt as if she had, truly, come home. Cord was gentle, teasing, relaxed. Despite the turbulent physical passion they shared, they could sit and watch television like friends, or talk about politics and current news events without quarreling. They had more in common than they ever had before.

Cord hadn't touched her again after the passion they'd shared in her bedroom. But he'd walked her to her door and touched her hair in the ponytail, and smiled down at her before he went to his own room. She felt cherished. Whatever came of their new relationship, it was a wonderful glimpse into a world she'd never known.

Maggie dressed in a neat navy blue business suit for work the next morning, arriving for breakfast with her purse and laptop in hand.

Cord was wearing slacks and a rib-necked silk shirt with a

sports coat. He looked powerful and very sexy. Maggie's hands itched to smooth over that shirtfront that revealed every muscular inch of his broad chest.

"You look nice," he remarked with a smile. "Very neat and professional."

"I'm a corporate woman," she informed him with a grin. "I have to project a classy image."

"You project a classy image in shorts," he said, knowing it would prick her temper.

It did. She glared at him over bacon and eggs. "I don't have to use sex to get clients."

"I don't remember insinuating that."

She ate a forkful of eggs with attitude. "I've seen women do it."

"Not you. Never you." He leaned back, his breakfast finished, with his coffee mug in his hand and just looked at her. "You do nothing suggestive. You don't wear clothes that even hint at the curves underneath. You walk in a businesslike way. You don't flirt. You don't entice." He sighed, frowning. "It's a good business image. But you're denying your sex appeal entirely."

"Business demands that," she replied quietly.

"A woman doesn't become a man just because she wears a pin-striped pantsuit and a blouse with a tie," he replied. "But it makes her look like a hybrid. Men work in previously feminine job slots, like florists and fabric salesmen, but they haven't started wearing skirts. I think a woman should be able to take pride in her femininity without being accused of using it to further her career. But that's not the problem with you, is it, Maggie? Your prickly hang-ups show even in the way you dress," he said gently. "It amazes me that it took me almost eighteen years to see it."

She didn't know how to handle the conversation. He was getting into uncomfortably personal areas. He was a gifted interrogator, and he knew people very well, right down to their bones. She didn't want him delving too deeply into her past.

"Logan gave Kit hell yesterday about that photo," he remarked.

"They have a little boy," she recalled. "I guess he was upset that she'd done something potentially dangerous."

"He wasn't the only one," he replied solemnly. "I'm the risk-taker in this family. I've handled dangerous situations most of my adult life, and I'm damned good at it. You stick to your stock quotes and leave detective work to the experts."

He was right, but she didn't like admitting it. "Oh, right, let's keep fragile little women out of the line of fire!"

"Fragile, hell," he said with an amused glance. "You're exactly the sort of companion I'd want in a firefight. You've got nerve, and you don't back away, ever."

That surprised her. She stared at him with evident confusion.

"But this isn't a firefight, it's a covert covering action," he continued. "And you're outgunned. Gruber has hired thugs in his organization who have a genius for getting into and out of protected places. I've had to call in markers from half a dozen colleagues just to keep the ranch safe."

"Huh?"

He just smiled. "Ready to go to work?" he asked, checking his watch.

"Sure. Anytime you are."

She got her laptop and her purse and followed him out. He paused to speak to June on the way, cautioning her about keeping doors locked and windows shut. He put on his dark glasses before they went outside.

They moved to the garage just in time to see a tall man in dark clothing carrying some sort of electronic device leading a huge black-and-brown German shepherd out of the building. He gave Cord a curt nod, but didn't stop to speak.

"Thanks, Wilson," Cord called. The other man threw up a hand.

"What was he doing?" Maggie asked warily when Cord walked to the driver's side of the black sports car he drove.

"He was checking for nitrates," he said.

She frowned. "Fertilizer?"

He pursed his lips and looked amused. "Something like that."

Her eyes narrowed. "I don't know anything about that electronic device he had, but I do know that they use a wand like the one he was carrying at the airport. They aren't checking for fertilizer, either."

"You're too sharp for me, honey," he drawled, without even realizing he'd used the endearment. But he noted her soft flush with pleasure. "He was checking for a bomb."

Her gasp was loud in the silence.

"I won't hide things from you," he said. "You're a grown woman. You can handle this. Gruber is the sort who wouldn't think twice about setting a bomb here, and he wouldn't mind killing innocent people to get to me, or to you. From now on, until I settle with Gruber, I'll have to have the cars and the machinery, the outbuildings and especially the house, swept for bombs and bugs constantly."

The danger came home to her in that instant. She looked at Cord and remembered the bomb that had almost killed him. The fresh wounds were stark against his olive tan. They weren't disfiguring. In fact, they gave him a roguish look.

Her hands clenched. "I've been very naive," she confessed.

"You aren't used to this sort of thing. I am," he said. "And because I am," he added, tossing her the car keys as he slipped a pair of dark glasses on, "you're driving and I'm blind."

"You've never offered to let me drive you before," she remarked, her eyes on the keys.

"Trust takes a little work. And a little time," he said gently.

She looked up at him worriedly. "I'm not used to trusting people."

"Neither am I," he remarked. "But we can learn. Can't we?"

Hesitating, she nodded. Then she smiled and got in behind the wheel.

She loved driving the sports car. She'd have loved one of her own, but she'd never been able to afford such luxury. She almost laughed at the irony of her position, driving the one man in her life who was more than capable of taking care of himself and everyone around him. But, as he said, the fiction of his injury had to be maintained if he was going to get the best of Gruber.

She glanced at his profile when she stopped to turn onto the main highway. She'd never let herself think too deeply about his work. They'd lived separate lives for a long time. She'd never seen him in action, although she heard from Eb Scott, among others, about the chances he took, the cases he worked. She remembered when he'd been shot, when Patricia had committed suicide. It had been Maggie who had stayed in the hospital waiting room day and night, for the three days when he was in intensive care. She'd tried to phone his wife, but Patricia hadn't answered the phone, and Maggie had assumed she was out of town. She hadn't been able to find anyone who knew where she was. The tragedy didn't reveal itself until Cord was released from the hospital, and he'd found her body. It had changed him terribly. After that, he quit the FBI and took freelance jobs that most other mercenaries wouldn't have touched—mostly involving demolitions. He was an expert at defusing bombs.

He felt her inner turmoil. "You don't like what I do for a living, do you?" he asked.

"No," she said honestly.

She stopped for a red light and he studied her stoic expression. "I've never thought seriously about giving it up. Those adrenaline rushes are addictive. The greater the danger, the bigger the rush."

"I noticed that myself." She laughed shortly. "But you've never been family-man material."

He frowned. "Why do you say that?"

"I can see it now, you, with a wife and baby, rushing off to defuse a ticking bomb somewhere," she said with no real mirth. "I don't think there's a sane woman on earth who could live with that sort of uncertainty. It would kill a marriage at the outset."

He was silent while they waited for the light to change. His lean, strong fingers traced the dash absently. "I've never thought about my job in that light."

"No reason to," she said easily. "You have no one to consider except yourself. You can do what you please without worrying about anyone else's reactions."

His eyes narrowed as he looked at her averted face. She was speaking conversationally, but her body was giving away secrets. She was rigid. Her hands were tightly clenched in her lap, the nails biting into her palms. It occurred to him that she'd known about some of his more dangerous exploits, and that she'd worried about him—worried a lot. He thought he didn't have to consider her feelings, but if she cared about him, certainly she'd brood on the dangerous chances he took. He reversed their positions and thought how he'd react if Maggie defused bombs and took mercenary jobs in high-risk cases. Amazing, how sick it made him.

He noticed that the light had changed. She stepped on the gas a little too heavily, jerking the car. He was thrown off balance by his worried thoughts and barely kept from pitching forward against the seat belt.

"Sorry," she said tersely.

Cord never made ungraceful movements. She wondered what he'd been thinking to unsettle him. Probably about Patricia, she thought miserably. Poor Patricia, who'd loved him, too.

When they got to the Lassiter-Deverell Building, Cord walked beside Maggie into the elevator, sunglasses in place and holding her arm as if he needed it to guide him. He stood beside her without speaking as they rode up to her floor. His lack of conversation made her uneasy. He was brooding.

They got off on her floor and walked down the deserted hall to the wooden door with a brass plate announcing that this was the office of Deverell Investments.

"Thanks for coming in with me," she began.

He touched her cheek gently. "There's an old saying, about not judging people until we've walked in their shoes," he said out of the blue. "I've gone through life without considering how I affected other people's lives with my actions."

"We just agreed that you didn't need to," she pointed out.

His face was drawn. "How many sleepless nights have you spent over the years, worrying about me?"

Her eyebrows shot up. "I'll have to check my diary," she said lightly.

His fingertips went to her mouth and traced the upper lip. "I wish you wouldn't wear red lipstick," he murmured quietly. "If I kiss you, they'll think I landed the lead in *Cabaret*."

Her heart skipped wildly. "What did you drink for breakfast?" she asked wryly.

"Coffee, just like you." His fingers didn't move. He scowled at her mouth with visible curiosity, with a growing hunger to bend and catch her lips under his. He felt his breath choking him as he recalled unwanted memories of her soft breast under his lips, her faint moans like music to his ears...

He jerked his hand back and looked more formidable than ever. "I could retire on what I've got in the bank," he said absently. "Demolition work isn't much more than a hobby these days. I like breeding purebred bulls."

"Are we having the same conversation?" she asked. "We were talking about coffee, as I recall?" she prompted.

He smiled at her, with genuine warmth. It made his eyes soft, crinkly at the corners. It made his hard mouth look sensuous.

"You look elegant with your hair in a braid," he remarked, "but I like it long and soft around your shoulders."

"I work here," she pointed out. "I don't want to divert the clients by flaunting my sexy hair. Think of the complications if I had to toss someone out the window for getting fresh over AT&T preferred!"

He chuckled deeply. "You don't resort to those methods with me."

She shrugged. "You're special."

The smile faded. His eyes darkened, as if the glib remark

touched a sensitive spot. “So are you,” he said in a rough, husky tone. “More special than I ever knew.”

“Stop it,” she chided, trying to ward off more complications. “You’ll make me blush.”

He bent unexpectedly and brushed his lips tenderly over her eyelids, closing them in a flutter of long lashes. “You don’t leave the office unless someone goes with you,” he whispered. “You wait for me to come and get you when you get off work. I’ll have Davis drive me, to make it look good. If anything happens in between that worries you, you call Lassiter’s office or you call me. Or else.”

“Or else what?” she asked huskily.

“Or I’ll carry you down to the car and take you home right now.” He lifted his head to search her misty eyes. “Considering the state I’m in just at the moment, that might not be my best idea to date.”

“The state you’re in?” she murmured drowsily.

He glanced up and down the hall, found it deserted, took her by the waist and gently pulled her against him. “This state.” He smiled ruefully.

She jerked her hips back from his and a film of color lay along her high cheekbones.

He shrugged. “Think of it as an unavoidable response to an attractive woman,” he murmured with helpless pride.

“More likely, it’s a response to enforced abstinence!” she shot back.

His eyebrows lifted. “How do you know I’ve abstained?”

She colored even more. "Your private life is none of my business!" she muttered, glaring up at him. "I don't care how many women you have sex with! You can sleep with every woman in the building for all I care, from the cleaning lady up!"

He was suddenly looking over her shoulder with unholy amusement.

She groaned inwardly and turned. Logan Deverell was standing in the open office door with a speaking glance.

Logan cleared his throat. "The, uh, cleaning lady is fifty-two, twice married," he remarked, "and she only has three teeth..."

"Lead me to her," Cord enthused. "Experienced women turn me on!"

Maggie choked back laughter, dashed past Logan and shot into her own office with a speed that left Cord chuckling merrily.

Cord was shown into Lassiter's office by the secretary. Dark-eyed, dark-headed Dane Lassiter rose from behind his desk and moved around it with traces of a limp to shake hands.

"As you might notice," Lassiter said dryly, "I've had my own share of physical trauma. I let my attention wander during a shoot-out when I was a Texas Ranger and got shot to pieces. I lost my job, but I ended up with something almost as good." He indicated the office with a bland smile. "An infrequent limp isn't a bad trade-off."

Cord smiled and removed his dark glasses. At least here on

this floor, there was no need to pretend. "You can see my latest mishap in my face. I'm damned lucky to be alive and still have my sight."

Lassiter noted the scars around the other man's eyes and nodded slowly. "Defusing bombs is suicide. Why do you do it?" he asked with customary bluntness.

Cord shrugged. "My wife committed suicide and I felt responsible. I guess I've been punishing myself for it."

Lassiter gave him a meaningful look and moved back around the desk. On it were photos of a blond woman and a son of about eight, along with a blond girl not much younger. He noted Cord's curiosity and smiled as they sat down.

"Our son and daughter," he said with noticeable pride. "Tess and I didn't think children were even a remote possibility." His face tautened. "She almost lost her life with our first one. You never know how you feel about a woman until you're faced with losing her forever. I got my priorities straight in about ten seconds flat."

Cord wondered at the emotion in the other man's deep voice. He had a feeling Lassiter's road to fatherhood hadn't been an easy one, but he certainly looked like a happy man now.

"They both want to be detectives," Lassiter added with a look of absolute disgust. "And my wife," he added with muted outrage, "is out right now with one of my own damned operatives—who won't be an operative very much longer, I promise you!—trying to get tape of Gruber and Adams in the JobFair office!" He threw up his hands. "They bugged it and staked it out without even bothering to tell me, and Tess is supposed to be at a staff meeting here in two hours." He stared at Cord, who was struggling not to laugh. "They say marriage and motherhood settles women. Hell!"

Cord gave it up and burst out laughing. So much for his illusions.

8

It was all Cord could do not to roll on the floor laughing at Lassiter's expression. "How did they bug the office?" Cord asked the older man.

Lassiter sat back heavily. "Posing as exterminators," he said with barely concealed irritability.

Cord grinned. "Should I ask why an exterminator was called in?"

"Why the hell not?" Lassiter exclaimed. "Tess and Morrow went to a pet shop and bought thirty hissing cockroaches, put them in a box, and shot them into JobFair during lunch when the office was closed! That's when they spliced into the telephone line. When the call went out for an exterminator, they intercepted it, moved in, and planted bugs everywhere. Apparently Gruber and Adams didn't even suspect them, because they haven't swept the office today. I expect them to, any minute," he added icily.

Cord grinned. "Well, it's innovative."

Lassiter shrugged. "Hissing cockroaches." He thought about it for a minute and chuckled. "I suppose it is. Tess isn't bad at detective work. But she's setting a bad example for our kids," he added. "They put a listening device in the teacher's desk and had tape of her making a steamy cell phone call to her boyfriend during lunch. God knows what they planned to do with it. Fortunately we caught them before they had time to make plans! We grounded them for two weeks, and laughed into our hats for days afterward," he confessed amusedly.

"What a formidable duo they'll make later on."

Lassiter nodded. He leaned forward then, solemn. "I'd like to know what you have on Gruber."

Cord pulled a thick padded envelope out of the inner pocket of his suit and pushed it across the desk. "Documents, photos, background information on both Gruber and a man named Stillwell, the figurehead president of Global Enterprises, Limited, which is the multinational corporation founded, we believe, for the express purpose of exploiting child labor in developing countries," he said, explaining the contents.

"There's a CD in there as well, with what I downloaded from the CIA and Interpol files," he continued. "We suspect that JobFair and Global Enterprises are connected, and that both have a direct link to Gruber, but nobody's been able to prove it so far. The photo Kit Deverell took is the first break we've had. But it won't be enough without hard evidence that Gruber is the real head of Global Enterprises. That would give us an airtight case if we could. The corporation is known to deal in child exploitation for profit, with JobFair as its supplier, and it's recently been under fire in Africa. I was investigating JobFair when Gruber caught me off guard and damned near blew my head off with a planted bomb in Miami."

"How about the corporation's board of directors?" Lassiter asked.

"That's a possible back door," Cord told him. "I've got somebody working on it right now. One of the directors lives in Amsterdam and has been accused, but not convicted, of heading a child pornography and prostitution ring. Another is Spanish but lives in Morocco. He deals in prostitution, as well. Pity we don't have somebody who could go overseas and ferret these guys out. We might make a connection to Gruber if we dug hard enough."

"How did you get CIA and Interpol files, if I might ask?" Lassiter murmured with admiration as he examined the papers.

"Don't," came the dry reply.

Lassiter gave him a curious glance. "It's only illegal if we're helping the bad guys," he rationalized.

"Now, that's just what I tell myself every time I do it," Cord agreed.

Lassiter's gaze went back to the papers on his desk. He was scowling. "This is interesting. Alvarez Adams has financial ties to Global Enterprises, Ltd., although JobFair doesn't—at least on paper. Do you know much about it?"

Cord shook his head. "Only what's there. It's hard to

research, even for specialists. They cover their tracks very well electronically."

"I wouldn't know either, except that a former agent of mine works for the FBI out of Washington, and a friend of his is with a—" he hesitated "—shall we say covert organization with underworld connections. Global Enterprises runs a huge cocoa plantation on the Ivory Coast, as well as mining operations and cattle ranches in South America. We know that thousands of children are employed without pay in these enterprises. The problem is that, even though the countries where they're located are willing to help, they don't have the financial resources to combat a multinational corporation worth billions."

"That's the crux of the situation," Cord agreed. "Money. It always comes down to money."

"Sad commentary on the world, isn't it?" Lassiter replied. "But while we're feeling sorry for those poor kids, how about the Hispanic women who are brought into this country illegally to work in sweatshops or prostitution? They lure them in with promises of money, and when they get them here, they threaten them with disclosure and prison.

"I never knew how widespread the problem was until I started investigating Adams," Lassiter concluded with a heavy sigh. "It turns my stomach. Even if I weren't getting paid for the investigation, I'd take it on. These people need to be stopped."

"They do," Cord agreed. "But you can't go at an organization with this sort of money and power head-on. You have to slide in the back door when they're not looking. It's going to take a lot of manpower, and help from some powerful government agencies."

Lassiter grinned. He pulled a file out of his desk drawer and slid it across to Cord. "You didn't see this," he added.

Intrigued, Cord opened it. He whistled under his breath. "And I thought I had connections," he murmured as he went through the list of contacts.

"They're not all contacts, just yet. That's where I thought you'd come in handy. See the one at the very bottom?"

Cord did. He chuckled. "That's right. I'd forgotten that I had a cousin who works in imports and exports in Tangier. Until recent years, when I started searching for family," he confessed on a more somber note, "I didn't know there was any left except an elderly cousin in Andalusia, not too far from Málaga."

"You lost your parents here, didn't you?" Lassiter said.

Cord nodded. "In a hotel fire. I had no close relatives, although I had American citizenship through my mother," he added. "But if Amy Barton hadn't come along, I don't know what I'd have done."

"I don't remember the hotel fire personally, but I read about it. There wasn't a lot about it in the newspapers because of a high-profile sex scandal here in Houston about the same time," he added. "Two men were arrested for trafficking in child pornography. It was a heartbreaking case, and there was a lot of public outrage. They were sentenced to life in prison, but one of them was killed in a prison riot not much later." He shook his head. "We live in a perverse world."

"We do, from time to time, but..."

Before he could get the sentence out, the door opened, and a young woman with long blond hair and dark eyes burst in with a tape in her hand.

"Dane, guess what we got...?" she burst out.

The change in Lassiter was sudden and stark. His genial expression eclipsed into one of tormented relief. He jerked out of his chair and came around the desk with hardly any evidence of a limp.

"You crazy, half-witted, stubborn...!" Before he got all the words out, he had the woman up in his arms and he was kissing her with a violence and passion that knocked the breath out of Cord. He'd never seen such stark emotion erupt out of a man, especially one who seemed as cool and self-possessed as Lassiter.

The woman kissed him back just as hungrily and then seemed to notice Cord, and pulled away a little with a self-conscious smile.

Lassiter didn't let her go. His face slid into her throat and he still held her close. "Hissing cockroaches, for God's sake, telephone repairmen...!" He cursed once, harshly.

"Now, now, darling, I'm fine," Tess Lassiter said gently, smoothing his dark, dark hair. "I had Morrow with me. You stole him from the FBI. He's very good."

"Damn Morrow! I'll have him for breakfast!" Lassiter raged, and Cord noted with some amusement that the older man looked perfectly capable at that moment of roasting his erstwhile employee over a slow fire.

Tess grinned. "I was never in danger. Dane," she added, patting him on one shoulder, "we're not alone."

The man seemed only then to realize where he was and what he was doing. With a groan he pulled back from her, but his dark eyes couldn't let go. Cord felt like a voyeur just looking at the two of them. What they felt for each other was so tangible that it filled the room. And they'd been married almost nine years, he recalled with faint shock. Imagine an emotion so powerful that it still burst its bonds like that after nine years! It unsettled him.

Lassiter went back around his desk, leading Tess by the hand. He sat down, with her beside his chair, her hand on his shoulder.

"Sorry," he said stiffly. "She takes chances. Morrow won't, anymore, by God, when I'm through with him!" he added tersely.

"Morrow's nice, and I talked him into it. He said you'd shoot him, but I promised you wouldn't. Here," she added, placing the tape on the desk. "We got good tape. You're going to love the information you get from this. Hello," she added shyly, glancing at Cord. "I'm Tess, Dane's wife."

"The source of my only ulcer," her husband replied dryly, a little calmer now.

"Us and the kids," she added with a proud smile. "But we try not to get on his nerves too much."

"This is Cord Romero," Lassiter introduced.

"Oh," Tess exclaimed. "You're Maggie's brother!"

His face tautened. "We were foster children together," he corrected. "We're no relation to each other."

"Sorry!" Tess said at once, and blushed as she smiled. "Maggie didn't explain."

That was damned irritating, and he was going to have something to say to Maggie about it later.

"That's it, walk in and start trouble," Lassiter told his wife when he noted Cord's expression. "Never mind, what's on this famous tape that you think would have compensated me if something had happened to you?"

Tess grinned proudly. "A clue that may tie Gruber to that multinational corporation Adams is working with. It's right there, on tape, in his voice. The corporation's president is a man named Stillwell, and he's on the tape, too!"

Lassiter burst out laughing. "You little torment," he murmured, but when he looked up at her, his face was beaming.

She bent and kissed his forehead. "I love you, too. Now I'm going to have breakfast. Don't be hard on Morrow, okay? He's really sorry already."

"We'll talk about it later. Bring me back a bear claw, will you? Want anything?" he asked Cord.

"Thanks, but Maggie and I had a big breakfast."

Lassiter stood up and dug into his pocket for a bill. He handed it to Tess, smiled faintly and nudged her toward the door. "Don't get into any more trouble today," he instructed.

"And I was going to stand outside the bank with a pocket full of twenties and fish for pickpockets!" she scoffed.

"Out!"

She wrinkled her nose at him, exchanged a look that could have heated cold water, and left. Lassiter sat back down when the door closed, and it took him a minute to get his mind back on business.

"You've really been married nine years?" Cord had to ask.

"Almost." He shook his head. "It doesn't seem like even a year. Okay. Let's listen to this tape!"

He put it into the player and Cord sat back, his mind troubled with images of Lassiter and his wife in that unexpected, furious embrace. It had never occurred to him that marriage wouldn't take the edge off passion, leave the relationship lukewarm and complacent. He was having to mentally rewrite all his former opinions of it.

He had to force himself to concentrate on the tape when it began. He listened absently until something caught his attention. There was a new voice on the tape, identified by Adams's voice as someone called Stillwell.

Lassiter stopped the tape. "Stillwell is the visible president and chief stockholder of Global Enterprises, Ltd.," he told Cord. "If it had offices in this country, every government agency we have would be investigating it. Its headquarters are in Morocco, in North Africa, and all efforts by the West African governments on the Ivory Coast to prosecute it for exploitation of children, and women, have failed. Money and power give immunity on a continent where the annual wage is less than $300 per household.

"Some parents sell their children without even realizing they've done it. The company gives them money in advance of a child's wages, being told that the children will earn a fortune in jobs abroad. By the time they realize that the child isn't coming back, it's too late to do anything. Most children can't even be traced," he added with disgust. Before he started the tape again, he added, "The corporation lies low in Morocco, out of reach of legislators in the poorer countries."

On the tape, Adams was telling other people in the office that he'd looked into the identity of a young woman who came up and spoke to him and his companion outside a restaurant the day before, that she was the foster sister of an old enemy, a man named Cord Romero.

Cord exchanged a worried glance with Lassiter.

The tape continued. A voice quickly identified by Lassiter as corporation president Stillwell informed the others that he was certain that he was under investigation by the Interpol, but that he was certain they hadn't been able to connect him to anything illegal. He'd made certain of it, he added in a dark, ominous tone.

Gruber spoke now. Cord recognized his voice and told Lassiter who it was. Gruber mentioned an investigation by the Lassiter Detective Agency being conducted against Adams. He said that he'd observed a second dark-haired woman in the doorway of the restaurant taking his photo with Adams while the first woman detained them by pretending to recognize Gruber. He described the photographer and Adams identified her as Kit Deverell, an agent with Lassiter's agency. There was a profane curse.

Gruber said that he'd assigned a man to get rid of Cord Romero because he was helping a friend in a government agency investigate an illegal immigrant smuggling operation in Miami that could link Gruber to Global Enterprises. A bomb had been planted and Cord had been diverted to defuse it. Sadly it hadn't killed him. Now they had to take care of Romero before he came at them again. Even blind, he was formidable and he never gave up. It wouldn't be a bad idea, Gruber added, to take out Maggie Barton, as well. The Lassiter Agency was too high-profile to target, it would get the Texas Rangers involved as well as the Houston police if they tried. But Romero was a different proposition, and accidents did happen. They could target his foster sister and make Romero think twice about opposing them. He knew a man who could assist them, a professional.

Cord almost flew out of his chair as he registered the threat. Lassiter turned off the recording and the men exchanged glances.

"I hadn't anticipated that," Lassiter said darkly.

"It was his next logical step," Cord replied. "Damn the luck! If Gruber calls in a professional hit man, all the mercs I can hire won't guarantee Maggie's safety." He sighed heavily and ran a hand through his dark hair while he brooded. He glanced at Lassiter. "Suppose I get her out of the country?"

he said, thinking aloud. "And you back off your investigation of Adams at the same time. They'll be confused. Adams might think he was wrong about being targeted. He might even get careless."

Cord began to nod, his eyes glittering. "Maybe I can do some investigating. We know Gruber has connections in Tangier and Amsterdam, as well as Madrid." He pursed his lips, thinking fast. "He thinks I'm blind. Maybe he'll assume that I'm getting myself out of the line of fire because he tried to have me assassinated in Miami. He might also assume that Maggie was going along to nurse me. He obviously thinks I'm blind, thank God." He nodded slowly. "It just might work. If it does, Gruber might even give up his assassination plot. Suppose I go to visit my elderly cousin in Spain, with Maggie?"

"That could put you both in even more danger," Lassiter pointed out.

"But it could also throw Gruber off balance," came the reply. "If he and Adams relax their guard and get careless, you've got a chance to catch them in the act with that bug they haven't discovered. We can tie them to Stillwell, with that tape. And I can have the freedom to do some digging into Gruber's business connections in Europe and Africa. I'll wear my dark glasses and let Maggie lead me around. Even if Gruber follows us, he won't think I'm capable to getting up to much mischief. Meanwhile, you can have one of your contacts in that covert agency do a little digging on the Ivory Coast to see if they can connect JobFair and Global Enterprises. Can't you?" he prodded with a grin.

Lassiter chuckled. "I like the way you think. Lie low and carry the war into the enemy's camp. Attack when it's least expected."

"Exactly. Besides," Cord added thoughtfully, "I can call in markers from old comrades who'd love to see Gruber go down for that coup attempt a few years back. We've all got scars from it. Once we're out of the States, the odds become even. I have contacts overseas who can't operate in this country."

Lassiter nodded slowly. "It might work. Not that it isn't going to be dangerous," he added. "What if Maggie doesn't want to go?"

Cord lifted both eyebrows. "You don't know Maggie," he said with a soft laugh. "The more adventurous it is, the more she'll like it. She has a reckless spirit and she's said more than once that she'd love to do something dangerous. Not that I'll let her get into trouble."

"A unique woman," the other man remarked.

"Very unique, and good company under fire," Cord added. He got out of the chair and shook hands. "I'll start the ball rolling."

"Keep in touch."

"I'll certainly do that."

Cord put on his dark glasses and sat in the waiting room until he got Red Davis to come and pick him up and take him back out to the ranch. Lassiter waited until he left before he went back into his office and, on a whim, turned the tape cassette to the flip side, expecting nothing more. But the next words that were spoken caught him like a blow in the throat.

"We can't target Lassiter, and Romero is formidable," Stillwell agreed with the other man on the tape, "but it may not be necessary to use a hit man. I know something about Maggie Barton that you don't. I've got clippings, videos, still photos. It cost me an arm and a leg to turn them up, but they'll stop her dead. She has a past that she'd die to keep quiet. All we have to do is tell her what I've got, and she'll stop Romero doing any more investigation into our affairs. I guarantee it. We'll be safe."

"You're sure of that?" Gruber asked contemptuously. "I can't think of anything that would stop Romero, short of a bullet. Even blind, he's dangerous. What if Lassiter teams up with him? There's some sort of connection there. Besides, Romero knows a lot about me. Too much."

"He must have some affection for a woman he was raised with. If we scare her enough, she'll find a way to make him back off."

"You can try," Gruber said, unconvinced. "But if your way doesn't work, mine will," he added ominously.

Lassiter listened to the rest of that side of the recording, but it was brief and nothing else of interest turned up. He pondered his course of action while he and Tess shared pastries and coffee. Tess, dared to do anything else that was reckless for the day, went back to her desk to work on cases and Lassiter went downstairs to Logan Deverell's office to see Maggie.

She was just saying goodbye to a client when Dane Lassiter walked in and asked to speak to her in private. She invited him into her office, aware of curious looks from Logan's secretary.

"Has something happened to Cord?" she asked immediately when the door closed behind them.

"Cord's fine," he assured her. His black eyes narrowed. "We have tape of a conversation in Alvarez Adams's office. One of his cronies has some potentially damaging information about you—videotapes and still photos..."

Maggie went white in the face. Lassiter helped her into a chair and got her head down between her knees just before she passed out.

He cursed silently. He'd hoped Stillwell was lying. Obviously he wasn't.

She moaned, with her head in her hands. "Did Cord hear?" she whispered.

"No. He'd already left the office."

She swallowed hard, twice, and slowly sat back up. Her face was flushed now from the rush of blood, but she looked worn, and defeated.

"I deal in confidentiality," Lassiter told her at once. "I never reveal personal information, not even to Tess. Nothing you say to me in confidence will ever leave this room."

She could see why Kit Deverell liked this taciturn, quiet man. She hesitated, but only for a minute. "I know the photos and videotapes he's talking about," she said huskily. "They could destroy my life." She swallowed. "I would rather die than have Cord see them," she added simply.

"That bad?" Lassiter asked.

"Oh, yes," she assured. "Definitely, that bad."

"Tell me about it."

She hadn't expected that she could ever tell anyone. It was surprisingly easy to tell Dane Lassiter. The agony of the past burst from her. It was like lancing a boil. It felt good to finally be able to tell someone what had happened. Lassiter sat quietly, uncondemning, and listened until she was through. He was pale by the end of the story, but he didn't look at her with contempt, or disgust.

"Cord doesn't know?" he asked after a minute, surprised.

She shook her head. "Amy never told him. I tried to, once, but I couldn't. It would...change things between us. He might hate me..."

"For what?" he exclaimed. "God in heaven, it wasn't your fault!"

She grimaced. "That's what everybody said. But they looked at me as if I was too dirty to ever come clean again."

His black eyes glittered. "Cord wouldn't blame you. He'd be homicidal, but not at you."

She met his eyes levelly. "That's a chance I'm not willing to take, Mr. Lassiter," she said quietly. "Cord has resented me for a long time, actively disliked me even longer. Until very recently, I was a thorn in his side and nothing more. He's been kind to me since I came home from Morocco. I couldn't bear to lose his respect."

He could have told her that it wouldn't happen, but she was terrified. It was in her wide eyes, her strained face.

"I'm not going to tell him," he promised her. "But there is another thing you should know. Gruber is convinced that nothing short of murder will free him from Cord, and he mentioned targeting you, as well. But this other man thinks blackmail might work better."

"What can I do?" she asked miserably, near tears.

"Nothing, by yourself," he said. "But Cord has a plan. He can tell you about it. Don't panic," he added firmly. "Gruber's a rat, but he's not invulnerable."

She wasn't really listening. She knew now that Cord's enemies had information about her that Cord didn't. They would always have it. She felt like screaming with rage.

Watching her, Lassiter read her concern. "Stillwell's evidence can be eliminated," he told her. "I can't have anything to do with it officially, but I can talk to some people on your behalf."

"Great," she muttered. "We can take out an ad in the paper. Tell everybody!"

He shook his head. "It won't be like that. You have no idea what I know about some of the most influential people in the state. I share the information with several contacts, and all of them are as tight-lipped as I am. It's why I'm still in business. Leave it to me, Miss Barton," he added quietly. "I'll take care of it. You have my word."

Tears stung her eyes, but she was too proud to let him see them. She lifted her chin and blinked them away. "Thanks," she managed.

"You should have therapy."

She ignored that. "I appreciate your telling me what you knew." Her face tautened. "You won't tell Cord?"

"I won't tell Cord," Lassiter assured her. "But don't underestimate him, either. He's formidable under fire. If Gruber comes at him head-on, he'll regret it."

"He does dangerous work. I know he's good at it. I just try not to think too hard about the details," she added.

"You can take it from me that Romero is a dead shot and a formidable adversary in intelligence work," he said. "You're safe with him."

"I know that." She smiled up at him. "Want to give me a job? I might as well learn the trade if I'm going to become a walking target for international criminals. I can shoot a gun if I have to." She pursed her lips and her eyes twinkled. "And I look really great in a trench coat."

He chuckled, relieved to see her bounce back so quickly. "Dig it out. I'll keep you in mind. Meanwhile I'll do what I can to get enough evidence to go after JobFair and Global Enterprises at the same time."

She didn't say what she was thinking, which was that

exposure of the criminals would inevitably lead to her own exposure. They were the sort of people who'd take revenge any way they could get it, and Maggie was vulnerable. "Thanks, Mr. Lassiter," she said solemnly.

He shrugged. "We all have secrets that we'd rather not reveal to the world," he said, his eyes dark and quiet. "Too often, that information is potential for blackmailers, especially for people in the upper levels of society. Pain and suffering mean nothing to some people if there's a profit to be had."

"That's the truth."

"Don't worry about Stillwell's file," he repeated. "But it would be to your advantage to tell Romero everything," he added with genuine concern. "Just in case."

She smiled wanly. "That would take more courage than I have," she confessed.

He felt sorry for her. He wished he could do more. He wanted to tell her what Cord had in mind, but she'd find out soon enough. He said goodbye and left the office, determined to find a way to get that file out of Stillwell's office.

Maggie hadn't considered a direct contact from Cord's enemies, but a phone call soon before quitting time stopped her heart in her chest.

"If you're smart," the sly voice said when she picked up the receiver and identified herself, "you'll make Romero back off. We have some interesting video of you in, shall we say, compromising positions? Think how Romero would react if he saw it. What a nasty girl you are, Miss Barton!"

"You bastard," she choked, furious. "You utter coward! If I could get my hands on you...!"

"Don't push your luck!" the dark voice snarled. "Make Romero keep his nose out of JobFair. Think of some way to make him back off investigating us, and do it quick. Or you're going to be a star on the evening news!"

The receiver clicked. Maggie got up from her desk like a zombie, stumbled into the bathroom, locked the door, and threw up.

Maggie gathered her seared nerves by the end of the day and forced herself not to consider how devastating the threat of disclosure was. She had to think positively. She had to think about the helpless victims of JobFair and its major client, Global Enterprises. But all she could consider was the horror, the disgust, in Cord's beloved face if he ever saw those videotapes. She knew he'd never forgive her. Even his past hostility would pale by comparison with what she'd suffer. She had to hold her head up and pretend that nothing had happened.

But that was almost impossible. When Cord came to pick her up at quitting time, wearing dark glasses and with Davis behind the wheel of a ranch pickup instead of the sports car, she was quiet and remote all the way to the ranch. If she only knew how to tell Cord the threats that had been made against her. Lassiter said Cord was going to take her out of the country, but she wasn't convinced. Cord wasn't the sort to run from a threat. What if she couldn't convince him to leave town? The idea of her past being revealed in color video on the evening news made her sick at her stomach.

"You're brooding," he remarked when Davis parked Cord's car in the garage and left them to go back to work.

"I've had a hard day," she told him with a forced smile. "Nothing to worry about." She gave him a long look and felt near panic. "I don't suppose you'd like to go off to Tahiti with me and become a beach bum?" she added wistfully.

He chuckled warmly. "Why not?"

She shrugged. "I guess we'd be in even more danger there."

He studied her closely. "Tahiti is in the wrong direction. Too hot. But how would you like to go to Spain instead?" he asked out of the blue.

Her heart jumped as she looked up at him. "Spain? You mean it?"

He linked his long arm across her headrest and looked down at her. "I mean it. I understand that Gruber has made some veiled threats against both of us," he said, without revealing how he knew it, and unaware that she'd spoken to Lassiter. He saw her pale, but he didn't understand what she was thinking that led to such a sharp reaction. "I want to throw him off the track, make him back off, while Lassiter appears to do the same. If we can make the men careless, we've got a chance to stop them. If we leave the country, Adams and Gruber and Stillwell will think the pressure's off. I have an elderly cousin in Spain. We can go visit him, or at least, appear to."

"What if Gruber follows us to Spain?" she asked.

"I'm a blind man," he said blithely. "What danger could I pose to him?"

"That's a thought," she had to admit.

"It might get dangerous, there's always that possibility. But I can protect you. I've got a few friends who won't mind tagging along at a discreet distance. In any case, you'll be safer out of the United States than in it right now."

She didn't think about the wording. She peered up at him with twinkling eyes, forcing her worst fears to the back of her mind. It would be an adventure. She would be with Cord. It was one last chance to share something with him that no woman in his past ever had. And if worst came to worst, if she was...shot...she'd have had the time with him to carry into the dark with her.

She looked into his eyes with faint hunger. He would never have to know the truth if anything happened to her. But she would have such memories...! The prospect became exciting.

"I can see me now, with an official number and a trench coat and a gun," she told him with a gleeful grin. "I've almost talked Mr. Lassiter into hiring me, but this sounds much more adventurous. Call Interpol and tell them I'm available! Does the job come with one of those cyanide pills, just in case?" she added.

He laughed, delighted at her response. She had courage and spirit and style. He admired her more than any woman he'd ever known.

He touched her cheek with a teasing finger. "It comes with a damaged mercenary and a .45," he chided.

"Not so damaged," she said gently, and reached up to touch, lightly, the skin beside the fresh scars around his eyes. She winced. "And very lucky!"

He was watching her face, drinking in the helpless affection her actions betrayed, her visible longing for him. "Very lucky, indeed," he said under his breath.

She hesitated, frowning thoughtfully. "Cord, you aren't just planning a visit to an elderly relative. Are you?"

He traced her nose. "Leave it alone for now. We're going on a blind man's holiday. You'll be my eyes. We'll leave the country and let them think they've frightened us off. Then we'll give Gruber some rope and see if he'll oblige us and hang himself!"

9

Maggie packed just enough to fill a carry-on bag, excited at the prospect of an escapade with Cord, even under the circumstances. She didn't question why Cord, a man who never ran from trouble, should be so anxious to get away from an investigation of the man who'd almost killed him. But it saved her, momentarily, from fear of disclosure by Adams and his associates. They'd think that she'd convinced Cord to leave the country and back off, and they'd be placated, if only temporarily.

For the moment, JobFair and its threatening file could be left far behind. For a while, at least, she would be safe from reprisals. In that brief time, she could indulge her long-standing fantasies of Cord, being with him, traveling with him, being part of his life. She could share the danger, the chase, the excitement. However long it lasted, whatever the cost, she thought, it would be worth it!

He looked up when she came into the living room in slacks and a T-shirt under a jacket, her long dark hair in a braid down her back, her one piece of luggage carefully packed and tagging along behind her on its rollers.

"You do pack light," he remarked approvingly.

"I don't really have that much stuff," she reminded him. "Except for my photos of my parents and a couple of pieces of costume jewelry that belonged to my mother, which I'm leaving here, my clothes are all I own."

He'd never considered the scarcity of her memorabilia. Of course, his was similarly restricted. Everything his parents had with them was burned up in the fire. There were no relatives except his elderly cousin. His parents' home had been a rented one, and whatever they had was sold at auction after they died. The authorities assumed that Cord had died with them, not being informed to the contrary until Cord was of age and able to contact them.

He was looking at Maggie oddly. "No heirlooms?" he asked abruptly. "Not even from the great-grandmother who rode with Villa?" he teased.

She shook her head, not wanting to tell him that everything in her home had been confiscated by the authorities long ago. God knew what had happened to it. She'd never asked, afraid to prompt new curiosity about the case.

That was curious, Cord thought. She had a strange attitude toward possessions. She didn't accumulate things. In fact, she was like him in her Spartan attitude toward home.

"We'll probably have kids who are pack rats," he remarked absently.

She forced herself not to react to the painful remark. She even smiled. "Speak for yourself. My kids are going to be neat freaks."

He cocked an eyebrow. "When do you plan to have these mythical spotless children?"

"About the same time you start your own family with someone," she returned. "And God help her, the poor woman. She'll be stuck at home while you're off trying to get yourself blown up."

He didn't react with amusement, as she expected him to. He looked very somber. "If I married again, I'd come home and raise purebred Santa Gertrudis herd sires. Maybe I'd do a little consultant work for Eb Scott in my spare time at his anti-terrorism school in Jacobsville."

"That'll be the day," she said absently.

"You never know," he replied. "I do dangerous work. I told Lassiter that maybe I did it to punish myself for Patricia's suicide. Perhaps that was closer to the truth than I realized. I felt guilty."

She didn't know how to answer him. He'd loved Patricia. She'd loved him. Maggie knew nothing of mutual love affairs. She'd never had one.

"Marriage is a risk, even when you love each other," she said, remembering her brief marriage with anger and pain. "Do it in a hurry and you pay the price."

His eyes narrowed coldly as a wave of unexpected jealousy racked him. Her husband had been abusive, but she'd rushed into marriage with the man just the same. "You'd know, wouldn't you?"

She blinked, coming out of her bitter reverie. "Yes, I would. Shouldn't we go?" she added, turning away from him.

Amazingly, she felt his warm, steely hands on her shoulders, staying her retreat. His breath sighed out against her nape. "If I'd known what he was doing to you," he said carefully, "I'd have torn him apart!"

"Why would you have bothered?" she asked. "You didn't care where I went, as long as it was out of your life. You said so."

His eyes closed. The memory was agonizing. He'd said a lot of things, insulting things, that he hadn't meant. He'd been shocked, ashamed, disgusted with himself. He took it out on Maggie.

"I'm...sorry," he bit off.

"Oh, that's great, we should call the news people," she murmured dryly. "Another apology from Cord Romero. Wow! I'll bet they're wearing overcoats in hell right now."

He laughed softly. "I suppose they are. I'm not very good at apologies."

"You don't need to be. You're never wrong," she agreed with a wicked glance over her shoulder. "Shouldn't we go?"

"Is there a fire?"

She pulled away from his hands and turned toward him unflinchingly. "Broken mirrors can be patched, but they're always distorted afterward. I think relationships are like that," she told him quietly. "You don't really like me. Gruber's made threats and you're protecting me, because it's the way you're made. But once the danger is all gone, it will be just the way it was before. You'll tolerate me on the outskirts of your life." She smiled sadly. "I've had years of that. I want a new start, somewhere else. I want," she hesitated, averting her eyes, "I want to be free of the past."

"Running away isn't the answer."

She looked up into his irritated face with real pain. "Yes, it is, Cord," she said huskily, seeing dreams die as she remembered Stillwell's threat and the information he had about her. "Sometimes it's the only way there is."

He didn't understand her attitude. They'd been growing closer, physically and emotionally, since his brush with death. She was taking giant steps backward, just when he wanted to begin again with her.

"Why don't you take one day at a time?" he advised.

She laughed. It had a hollow sound. "It won't help. Nothing will help anymore. Please, can we go?"

"I'll have a quick word with June," he said.

"I'll take my case out..."

"You will not," he said firmly. "Wilson's in the barn with one of his men, and June's father and Red Davis aren't here.

There's no one right outside the door. You'll stay right in this room until I go out with you."

"All right, Cord," she agreed easily. She sat down on the arm of the sofa and waited patiently.

"What, no argument?" he asked with mock surprise.

"I don't have a gun yet," she reminded him.

"Don't hold your breath waiting for me to give you one, either," he mused. "The one time I tried to teach you to shoot a rifle, you dropped the damned thing on my foot."

Because being close to him shook her up. Because her whole body had reacted with predictable delight. She couldn't tell him that.

"It weighed half as much as I do, and you didn't hand it to me, you tossed it at me," she replied. "I couldn't even figure how to get the safety off."

She didn't add that she'd since learned to shoot a pistol with quite good accuracy. Eb Scott had taught her, during their very brief engagement.

"You were engaged to a professional soldier," he remarked. "Eb should have taught you."

"Eb was busy saving the planet from evil," she returned facetiously.

"Do you ever regret not marrying him?" he asked abruptly.

She shook her head. "We were good friends. It was never more than that."

"Then why get engaged to him in the first place?"

Because you married Patricia, she thought, feeling the anguished pain all over again. Cord had walked into Amy's living room with the petite blonde on his arm, ignoring Maggie, and announced that they were married. He had his arm tight around Patricia's thin shoulders, and they were both beaming. Maggie had smiled with her heart breaking inside her. She smiled now. She wasn't going to let him know.

"He was a dish," she said airily.

He glowered at her for a minute before he went out the door and down the hall to the kitchen, leaving Maggie time to collect herself.

Cord had a twin engine plane, and he frequently flew himself to cattle auctions and business meetings, but with the fiction of blindness, nobody would believe he could fly. So this time he put Maggie in the car with him and had Red Davis drive them to the airport to catch a flight to Spain.

"Is this a safe way to travel?" she asked as the jet lifted into the air over Houston.

"Relatively safe," was all he'd say.

They flew first-class, something Maggie hadn't expected, to Madrid. She sat beside Cord in the area of a plane she'd never graced in her life. She always traveled coach, because she didn't have the money to afford such luxuries.

Cord had apparently arranged for them to change planes to travel to Spain from New Jersey. The flight was long and Maggie couldn't sleep. She accepted water every time the flight attendants offered it. She got up and walked down the aisle, stretching her legs. She listened to music on the headphones. The movie—ironically, a disaster picture—didn't interest her. Apparently it didn't interest Cord, either, because he was plugged into a laptop computer and the Internet. Since he had the window seat, she couldn't look past him at the aisle in a covert attempt to see what he was doing. He wasn't inclined to talk, and she was. But eventually, she closed her eyes and, amazingly, fell asleep.

He shook her gently when they landed at the busy Barajas Airport in Madrid. She opened her eyes, stretched and yawned, and eased into the aisle when the plane taxied in to its concourse. She tugged her carry-on bag from under the seat in front of her and waited for Cord to move out with his own carry-on, the laptop neatly tucked inside it. They immediately got on to a charter flight to Málaga, in southern Spain.

After the flight, they walked up the long ramp into the concourse and Cord stopped unobtrusively and nudged her in the right direction. She glanced around her at all the travelers and remembered her trip to Morocco with Gretchen, because many of the passengers were Muslim. It wasn't unusual to see men in long robes and women with head scarves among the jeans and pantsuits of the other travelers.

The walls had travel posters and she found herself reading them without hesitation or difficulty. That ability to understand Spanish brought back painful memories of her first years with Cord, when a shared knowledge of Spanish had given her a special place in his life. In recent years, it hurt her just to hear it. But now it all came back in a rush.

"You don't speak Spanish much anymore, do you?" Cord asked suddenly, glancing at her.

"Not for years," she confessed.

"Not since you grew up," he corrected. He searched her taut face. "You had the most unique accent," he recalled with a smile. "Mexican mixed with a deep Southern drawl."

She wrinkled her nose. "I've still got it. They'd flog me here if I spoke Spanish, with my accent," she agreed.

He chuckled. "People are more tolerant these days. You haven't lived until you've heard someone from Russia speak it."

That amused her and she laughed.

"That's better," he said gently. "You were looking a little fraught there for a while. I shouldn't have ignored you on the way over."

Her face closed. "I don't need babysitting."

"Don't you?" He looked around them, as if he were searching for someone. "I phoned my cousin before we left the States. He offered to send a man to pick us up, but I told him we'd rent a car and drive up. I don't like the idea of a stranger meeting us—he could be anybody."

"Do they have rental cars here?" she asked, feeling lost.

He chuckled. "They have them everywhere. Come on."

He let her lead him to passport control and then onto the ground floor where the rental car counters were lined up. He waited with the suitcases while she filled out the form and got the key. Then she led him out into the scorching summer heat of Madrid.

"Cousin Jorge lives north of Málaga," he told her. "Picasso was born in Málaga," he added. "Jorge has a big farm—they call them *ganaderias* here in Andalusia. Jorge still raises fighting bulls for the *corrida,* the bullfighting ring. A Romero from Ronda, not related to us, was the father of modern bullfighting. Jorge has fewer bulls now, and since he's a bachelor, when he dies the *ganaderia* will have to be sold."

"It's a shame," she remarked.

"Life goes on," he said without sentiment. "You'll like him. He can tell some incredible stories about the old days of bullfighting, when my grandfather was a matador."

"I like history."

"So do I."

"Andalusia is the home of the flamenco," Cord told her. "It has been traditionally performed by gypsies, and it varies in style depending on the area where it's performed. There are Roman ruins everywhere—there's even a small one on Jorge's *ganaderia,*" he added with a smile. "Nearby is the Costa del Sol, the playground of millionaires, and the famous 'white' towns. Farther along the coast is Gibraltar, still a British possession, and across the Straits of Gibraltar is Morocco. To be more specific, Tangier," he reminded her.

She grinned. "I loved Tangier. I'd love to see more of it."

"You'll probably get your chance later," he said mysteriously.

"Do they drive on the wrong side of the road here?" she worried as they reached the rental car.

"They do not. They drive on the right side, here and in Gibraltar," he added, smiling at her surprise. "There were too many wrecks when other Europeans had to switch sides of the road in Gibraltar, so they made it conform to Spain and Morocco's driving rules."

"Thank goodness!" she exclaimed with relief.

She didn't tell him that the most exciting thing about the upcoming drive to Jorge's home was sharing it with him. She'd never been so happy, despite the potential danger that surrounded the trip.

The countryside was exquisite, dotted with olive groves and cypress, with ancient buildings in the inhabited areas and cattle and horses grazing in picturesque pastures along the winding road. There was no real traffic outside the city, and Maggie relaxed a little as she drove. She didn't drive in Houston, preferring cabs to the difficult ownership and expense of a car.

Eventually they came to a wrought-iron gate with the name "Romero" on a painted board beside it. Cord got out and opened the gate. She drove the car through, and then he shut it again. Minutes later, they drove up between fenced pastures to an elegant arched home that resembled adobe structures Maggie had seen in Texas. The house was white with a red-tiled roof, and two shaggy dogs sat on the front porch next to a white-haired man leaning on a cane.

"Cousin Jorge was my grandfather's brother's son," Cord informed Maggie as she stopped the car. "Which makes him my cousin."

"He's very elegant, isn't he? He looks like an aristocrat." Maggie commented as the elderly gentleman made his way down the steps to greet them.

"He's a card," he replied, smiling. "You'll see what I mean when you get to know him." He got out of the car and let the old man come to him, hugging him warmly. They exchanged greetings before Maggie was introduced. The old man took her hand to his lips with a flourish.

"It is a great pleasure to meet the most important woman in my cousin's life," Cousin Jorge said in passable English, and grinned.

She laughed self-consciously. "I'm only his foster sister, but I'm very glad to meet you, too," she replied.

He gave her an odd look but he shrugged. "Please, come in. I have had rooms made ready for you..." He hesitated, both eyebrows coming together in a monstrous scowl. "You do not share a room?" he added suspiciously.

Maggie burst out laughing. "Oh, that will be the day," she burbled helplessly and didn't dare look at Cord.

The old man chuckled. "Forgive me. I do not, how does one say it, 'move with the times.'"

"Don't you feel bad," Maggie said easily, taking his arm. "I don't move with them, either. Sad that we can't say the same for some other people," she added with a meaningful glance at Cord.

When they were in the house, Cord took off the dark glasses. "I'm in disguise," he told the old man somberly. "I was injured in an accident, and the man who did this to me—" he indicated the wounds on his face "—wants to try again. I came out of the country to throw him off the track."

"You must tell me all about it," Jorge said with a smile. "I am no stranger to violence, as you recall. Come."

He led them out of the hall, into the living room. The interior of Jorge Romero's house was immaculate, like something out of a designer magazine. The floors were marble, old, elegant. The wood was stained oak. The carved ceiling was a work of art. There were Persian carpets on the floors and silk curtains at the windows. The furniture was covered in silk as well, except for the deep, high-backed armchairs, which were leather.

"Your home is beautiful," Maggie remarked.

"A bachelor's home must substitute for a wife and children," he informed her with a sad smile. "I lost my fiancée during our civil war here. She was a beautiful young girl whose smile lifted my heart. She was by my side in the thick of battle, and a bullet ended her life. I was never inclined to replace her."

"I'm sorry," Maggie said with genuine sympathy.

He shrugged and smiled at her. "We all have trials as we

go through life. Mine have been less traumatic than those of many other people," he explained. "Sit here," he offered her a seat on the dainty little sofa. "And I will have Marisa bring us hot chocolate. You like hot chocolate?" he added quickly.

"I love it," she agreed with a smile.

"That is good. As you drink coffee in America, we drink chocolate in Spain. I am fond of it."

He excused himself and walked toward the back of the house.

"I like him," Maggie told Cord.

"He likes you. I'm not allowed to sit there," he added, standing over her with his hands deep in his slacks pockets. "It's where his fiancée sat, when his father owned this house and Jorge was courting her."

"I'm flattered," she replied.

He searched her face quietly. "I wish we could share a room, Maggie," he said quietly.

She averted her eyes. "Don't."

His indrawn breath was low and impatient. "You won't let me in, will you?" he asked curtly. "You meet every overture with a mad dash for the door."

She studied her clenched fingers. "You said..."

"I lied!" He turned away from her. "I'm going out of my mind."

She didn't understand. Her green eyes followed him as he walked to the window and looked out.

While he was brooding, Jorge came back, and very soon

Cord's outburst was lost in conversation laced with delicious hot chocolate served in dainty china cups.

Jorge didn't own a television. That evening, they all went out onto the wide, long front porch and sat in rocking chairs, listening to the cattle low in the distance.

"This is wonderful," Maggie remarked dreamily, closing her eyes. "It's just like at Cord's ranch, late in the evening."

"You live with him?" Jorge queried.

"No. I'm staying there for a while," she replied. "It's rather complicated."

"She doesn't want to tell you that we're being targeted by the assassin I mentioned earlier," Cord told the old man, despite Maggie's attempt to hush him up. "He's buying and selling little children into slave labor, and we're trying to shut him down."

The old man became a stranger. He leaned forward, his lean face intent in the yellow light beaming out through the windows.

"Three of my men were with me in the Republican army," he told Cord. "We are old, but at your disposal."

Cord grinned. "Thanks. I may take you up on it. I brought along a few friends," he added to Maggie's surprise. "You'll find them bivouaced in your pasture, one of your grain storage sheds, and in the barn out back. I hope you don't mind."

Jorge chuckled. "Mind? It will be like old times. An adventure!" He hesitated. "But the lovely little one here...!" he exclaimed.

"She'd go right into the trenches with me," he told Jorge, "just as your Louisa did with you."

The old man and Cord shared a look that Maggie couldn't begin to interpret, but it made her feel warm inside.

"What I propose to do," Cord said, "with your permission, is leave a man here disguised as myself. I want you to appear to travel to Tangier with Maggie, as if you're showing her this part of the world. Are you game?"

"I live a boring and uncomplicated life," Jorge said with a twinkle in his dark eyes. "Adventure becomes the stuff of legends to such a man as I have become."

"I'm not leaving you!" Maggie said at once, her wide eyes riveted to Cord.

His heart lifted. "I'm not leaving you, either," he said gently. "I'm going in disguise, as Jorge."

The old man chuckled. "You must have silver hair and walk with a stoop," he pointed out.

Cord grinned. "One of my men was on the stage. He's an expert at disguise. My own parents wouldn't know me when he gets through working on me."

Jorge looked sad for a moment. "I remember your parents, very well indeed. Your father had magic in his hands, in his body. He was not Sanchez, but he was skilled."

"Sanchez Romero was my grandfather," Cord told Maggie.

"Yes. I have a poster..."

The old man opened a huge cabinet and took out a poster of a bullfight, vivid with reds and yellows under the thick black lettering. It advertised the final appearance of the great Sanchez Romero in the great bullring in Madrid. He removed a painting, a portrait of the same man.

"He was magnificent," Maggie said against her will, drinking in the elegant, muscular lines of the handsome black-haired man. He had an arrogance and grace of carriage, even in the painting, which was striking and attractive.

"He was gored as he stood on tiptoe to deliver the *muerte,*" the old man said sadly. "I was just behind the *barrera,* cheering him on." His eyes closed. "It was as if the bull had a bundle of colorful rags on his horns. Sanchez's *traje de luz* shone like pure gold in the sunlight as the bull ran around the ring, to the horror of the crowd." He glanced at Maggie, waiting for her reaction.

She only smiled sadly. "I had an uncle who died in a rodeo outside Houston," she said. "Dangerous sports are always life-threatening. But people die on football fields of heatstroke."

"You will wish me to remain inside during your absence," the old man said suddenly, glancing at Cord.

He nodded. "And away from your friends."

"I understand." He grinned. "I am to be 'undercover.'"

Cord chuckled. "You'll be safe, as well," he pointed out. "Some of my men will remain here. Two others will be with Maggie and me, also 'undercover.'"

"You are a brave young woman," Jorge told Maggie.

She grinned at him. "I've lived a boring life myself until lately. I've got a trench coat on layaway," she added with a mischievous glance at Cord.

He smiled at her with obvious pride. It made her heart fly.

10

Maggie listened while Cord outlined his plans for travel to Tangier the following day. They would drive one of Jorge's Mercedes to the ferry and go across to Tangier, car and all. In Tangier, they would stay with Cord's cousin, Jorge's grand-nephew, Ahmed, a Berber who owned a small import/export business there.

There was no time for a leisurely visit while Gruber and his friends worked at obliterating traces of their collaboration. Cord would have to work fast. Meanwhile, the visit to his cousin would give the impression that he was staying with family during his recuperation, and Maggie was taking advantage of the holiday to see Morocco as well as Spain in the company of Cord's cousin Jorge. If Gruber checked, Cord told Maggie, he'd find out that Jorge had cousins in Tangier, which was true. In fact, Cord—disguised as Jorge—

and Maggie would be staying with one of them who lived in the city.

She tried not to be concerned about the masquerade, but it worried her. She wasn't afraid for herself. She was fearful of what might happen to Cord if Gruber discovered his disguise and his real intent. The headquarters of Global Enterprises was in Tangier. If Gruber realized that she and Cord were digging for evidence, their lives would be in terrible danger. Despite the company of those shadowy friends of Cord's, she had reservations. They were compounded by the knowledge of what Gruber and his cronies would do to her if they discovered her part in this. She knew they wouldn't hesitate to make public her most terrible secrets. She remembered Lassiter's stern advice, that she should tell Cord the truth. But not yet, she told herself. Not just yet.

It wasn't surprising that she had a nightmare after she went to sleep. The tension of the past few days, compounded by the threats of blackmail, brought back horrible memories of her childhood.

She was sobbing piteously when she felt strong arms lift her close to a warm, strong bare chest. She was cradled there, her nose ticking in the thick pelt of hair, while she cried.

"There, there," a soothing deep voice whispered at her ear while a big hand smoothed her long, wild hair. "You're perfectly safe. I won't let anything hurt you."

She became slowly aware that she was no longer dreaming. The spicy scent of Cord's cologne was in her nostrils, along with the prickly feel of the thick hair that ran in a wedge down his chest to his belly.

Her hands were flat against his body, feeling its strength. She'd been relaxed while he held her, but now she was nervous again. Her eyes opened and she drew back a breath.

The bedside light was on. The door was closed. She was sitting up in the concealing lacy white cotton gown she'd brought to sleep in, with its puffy sleeves and modest neckline. Cord was sitting on the bed beside her in a towel.

He lifted an eyebrow amusedly at her flush. "You've seen me without it," he reminded her.

She swallowed. She was still uneasy with him, with any man, like this. She realized that her inhibitions and distaste for intimacy had all but ruined her life.

He pushed back the thick hair from her cheek. "Don't you think it's time you told me the truth, Maggie?" he asked softly.

She bit her lower lip, hard. "I'd rather die," she said on a husky laugh, but she meant it.

"Why?"

Her face contorted. "Painful subjects are best left alone."

He tilted her eyes up to his. He was somber, stern-looking. He felt the tension in her hands and he smoothed them out gently, pressing her long fingers against his skin. "I was on the Internet, when we flew here," he remarked out of the blue.

"So?" she murmured noncommittally.

"Aren't you curious about why?" he persisted slowly.

Her eyes lifted to his and a flash of fear brightened them

momentarily. Surely he couldn't have found out anything there, not when the files were protected....

He drew in a deep breath. "I don't even know how to tell you." His fingers slid around hers, warm and strong. "Lassiter mentioned something to me while we were talking, about a criminal case that came up in Houston at the same time as the hotel fire that killed my parents." He searched her eyes. "I don't know why, but it started me thinking about criminal cases... So I dug into some old files, using codes I haven't resorted to in years, and I found out..." He hesitated, noting the look of stark horror on her white face.

She tried to jerk away from him, sick, horrified at having him see the photos, knowing the truth. She sobbed like a wounded thing as she fought his hands.

But he was far too strong. He eased her down onto the bed and pulled her against him, holding her gently but firmly, with her wet cheek pressed against his chest.

"You should have told me years ago," he whispered harshly. "God, when I realized what I'd done to you...!" His indrawn breath was harsh. His arms tightened, containing her helpless shivers. "I gave you hell. I hurt you, made you afraid of me—so afraid that you had to hide the truth. How do I apologize for what you went through because of the way I behaved? And I never even knew... You and your damned secrets, Maggie!" he concluded with fierce anger.

"Amy thought it best..." she began hoarsely.

"Amy?" He drew away from her, scowling. "Amy was dead when you married Evans," he said, misunderstanding.

Her eyes opened wider. She didn't understand what he meant.

He grimaced. He looked down at her with pain in his dark eyes. "We made a baby together, the night Amy died," he said unsteadily. "Evans caused you to miscarry, in a drunken rage." He ground his teeth together and there was anguish in his expression. "God, baby, I'd have killed him if I'd known...!"

She reached up and caught him around the neck, pulling him close, so close! He didn't know about the other! It was all right. She buried her face in his throat, clinging.

She felt something damp against her cheek. Tears stung her own eyes. "I never would have told you," she choked, her voice breaking. "I never wanted you to have to know. I knew it would hurt you, so much...!"

He groaned. His mouth searched over her face in hot, quick kisses that suddenly slowed and became breathlessly tender. His big body relaxed into hers, pressing her gently into the mattress. He whispered something she couldn't understand as one long, powerful leg insinuated itself between both of hers through the cotton gown.

Ordinarily she would have been intimidated by the movement. She would have been nervous, shy, hesitant. But he was sharing grief with her. She'd lost their child and now he knew. The pain was suddenly bearable, only because he knew.

"Oh, Cord," she whispered brokenly, accommodating the slow, sensuous brush of his body over hers. Her arms curled around his chest. "I wanted our baby," she said at his ear. "I wanted him so much. And Bart hit me and hit me! I remember...I remember lying there, bleeding and broken, cursing him at the top of my lungs for what I knew he'd done. I told him I'd tell you, and he'd never have a minute's peace for the rest of his miserable life." Her eyes stung with tears. "I told him I'd get even with him if it was the last thing I ever did...!" She swallowed. "He killed himself," she whispered. "I made him kill himself. I've had to live with that, too, on top of everything else...!"

"Damn him. If he hadn't committed suicide, I'd have killed him myself!" he choked.

"He was an alcoholic and I never knew until after I married him. I suspected I was pregnant. I wanted the baby to have a name, and I was afraid to tell you..."

"Yes. I was cruel to you. Horribly cruel."

She nuzzled her face against him. "You were shocked. I'd been engaged. You thought I was experienced. It's all right."

"It will never be all right," he said harshly. "I didn't even think about consequences."

"We'd both been drinking," she said quietly. "Don't beat yourself to death with it. It won't change a thing."

"It won't," he agreed heavily. "I'm sorry you had to go through that alone."

Her hands smoothed over his dark hair. "I phoned Eb."

"Yes, I remember you told me that," he said, and his tone was cold.

"I...was going to have him get in touch with you," she confessed, "in a moment's insanity. But then they told me about my husband's wreck, and I didn't make the call."

His big hands slid warmly against her body as he shifted slowly. His mouth brushed at her throat, stirring her. "I would have come immediately," he whispered. "In fact, I did come, soon afterward, the minute I heard that you were in the hospital. I never knew exactly why you were there." His hands contracted bruisingly. "You were at home by then but you wouldn't even look at me!"

She kissed his throat gently. "You'd have seen right through me if I had. I wanted only to spare you the heartache. It was over. Telling you would have accomplished nothing, except to hurt you."

He made a rough sound in his throat. His mouth found her breast through the thick cotton and pressed hard against it. "I deserved to be hurt."

She smiled through her excitement. It was drugging, to be held so close by him, so hungrily.

"I've never hurt you deliberately."

"I wish I could say the same."

Her fingers toyed with his thick hair. It was delightful to be able to touch him, lie with him, be with him. Her body tingled, and she felt no fear at all, only a sense of unreality. One of her long legs moved involuntarily, sliding against his. To her surprise, the tiny movement aroused him blantantly, and at once.

He stiffened. "I think you'd better not do that again," he said through his teeth.

"Sorry."

He let out a heavy breath at her ear. "I wish we were in a hotel."

"Why?" she asked curiously.

He laughed deep in his throat. "I could call room service for an emergency condom."

She laughed, too. Her mouth moved lazily against his hot neck. "I like feeling you like this," she said, her voice faintly surprised.

His big hand caught her hip and pulled it up into his, letting her feel the full power of the arousal. His fingers contracted and he shivered faintly. "I want to go inside you," he breathed at her ear.

Her soft gasp was audible. She couldn't believe he'd said something so blatant.

He moved lazily against her, while his mouth slid to the square neckline of the gown. He traced its line with his lips, nuzzling under it to draw his mouth against the petal-soft skin.

She moved restlessly, burning up with pleasure. "That feels good," she murmured dazedly.

His tongue traced a pattern on her flesh. "Let me take your gown off, and I'll show you something that feels even better."

"You never struck me as the sort of man who'd ask first," she teased breathlessly.

"Only with you," he replied. "Does this thing unsnap or unbutton?"

His fingers nudged buttons out of buttonholes while she laughed softly. He lifted his head and looked down into her eyes. He eased his forefinger under the edge of the fabric and teased a path halfway to her hard nipple, watching her like a hawk to judge her reaction.

Her lips parted. She was finding it increasingly hard to breathe normally. Her nails bit into his upper arms as he poised just above her. Impulsively, she looked down. The towel had fallen away from his hips, but they were pressed so closely together that she couldn't see anything.

"Want to look?" he asked gently, and lifted himself a few inches above her, to let her see.

Her breath caught. He was amazingly beautiful, like a sculpture she'd seen once. She lay still, just staring at the perfection of his lean, hard-muscled body. He looked formidable, but she wasn't afraid of him.

"You're very aroused," she whispered boldly and lifted her eyes back up to his.

His hand slid gently inside the gown to cover her soft breast. "Hard and hungry," he agreed. "But if you'll let me have you, I can promise you it won't hurt. Lovemaking is beautiful. It has a rhythm. It builds like a symphony. The pleasure is more exquisite than words can describe." He searched her eyes while he caressed her tenderly, feeling her helpless response in the lifting of her body toward his hand. "I want you very much."

"I don't...take anything," she managed to say.

His fingers found her nipple and tested its hardness, his forefinger brushing it gently until she stiffened with pleasure. "I don't have anything to use. It would be reckless. Irresponsible." He smiled slowly, his dark eyes flashing. "It would be delicious!"

Her expression was one of excited curiosity. She'd never had pleasure from a man. Even with him, it had been uncomfortable and frightening. She no longer felt the inhibitions or fear. The tenderness he'd shown her in recent days had changed her. Perhaps it had changed him, too, because he wasn't making demands.

Her fingers lifted to trace his hard, chiseled mouth. Her eyes gleamed with wonder. "Cousin Jorge wouldn't like it."

He only smiled.

Her body shifted, just a breath. It arched faintly.

His fingers went back to the buttons and slowly unfastened them to her waist. "Sit up," he whispered.

He drew her up with him and slid the gown down over her hips, tossing it off the bed along with his towel. Under it, she was wearing simple cotton briefs. He removed those, too, with his mouth making exciting forays over her belly, so that she didn't protest her sudden nudity.

He nipped her hip with his teeth and laughed at her hushed giggle. His lips opened slowly on her flat stomach while his hand found her in a way she hadn't experienced in her adult life. The touch brought back terrible memories and she started to protest when a shock of delight arched her hips. It reflected in the eyes that met his when he lifted his head.

He held her startled gaze while he coaxed her body expertly to permit even greater liberties.

"This is just the beginning," he whispered as she began to move involuntarily and whimper rhythmically with the deft touch of his hand. "I'm going to make you climax," he said huskily as his mouth lowered to hers. "And when you reach it, I'm going into you, hard and deep!"

She moaned into his mouth, the words as arousing as what he was doing to her eager, delighted body. Her nails bit into him. "It's...wonderful," she choked.

"It's fun," he breathed. "Glorious fun. Touch me."

Her hand found him a little shyly, and she made a husky little sound when he nibbled her lower lip and laughed huskily.

"I never thought...it could be like this," she managed, shivering with the increasing pleasure. "I never imagined... Cord!" She gasped, stiffening, shuddering as he took her faster and faster toward some impossibly pleasurable height.

"I love looking at you," he whispered, his eyes smoldering as he watched her body, delighting in its slender beauty. Her breasts were firm and pert, their crowns red and hard. Her legs were spreading wide as she watched his face and lifted to the touch of his hand. "Your breasts are beautiful, especially like this, with your nipples hard and red as wine."

She was barely hearing him. Her eyes were fixed, her body

shivering now with each touch, her arms beside her head as she watched him blankly and sobbed, praying that he wasn't going to stop.

"You won't...stop?" she whispered helplessly.

He shook his head slowly.

Her hips lifted to him. It was incredible that she could lie here, nude, letting him make love to her body, and not feel ashamed.

His touch became insistent. "It excites me when you whimper like that," he said gruffly. "Do you like it?"

"It's...so...good!" she bit off.

"It gets even better." He didn't stop touching her, but he did move, so that his body was poised over hers, his powerful legs pushing hers even wider apart. He eased down, his hips hovering while he increased the pressure and the rhythm of his hand on her.

She cried out softly, biting her lip as the pleasure came in sudden great waves.

"Yes," he said roughly. "Yes. I'm going to push you right over the edge now. Don't think, just let me have your body. Let me have all of you. Let me go into you, Maggie...!"

She stiffened suddenly under a crashing tidal wave of pleasure that reached a frightening level of pleasure, and yet there was still something more to attain! Her back arched as she looked into his eyes, drawing her knees up on either side of her body to coax him down to her as the glory of physical ecstasy convulsed her.

"God...!" he groaned helplessly, and his hips thrust down as his hand lifted to her waist.

He went into her body with a violent motion, aware that she was more than ready to accept him, to accommodate him, to swallow him up whole. He looked straight into her dilating eyes as he thrust fiercely into her prone body.

"Watch me," he choked. "I'll let you see me. I'll let you have me...!"

His voice broke on the explosive climax that stiffened him violently above her. His eyes were glazed. His breathing seemed to have stopped. His teeth clenched and he shuddered again and again and again.

"Oh...God...it's...like...dying!" he cried out. "Maggie... Maggie, darling...!"

His eyes closed and he convulsed so harshly that she was actually afraid for him. She reached around his hips with her long, elegant legs, surprised to find that the gentle shifting of her body made the convulsions worse. His fists clenched beside her head. He sobbed harshly, rhythmically, like the contractions of his powerful body.

"Cord?" she whispered, shivering in the aftermath of her own exquisite climax.

"Can't...stop," he gasped. "Can't...stop!"

"My darling," she whispered, kissing him everywhere she could reach, comforting him as he exploded in her arms. She heard his harsh breathing at her ear as he lay completely on her, his hips still moving convulsively. She felt him inside her, hard and warm and big, velvety soft over the hardness. She closed her eyes to savor the delight. She felt him in her body, felt the release that seemed to go on forever, and she sighed, cuddling him. She'd never felt so close to anyone, ever.

"Maggie," he groaned hoarsely. His hands went under her back as his mouth searched for hers. He kissed her fiercely, groaning helplessly into her open mouth.

She cradled him, smiling under his devouring kisses as he slowly, slowly, began to relax, shivering now in the aftermath of physical delight.

Her hands smoothed over his dark hair tenderly. They'd made love. She could give herself, without fear or shame. She could be a whole woman. She'd never thought it would happen for her, not like this, never with Cord.

His big hands smoothed the length of her, from her breasts to her hips, while his lips began to search tenderly over her face. He smiled. He laughed mysteriously.

"What's funny?" she asked drowsily.

He kissed her softly. "I'll tell you one day." He started to lift away and her arms caught him, protesting.

He looked down at her with breathless tenderness, his black hair damp with sweat as he studied her flushed face. Impulsively he moved his hips and felt her body open to him. He withdrew a heartbeat and then moved down again. She moved with him, her legs brushing his as she felt the pleasure begin all over. She lifted her hips, grinding them into his, as her teeth clenched. "Oh, dear Lord," she choked. "Cord!"

He moved then, fiercely, dragging his hips from side to side, watching her eyes widen with every hard brush. His face tautened with desire.

"I'm going to have you again," he said huskily. "Feel me swell, baby. Feel me deep in your body!" He groaned and his eyes closed as the fierce arousal burst through him and made him helpless to stop.

"I want you," she whispered blindly. "I want to feel you... explode...in me!"

He cried out, the words bringing a sudden, unexpected climax that wrapped the two of them in a hot, helpless tangle of movement.

"Cord," she whispered, lifting her mouth to his ear. "Cord...make me...have a baby!"

The words deepened the climax into unexplored territory. He felt his body whip helplessly above hers.

She watched him, her own excitement blazing up in the hot silence of flesh brushing flesh, the sound of the sheet brushing the mattress under them unexpectedly loud as they strained together in a frenzy of motion.

She felt herself throbbing, and then her own body matched the racking convulsions she felt in him. The whole world seemed to blur and fly away as the pleasure throbbed in her lower belly and suddenly burst. She felt the heat of it surge through her in waves of unbearable pleasure...

She heard Cord's strained breathing above her, felt the beloved weight of his powerful body as he shivered in the aftermath.

His arms cradled her as he rolled over onto his side, one long leg thrown over her hips.

"That was a first," he whispered, his voice deep with exhaustion.

"Hmmm?" she murmured, still dazed.

He kissed her eyes. "Do you know what an orgasm is?"

"No, but I think I just had one," she whispered back with a soft, secret laugh.

"I've never had an experience like this with anyone else."

Her leg curled into his. "Honest?"

"Honest." He kissed her soft mouth. "You whispered for me to make you pregnant," he breathed into her open lips.

She flushed, embarrassed.

He felt the awkward movement of her body and lifted his head to look into her uncertain eyes.

"It's too late now for you to unwhisper it," he pointed out. He pursed his lips and looked rakish. "I forget how many sperm a man's body can produce, but I think I just set a world's record."

She flushed, but she smiled, too.

"What the hell," he murmured drowsily. "The world won't end if you get pregnant."

"You shouldn't worry," she began. "It would be a long shot..."

He looked into her eyes curiously. "I'm not worried, Maggie," he said gently.

She grimaced. "You have a lifestyle..."

He kissed her eyelids closed. “We won’t solve all the problems tonight. Let’s face one problem at a time. Gruber is our priority.”

“Gruber. I forgot.”

He cocked an eyebrow and grinned. “Did you?”

“Don’t get conceited,” she chided. “Probably there are at least ten other extraordinary lovers in the world who could pleasure me almost to unconsciousness.”

“Don’t go looking for any of them,” he said darkly.

She sighed and looked down between their bodies. “I didn’t expect it to feel like that,” she confessed.

He pulled slowly away from her, watching her as she saw their bodies separate. She flushed a little, but she didn’t look away. He followed her gaze and smiled slowly.

“Think of it as sex education,” he teased.

She lifted her eyes to his face. “It’s so funny,” she tried to explain. “I know all about it, but I know nothing. I knew nothing, until tonight. I thought...” She hesitated. “It isn’t always like that, is it?”

“Not for me, no,” he said quietly. “I’ve never had sex this good.”

She frowned. “Was it just sex?”

He scowled thoughtfully and traced a pattern over her relaxed breasts. “It was lovemaking,” he said quietly, “in the purest sense.” He searched her eyes relentlessly. “I thought about making you pregnant, even before you whispered to me. It aroused me. It really aroused me. I’m not usually quite that...potent.”

Her face relaxed as she studied his lean face. He seemed confused, uncertain. "It's been a long time for you, hasn't it?" she asked.

His eyes shot back to hers. "You think abstinence could produce an experience like this?"

She sighed. "I don't know. Could it?"

He didn't speak. With a long sigh, he lifted his legs off the bed and searched on the carpet for his towel and her gown and briefs. He tossed them to her without quite meeting her eyes.

"What's wrong?" she asked gently.

He wrapped the towel around his hips. "I didn't mean to do this," he said, turning to stare at her with troubled eyes. "I genuinely came in to comfort you. After what I learned, about our baby," he added slowly, "I wouldn't have taken advantage of a nightmare to make you give yourself to me."

She held the nightgown to her breasts and watched him. "I know that."

He sighed. "Maggie, you thought I'd found out something else, something besides the baby, didn't you?" he asked out of the blue. His eyes narrowed as she stiffened. "What other secret are you keeping?"

11

Maggie held her breath while Cord studied her reactions to that bombshell of a question.

"After what just happened between us," he said persistently, "there shouldn't be room for a single secret."

She still looked worried. She wanted to trust him, but it was more frightening now to have him know about her past, after the tenderness they'd shared. It would make her...dirty, somehow.

He could see the torment in her face, and he backed down. He'd ferreted out the miscarriage. With time, he could find out the rest. It must be something terrible, for her to react like this.

"Here." He coaxed her into lifting her arms, and he slid the gown over her head. "Want a shower?" he asked with a slow smile. "We could have one together."

"Cousin Jorge..." she began.

"...is a man," he said complacently. "And he knows what it's like to be at the mercy of desire."

"So do you," she remarked, and looked uneasy.

He searched her troubled eyes. He traced her soft lower lip with a lazy forefinger. "When I was younger, before I married Patricia, I had my share of adventures with willing women," he said bluntly. "But I grew out of it. I don't have the same curiosity, and even if I did, I wouldn't use you to satisfy it. Okay?"

She bit her lower lip, feeling sad and not understanding why. "I don't...know a lot about this, on a personal level," she said, trying to make herself clear without resorting to the truth. "Tonight was sort of a first for me."

"It was for me, too," he replied quietly. "I've never felt anything like it. I want to be tender with you. I want to listen and touch and taste, even when it gets violent." His eyes shimmered with dark warmth. "What happened isn't supposed to be possible. A man spends himself and then it takes time, a lot of time usually, before he's even capable again. I managed it twice without stopping to breathe."

Her face brightened. "Didn't you, before?" She wanted to know.

"Hell!" He laughed, genuinely, at her mischievous expression. "No, I didn't, before," he confessed. "Satisfied?"

She stretched slowly, watching his eyes follow the movement of her body. "Very," she said huskily.

He drew in a long breath and got to his feet, wrapping the

towel back around his lean hips. "I'm leaving," he informed her. "Even if you're not sore after that, I am. I want a shower and a good night's sleep. Tomorrow, I have to age forty years and acquire a stoop."

She laughed delightedly. "I need a trench coat and a gun," she pointed out. "I'll ride shotgun for you!"

He looked down at her, drinking in her radiant face, the excitement mingled with tenderness in her green eyes. "You take my breath away," he said huskily.

The words confused her. She didn't understand.

He laughed at his own sense of wonder. He'd known Maggie for so many years, yet until tonight, he'd known nothing so little about her. They'd created a child together, lost it, and he'd never known. Now that he did, it...involved them, as they'd never been involved before. All the grief and pain of their lives had contrived to make them closer than ever. Perhaps that was what relationships grew out of, he thought while he studied her, they grew out of hardship and pain, making two people cling to each other and share their problems.

"What are you thinking?" she asked.

"That you and I are closer than most people," he said softly. "And I don't mean just in bed." One broad shoulder lifted. "We've shared some of the most painful episodes of our lives with each other. There's a bond. Until I knew about the baby, I never really faced it."

Her eyes were sad. "I should have told you."

He nodded. “You should have, but I certainly understand why you couldn’t. Nobody’s to blame for that except me. I pushed you away out of shame and self-disgust.” He sighed gently. “I’ll never do that again,” he added huskily. “And if you get pregnant from what we just did, you won’t be able to hide it from me. I won’t let you.”

She smiled faintly. “I might never be able to get pregnant again,” she said sadly.

He lifted an eyebrow haughtily. “Are you paying attention? I have industrial-strength sperm. In the history of the planet, there was never a man more inspired to produce them than I was tonight. And you think you can’t get pregnant? Ha!”

She laughed with pure delight. His eyes were twinkling. She liked the way they crinkled at the corners when he smiled.

He bent and kissed her gently. “I’m going to bed. You should, too. We’ve got a long few days ahead of us.”

“I know.” She watched him like a bird, her head turned to one side, her eyes bright and curious.

“Something bothering you?” he asked, because he didn’t understand her rapt regard.

She moved her shoulders and smiled shyly. “No.”

He lifted his chin. “Don’t hand me that,” he said, reading through the subterfuge. “Spill it.”

She toyed with her gown and didn’t look straight at him. “Lassiter said he’d give me a job if I wanted it.”

There was a long, heavy pause. She didn’t dare look up. She was fishing.

Finally he sighed. "Okay," he replied. "When this is over, and I've taught you the ropes, if you have to find out about detective work, he's a good place to start. But only until the kids come along," he added firmly, bringing her shocked eyes to his lean, solemn face. "While they're young, they'll need you at home, along with me. We'll give them a solid foundation, and then when they're in school, you can pick up your job again."

Her eyes were full of wonder. He was talking about a shared future. He never had, before.

"Don't look at me as if the whole thing is my responsibility," he chided. "You were the one screaming, 'Make me pregnant!'"

She flushed and burst out laughing. "You stop that!"

He grinned. "I like kids. They can all learn to be cowboys." He frowned thoughtfully. "But we won't let them learn about wires and listening devices," he added, remembering what Lassiter had told him about his own children. "Lassiter made a real mistake there, with his kids. We aren't going to repeat his mistakes."

She grinned back. It was all a pipe dream, of course. She couldn't get pregnant and he wouldn't settle down. They were daydreaming out loud. But it was such a wonderful picture that she didn't say a word in protest. Living with Cord, having his children, sharing his life...that was real fantasy. And even if she bought into it, there was still her past, the sordid horrible past that would destroy what was left of her life. Once he knew, he'd never want to touch her again.

The thought tortured her, but she kept smiling. She didn't let him see that she knew it was an impossible dream. He didn't know about her past, and he couldn't find out. Those records were sealed. Even if he had pass codes, they wouldn't do him any good. Stillwell had documents and videotape, but he wasn't likely to share those unless he had to. Maggie was going to make sure he didn't get the opportunity. If she had to, she'd go after Stillwell herself, once Cord taught her the ropes of this spy game.

"You look like you're plotting something," he said.

She chuckled. "I am."

He pursed his lips. "What a delicious thought. I like pink, if you're concocting seduction plans."

"I like pink myself. Wait and see."

He sighed and smiled ruefully. "Considering my present state, and yours, I'll have to. Sleep well, sweetheart."

"You, too," she replied in the same soft tone he'd used.

He left, reluctantly.

She got into the shower and put on a fresh gown, pausing to strip the bed and remake it. She worried that Jorge's maid might discover that hanky-panky was going on in the bedroom, but when she thought about the sheer delight of Cord's lovemaking, she couldn't manage to be ashamed of it. In all her life, there had only ever been Cord. Whatever happened now, she had one perfect night to tuck in with her memories.

Everyone was somber at the breakfast table. Cord's eyes were warm and gentle as he greeted her, but there was no opportunity for shared memories. He was there with two strange men, one wearing a hooded djellabah made of oyster-colored silk, the other, a tall Latin, in a conventional suit.

"This is Bojo," Cord introduced the silk-clad man who smiled pleasantly at her through an abbreviated mustache and beard, "and that's Rodrigo," he added, nodding toward the handsome Latin, who also smiled pleasantly.

She studied them. "Covert ops 101," she said finally, nodding. "I can't *wait* to see what the lab work involves!"

It broke them up. Everyone laughed, including Cord and Jorge.

"I told you she was game," Cord told the newcomers. He grinned at Maggie. "This is where you get your toy gun and practice dodging bullets."

"Lead me to it," she returned.

"First things first." Cord's eyes narrowed as he outlined the plan for his associates.

"We leave Peter and Don here, to watch over Jorge and keep things safe," Cord told the others. "Rodrigo, you're going to be my valet for the trip. Bojo," he sighed, shaking his head, "you're going to be our guide again, I'm afraid."

Bojo shrugged and smiled complacently. "If you ask His Highness, the Sheikh of Qawi, he will tell you that I am more than adequate to the task."

"I'll take your word for it," Cord told him. He glanced at Maggie. "Micha Steele heads up a group of mercs, of which Bojo is vice commander. I've worked in and out of it between government assignments."

She was amazed that Cord was sharing these intimate details of his life with her. It must have shown, because he smiled and grasped her hand tightly in his beside her plate.

"No secrets, remember?" he chided gently. He glanced at Jorge. "You'll be safe here," he told his cousin. "Peter won't let anything go wrong."

Jorge chuckled with delight, especially after noticing the close clasp of Cord's hand in Maggie's. "I still have my rifle," he told the younger man, "and I am still a dead shot. One must be, when one has bulls the equal of my own. I also have caballeros who work for me on the *finca,* most of whom served in the military before they came here. No, I am safe. It is the four of you for whom I worry," he added with a speaking glance toward Maggie.

"I'm in very safe hands," she told him, feeling warm all over at the expression in Cord's lean face as he looked at her.

"The safest," Cord said gently. He lifted her hand to his mouth. "Now," he said, releasing it. "Let's get down to logistics."

There were weapons, of course. Maggie was going to have to learn to endure them, she told herself, because they were going up against some of the most dangerous men on earth. A multimillion-dollar enterprise would arm itself to the teeth if it were threatened, and Gruber wouldn't hesitate to kill anyone who posed a threat. So when Cord ran her through the motions of loading, locking, and firing a .45 caliber automatic handgun, she paid attention.

He set up a target in one of the deserted pastures and stood behind her while she mastered the two-handed technique of balancing a heavy automatic weapon and sighting it without closing both eyes.

"Just relax," he chided at her ear, moving closer. "It's not the enemy."

She leaned back deliberately with a soft moan. "I can't concentrate," she murmured huskily, loving the feel of all that warm strength at her back. "I want to make love."

His breath caught and he laughed delightedly. "So do I," he murmured, kissing her neck fiercely. "But neither of us is in any condition for bedroom gymnastics this morning! Besides, we have a mission. That means no sex."

"That's for football players," she scoffed.

He nipped her ear with his teeth. "It's for mercs, too. You just joined the unit, so pay attention."

"Afterward," she said deliberately, with a twinkling glance over her shoulder into smoldering dark eyes.

"Afterward," he agreed huskily.

She shivered. Her eyes held his and she burned from head to toe.

He caught her waist firmly and shook her, his lean face evidence of a passion just barely restrained. "If I start kissing you, we'll have each other on the ground. People will stare. Really."

She laughed. "Okay. I'll behave. Show me again!"

At the end of an hour, she'd recalled her earlier training with Eb Scott, and was making inroads into the target.

"Very nice," he murmured. "You're a quick study."

"I never told you, but Eb showed me how to shoot," she said without thinking. "Cord!"

He released his suddenly bruising hold on her waist abruptly. "Sorry," he said at once.

She turned, her eyes apologetic as she lifted them. "I didn't mean to bring it up. But while we're on the subject," she added gently, "you must surely know by now that I'm in love with you. I have been since I was barely twelve."

He scowled, surprised by the blunt statement.

"Eb will tell you that I broke things off because he couldn't give up working as a mercenary," she continued bravely. "But the real reason was because I couldn't bear for him to touch me." She smiled sadly. "I wanted you..."

He caught her up in his arms and kissed her with slow, fierce passion, feeling his taut body rivet itself to every inch of hers. With a husky moan, she reached up to him and clung, her feet off the ground as he lifted her. For those few seconds, they were alone in the world, bound by forces stronger than either of them had realized. Time passed by in a heated fervor.

"I hope the safety is on," an amused voice murmured close by.

They drew apart at once. Cord looked at Bojo with his mind in limbo, and Maggie stared at him with equal blankness.

"The pistol?" he prompted, nodding toward Maggie's hand curled so tightly around Cord's neck.

"Pistol. Right." She cleared her throat and abruptly moved back from Cord, handing him the gun, handle first.

"Safety," he murmured. His hands were unsteady as he put it on.

Bojo laughed wickedly. "This is going to be the most interesting covert mission of my life," he remarked dryly, and walked off while they were still trying to regain their poise.

During a lull in the preparations, Cord led Maggie out to the barn and the large corral that surrounded it. He gestured across the hills toward the grazing cattle in the distance.

"The bulls that Jorge raises for the bullring," he pointed out. "He doesn't raise many these days. I think he's lost heart. In the old days, when things were different, there was almost a religion built around the art—notice I didn't say sport—of the *corrida.* My grandfather would stand, they said, in the center of the ring with the fighting cape and wait for the bull. Consider," he added with bright eyes, "that the bull weighs half a ton and is bred for aggression and stamina. My grandfather would wait for the charge and move not a muscle, not an eyelash, as the animal lowered its horns and came straight for him! Then, with a flick of the cape, he would distract the bull at the last instant and the audience would gasp as the huge animal brushed right against him in its furious charge." He sighed. "A brave bull would be spared, its life demanded by the spectators. While the losers would be fed to the community." He glanced down at her with a curious smile. "How would it be for you," he asked softly, "if you had to watch me dress in the *traje de luces,* the golden 'suit of lights' worn by a matador, and know that I went into the ring with only my cape and my courage to protect me from horns as sharp as spears?"

She drew in a slow breath and shivered in the hot sun.

He caught her gently by her nape and pulled her into his body, held her, comforted her against a phantom thought that he was ashamed for voicing. His hand soothed her neck. "My mother and my grandmother faced that agony most of their married lives. My mother was American. She had a brave heart, much courage, but she went white and threw up every time my father signed a new contract and went the rounds of the *ferias.*" He sighed. "I don't think I could do that to you," he said in a soft, absent tone.

She slid her arms around him and pressed tight into his arms with a soft moan. He belonged to her now. She wondered if he even realized it. Her heart almost burst with joy. She put all thoughts of tomorrow out of her mind and felt his arms close with wonder. She drank in the clean smell of his powerful body, the warmth of him so close. She closed her eyes with a smile, listening contentedly to his steady heartbeat under her ear while his deep voice continued about the old days of the bullfight. It was one of those few moments in a lifetime when everything is, for a space of minutes, absolutely ethereal, joy hanging like a drop of rain from a trembling dry leaf, the very hesitation pregnant with anticipation. She knew that she would remember it all her life, no matter what happened.

That afternoon, they were dressed in their various disguises, with the exception of Bojo and Maggie. Cord had acquired a wig that looked remarkably like Jorge's wavy white hair, along with one of Jorge's suits—fortunately they were of a similar height—and his silver-headed wolf's head cane. He also had a nice stoop that Jorge chided him for, although it was accurate. Jorge had crippling arthritis of the spine.

Rodrigo, the Latin, was wearing the elegant suit of a valet and hovering near Cord. Bojo put on his dark glasses and pulled the hood over his short black hair. Maggie, in a neat white pantsuit with low-heeled shoes, a lacy scarf over her long hair, which was loose down her back, and dark glasses covering her eyes, clung to Cord's arm. Wearing a dressy hat as Jorge did, with dark glasses over his eyes to help the disguise, Cord stooped and walked along beside Maggie toward the car.

Minutes later, they were down the long paved driveway, through the wrought-iron gate that closed and locked behind them, and on the road to the Costa del Sol and Gibraltar, and the ferry that would take them to Tangier.

After passing through passport control twice—once arriving at Gibraltar and then again for entrance to Morocco—Rodrigo, with Bojo in the front seat beside him, drove them into the city of Tangier. It wasn't Maggie's first glimpse of the exotic place, having been there with Gretchen Brannon only weeks before. She'd lost touch with her friend, and she hoped that the job she'd given up in Qawi was working out for Gretchen. Like everyone else, she'd maintained the fiction of Cord's blindness. If Gretchen knew anything of them, she'd been told that Cord hadn't regained his sight. Hopefully Maggie would get to correct that false impression in the months ahead, if everything went well.

She glanced at Cord beside her in the back seat, getting a good idea of how he would look as an old man. She would have given anything to share her life with him, to grow old with him. She loved him more than her life. She always would. But if her sins were disclosed, Cord wouldn't want her anymore, she was certain of it. She'd best pay attention to what she was learning of firearms and covert ops, so that she could do as she threatened, and beg Lassiter for a job as a private investigator when this was all over. If she could stay in Houston, she added miserably. It might be too painful, if the truth came out. There were other cities, she consoled herself. But none of them would contain Cord.

They came into sight of a pretty little villa with a wrought-iron gate reminiscent of the entrance to Jorge's *finca* in Spain. There were flowers everywhere once they got inside it. The house itself was two stories high, white adobe, with red tiles on its roof. The entrance led down a hallway through a wooden door and opened to inside balconies, dripping flowers, and a courtyard where a fountain pulsed with watery music, in a patio of blue and white ceramic tiles in elegant patterns. The tiles went halfway up the walls, as well. Everywhere in Tangier was the sweet scent of musk.

A tall, elegant young man came out to meet them. "Cousin Jorge!" he said loudly, taking the "old man's" hand in both of his. "How wonderful that you could come to visit! And this must be Maggie, of whom you have spoken, who accompanied poor Cord to Spain. Welcome, welcome!"

"Thank you for your hospitality, Cousin Ahmed," Cord said in a nice approximation of Jorge's husky deep voice, speaking loudly enough that the servants could hear him without straining. "Cord thought it might be good for Maggie to see something of Tangier, while he rested for a day or so. I think he craved some solitude. His lack of vision troubles him greatly. This is my valet, Rodrigo," he introduced their companion, who bowed, "and our guide, Bojo."

"They are both welcome, also. Come, let me show you to your rooms! Carmen! Come and meet our guests," he called as they entered the open door of the living room, a spacious expanse of polished wood floors and antique furniture with brocade draperies.

A pretty young woman came forward with a baby in her arms. She greeted Maggie effusively, and the men with a somewhat subdued manner.

"Carmen and our son, Mohammed," Ahmed introduced his family. "She is on her way to her sister's house for a visit, but she wanted to meet you before she left."

As they spoke conversationally, it was very obvious to Maggie why the young woman was being moved, with her child, from the premises. It would take her out of the line of fire, if there was trouble.

Carmen was escorted out by her husband to a waiting limousine, put into it, and waved goodbye. The servants, a woman and a man, both small and dark and apparently not Muslim by their apparel, led Maggie to an upstairs bedroom next door to the one that would be occupied by Cord and Rodrigo. Bojo was down the hall. Maggie was rather sad about the arrangements, because she wanted to be in Cord's arms in the darkness, as she had the night before.

They had a light lunch and went to sit in the enclosed patio and drink hot chocolate and talk. It was a lazy, pleasant afternoon. Soon afterward, Ahmed announced that he would have to make an appearance at his office, where he worked in the import/export business, since he'd taken off half the day to spend with his arriving guests. He left his visitors in the care of the servants, who were obviously not in on the masquerade, so Cord and Maggie had to be very careful not to give the game away.

Later, when Ahmed had returned, supper was served, and it was time to retire, Cord went into Maggie's bedroom to caution her about talking to the servants.

"We can't trust anyone," he said gently. "It has nothing to do with credentials. This city was always known for international intrigue, and it still is. There are conclaves of people from all over Europe here, and some of them are shady characters. We can't possibly know these people who work for Ahmed. He doesn't trust them, either, for what it's worth."

She traced a pattern on the front of his white shirt. "So we can't sleep together," she agreed.

His big hands spanned her waist. "You don't regret that any more than I do," he said gently. "I can't think of anything I want more than you in my arms all night, close and safe." He bent and kissed her tenderly. "It isn't just sex, either," he whispered, "although it's great between us."

"I understand," she said, and she did. There was a need to be with him all the time. It was overpowering, breathtaking. She searched his dark eyes. "I feel odd today," she said huskily. Her fingers reached up to touch his mouth. "I hate being away from you, at all."

He bent and brushed his mouth over her eyelids. "It's very natural when people become lovers," he told her. "Or even when they don't. Feelings, emotions, like this become irresistible. I tingle all over every time I look at you. All I want to do right now, in fact, is ease you down on that bed and kiss you until my mouth hurts." He smiled ruefully.

She pressed close, but not too close, and laid her cheek against his broad chest with a sigh. "I just want to hold you," she said, her voice choked with emotion she couldn't contain.

He moaned softly and lifted her close, carrying her to an armchair in the corner. He cuddled her against him and kissed her face with breathless tenderness while he cradled her in the warm darkness.

"We have to stop," he said after a minute. "God forbid that one of the servants should snoop around here and wonder why you're kissing a man old enough to be your grandfather."

She chuckled softly, tracing the white wig on his head. "Why not, when he's so sexy?"

He kissed her one last time and, regretfully, got to his feet, setting her firmly on hers. "Keep both doors locked, the one onto the balcony as well as the one leading into the hall. Here." He pressed something small into her hand. "It's a listening device, disguised as a button. Put it on the bedside table. If anything happens, talk loud."

"I'm not armed," she pointed out.

"And you won't be, at night," he replied. "I almost shot Bojo one dark night when he came in unexpectedly, and I've been handling a gun most of my adult life."

She grimaced. "I get the point."

He tilted her chin up and studied her flushed face with appreciation. "You look loved."

"So do you," she chided softly.

He chuckled. "I'm going to bed with Rodrigo."

"My God!"

He glared at her. "Not like that!"

She sighed. "Thank goodness."

He laughed, shaking his head. "You're going to be the death of me."

"Don't even joke about it," she said. She stared up at him solemnly, as she had when she was ten and he was eighteen, and he was in trouble. "You have to be careful. I wouldn't want to live, if anything happened to you," she added with a simplicity that was profound in its lack of emphasis.

His face tautened as he looked at her. He felt again, that unwelcome sense of aching fear that he could lose her, the knowledge that this woman was all he had in the world. His fingers brushed her cheek lightly and he fought for self-control.

"I'm not reckless," he said softly. "And even when I take chances, they're weighed and calculated. You're my loose cannon. You have to do exactly what I tell you, no hesitation."

She smiled. "Haven't I always?" she teased.

He drew his fingers back. "That's a can of worms I'm not opening tonight," he teased. "Sleep well. Lock everything."

"You bet, boss!" she said brightly.

"Oh, doesn't that sound sweet and submissive?" he drawled. "If I didn't know you better, I might even believe it."

She curtsied.

He made a face and left, closing the door firmly behind him.

12

The next day, Cord and Maggie lounged around the villa, with Cord still in his disguise. Meanwhile Bojo went into the city with Cousin Ahmed for a tour of the city—but actually to do some undercover work for the mission. Both men were gone until very late.

When Bojo returned, he went immediately into "Jorge's" room, where Cord was lying down, Rodrigo was moving clothes from a closet to a chair and Ahmed's determined little male servant hovered with no apparent excuse.

"Ahmed asked me to send you to him," Bojo told the small man, with a smile. "We are going out for the evening, and he wishes you to help him select his clothing."

"Sí, señor," the little man replied, but he cast a suspicious glance at the newcomer before he closed the door.

Immediately when he left, Cord sat up in bed and snapped a

nod at Bojo, who pulled a small electronic device from his pocket in the slit at the hip of the djellaba, and began sweeping the room.

Their worst suspicions were confirmed when the detector found two bugs, one in a table drawer beside the bed, the other in the bathroom. Both were left in place, so as not to alert the person who had placed them.

Cord grimaced, furious. Bojo shrugged, curious as to how to proceed with a third unknown person "in" the room with them.

Rodrigo put down the jacket he was holding and began making hand gestures. Cord's eyes brightened. He grinned. He nodded, and replied to the gestures. Bojo was puzzled. Later, Cord would explain that Rodrigo was adept at Plains Indian sign talk, and had taught Cord once on a surveillance mission. They liked to use it to confound other mercs in their group. But now, it became a very handy tool.

With it, Cord told Rodrigo in simple terms that he and Maggie were going to break into the offices of Global Enterprises that night while, apparently, in a fancy restaurant with Ahmed. Rodrigo and Bojo would cover for them. Rodrigo was to get out his night gear, in a hidden compartment of his suitcase, and a matching one he'd brought for Maggie. He was to get Maggie in here on some pretext so that she could don it. He was also to sweep Maggie's rooms for bugs, not missing the one he'd told her to place beside her bed disguised as a button.

That done, Rodrigo began speaking in lazy Spanish about the coming evening affair and what would "Jorge" like to wear. Bojo just shook his head.

Maggie was surprised when Rodrigo requested her presence in "Cousin Jorge's" room, but she went without asking any questions. Once the door was closed behind them, she found Cord in a skin-close black outfit of pants and long-sleeved turtleneck silk shirt, with a shoulder-holster containing the same .45 caliber automatic weapon he'd been teaching her to shoot.

He wasn't smiling, and he didn't look loverlike. He was taciturn and formidable-looking. Maggie got a glimpse of the man he must be when he was on a mission, and it chilled her almost as much as the sight of the gun. He wasn't an obviously muscular man, but in those garments, every powerful inch of him was lovingly outlined. She caught her breath at the expanse of muscle and the sheer animal magnetism that he radiated. She knew the warm strength of him intimately, knew the inexhaustible endurance of that body, and had to fight blushes as she stared at him.

He moved forward with quick, economical steps and drew her out of view of the window to a walk-in closet. He handed her an outfit that matched his and nodded, pushing her into the closet and closing the door behind her.

Dressing in the confines, while the men spoke of commonplace things outside the closet, was amusing and she had to try not to laugh. When she was enclosed in black silk, she opened the door and walked into the room, pulling her hair out of the neck of the shirt absently. The silence got her attention. She looked up to find three pairs of exceptionally masculine eyes helplessly drawn to her figure. Cord was almost vibrating with the exquisite desire she kindled in him. Bojo and Rodrigo were just as entranced and staring like fiends.

Cord swatted the other two men with the tie he was just putting into place over the vested black suit he'd donned. They grinned sheepishly and made excuses about dressing, so they could leave.

Maggie grinned at Cord. He didn't grin back. His gaze was somber. He was wearing the white wig.

"Por favor, niña," he said in an imitation of Jorge's deep voice, for the benefit of the eavesdroppers. "Could you help me with my tie? Do excuse me, but I must listen to the news. An old man's whim!" he added amusedly, and turned up the radio.

"Of course, Cousin Jorge," she said, and drew close as the radio boomed in Spanish.

"I'll do this," Cord said into her ear. "You'll need to put your dress over that. Good thing you like long sleeves and skirts."

"Isn't it, though?" she teased as she went back to the closet and dug out the dress she'd worn into the room. She pulled it over her head and fastened it, careful to tuck away any revealing traces of the suit under it. She glanced at Cord, whose tie was now immaculately done up, and he surveyed her narrowly and nodded.

"We must not stay out too long," he continued in his disguise. "I grow fatigued easily. And I fear that in a day or so, we must go home. Cord will be missing us. I do not like leaving him alone in his condition."

"It amazes me that he didn't mind being left while we came here," she added, in her role.

"He knew, as I did, that you would love a glimpse of the real Tangier, the one the tourists never see," he replied with a soft chuckle.

"I am enjoying it," she agreed with a pursing of her lips.

He cocked an eyebrow. "As am I," he said softly.

The knock on the door made them start. Cord called for the person outside to come in, and the little servant entered, his black eyes everywhere as he carried a black mantilla to Maggie and placed it in her hands.

"Señor Ahmed thought you might need this, against the chill of evening," he told her. "Can I be of service, *señor?*" he added to "Jorge."

"No, my son," Cord replied with a polite smile. "As you see, my young friend has sorted out the tie!"

"Sí," the little man replied. "You go to a late supper, yes?"

Cord yawned. "Not so late," he replied with a chuckle.

"Of course! *Que tienen un buen noche,*" the servant added, with a bow, and left them.

Cord drew Maggie close to whisper in her ear, "He's thrilled. He wants time to go through our luggage!"

"More luck to him, if he can find anything!" She giggled.

He tweaked her hair. "Go comb your curly locks and come down to the living room."

"On my way," she agreed.

The brief ride in the car gave them no time to talk, because the driver listened carefully, though not blatantly, to every word they spoke.

But once inside the restaurant, in the foyer where Bojo quickly and unobtrusively checked for bugs and found none, they could speak freely.

"Just after we order," Cord told Ahmed and Bojo, "Maggie will ask me to escort her into the garden to see the flowers and the fountain, which are famous, while we wait for the food to be prepared. We will order a special dish of mutton which takes at least forty-five minutes to prepare. That gives us a window to get to Global Enterprises, only a block away, and use Bojo's information to get in."

"What about the safe?" Bojo asked.

Cord only grinned. "If I can't open a safe, I'm in the wrong business."

"Sorry," Bojo murmured.

"There will be security guards," Cord added. "But one of them was replaced this morning because the regular man had colic." He contrived to look innocent of helping the man acquire it. "He's on our payroll and will divert the other guards." He glanced down at Maggie. "I wanted you along because you're slender enough to fit inside an air-conditioning duct that leads down into the office. We can't walk through the front door. And there are steel doors front and back, bolted, not electronically locked, that separate the front hall and the kitchen from the rest of the house."

Now she understood her role, and she grinned. "Bojo's thin, too," she pointed out.

"Yes, but his presence would be missed. Yours won't. Who would suspect you of being a secret agent?" he teased gently.

Her eyes sparkled. "Good point."

"Check your watches." He gave the minutes, the seconds, and then the signal to synchronize them.

By that time, the waiter was ready to seat them. They followed him to a table near the double doors that led into the garden, and Maggie saw a colorful bill of large-denomination Moroccan paper money slipped from Bojo's hand into the waiter's. It was a very convenient location.

They talked conversationally of Morocco and its dispute with Spain over illegal Moroccan immigrants trickling across the Straits of Gibraltar onto the Iberian Peninsula.

"Another example of slave traffickers at work," Ahmed said quietly. "They agree, for a price, to smuggle illegal immigrants over the Straits, and not just to relocate. Many of them are young women, children, used in prostitution. There is also a link to Amsterdam, to the district where more trafficking goes on. Our government, in conjunction with the other countries, has tried to stop it, but we have been unsuccessful."

"Money and power make formidable adversaries," Cord replied. "I've seen it in plenty of other places, especially in Africa."

"Where some friends of ours were involved with Gruber, to their cost," Bojo added darkly. "Colleagues died in a firefight when Gruber sold them out to the government forces."

"He'll pay for it," Cord promised darkly. "And for his other sins. He isn't walking away again."

"D'accord," Bojo agreed curtly in French.

The waiter came and they ordered the exquisite mutton dish, exclaiming to Maggie its perfection. When the waiter left, "Jorge" offered Maggie a walk in the gardens, at the same time apologizing for his advanced age making him a barely acceptable escort for such a lovely young woman.

She laughed and took his arm, and they strolled out through the French doors into the garden.

Cord drew her along to the thick growth of olive trees and suddenly whisked her through a wrought-iron gate and into a hidden alcove. He ripped off his tie in the dim light from the restaurant.

"We'll leave our evening clothes here. Can you run in those shoes?" he added, nodding toward her feet.

"They're almost flat heels, and rubber-soled," she assured him. "I can keep up."

"Good girl. Ready?" He pulled the .45 from his holster, checked it, cocked it, put on the safety, and replaced it. That was when she noticed the thin leather sheath under his other arm on a holster. It contained a knife.

She didn't dare react to these tools of the trade, but she hoped against hope that she wasn't going to be in the middle of a firefight. She hoped she had enough courage not to let Cord down. She didn't know for sure. Nobody did, until they were in the situation.

He darted down a side street with Maggie right behind him, keeping to the shadows. The offices of Global Enterprises were only a quick walk from the restaurant, a two-story adobe building that wasn't modern or pretentious. It was rather like some of the shops in the *grand socco,* the bazaar, that Maggie had seen when she went on the walking city tour with Gretchen.

"It doesn't look imposing," Maggie whispered at Cord's back.

"Neither does a black widow spider, at first glance," he replied. "Careful now. No talking."

"Okay."

He led the way, stealthily, to the back of the building. There was a surprising array of electronics at the door, which he bypassed with a small device. But beyond that door was a steel door, with more locks. Cord led her around it and into a small kitchen, deserted now.

He got a chair and unfastened a grated duct, obviously a modern air-conditioning conduit. He put it down carefully, stopping to listen.

He pulled Maggie to him. "You go that way, to the next grating," he told her, pulling out a hastily drawn diagram and showing it to her. "You have to be careful not to make noise. You saw me take this grate off. It's just a matter of pushing, it's not secured with screws. But don't let it drop! Then you're going to have to hold on to the ceiling and let yourself down, so that you can come to this door—" he indicated the closed and locked door at the end of the kitchen "—and unbolt it for me. Think you can do it?"

"I can do it," she assured him. "I haven't spent all those years working out for nothing." Her heart was racing. She looked up at him. "There are men with guns somewhere in here, aren't there, Cord?" she asked huskily.

His face was hard. "Yes," he said. "If you don't want the risk..."

She put her fingers over his hard mouth. "I'm only afraid for you, not for myself. I've done martial arts, and not too long ago. I can climb, and I can jump. I know how to do this."

"I know that," he said tautly. "But somehow it was easier when I was just planning it."

She smiled. "Don't worry. I won't let you down. Here goes."

She stood in the chair, caught the upper edges of the duct, and pulled herself up with painstaking effort. She was months away from her training, but she was strong and athletic. As an afterthought, she took off her shoes, and dropped them carefully down to Cord. She gave him a thumbs-up, got her bearings, and began to crawl stealthily, aware that time was limited and they might not have enough.

It was dark and cold in the duct. She hoped that the guards

wouldn't notice the change in pitch of the air stream with her body inhibiting it. She moved quickly in the direction on the map, pausing to look for the grates.

Her heart stopped when she found not one, but two of them, each in a different direction. Now what?

Cord, waiting in the kitchen with his .45 automatic now in his hand, was listening for movement anywhere around him. There was a flash of light through the window and he ducked down, moving the chair aside, so that no evidence of tampering was visible. It was one of the outside guards, and not the small one he'd hired to replace the regular guard. The man outside wasn't on his payroll.

The man moved close to the window and aimed the light in again, as if he suspected something. Cord plastered himself against the wall and waited, praying that Maggie wouldn't choose right now to open that kitchen door. If she did, the light would reflect the movement, and they'd be in a shooting battle with nothing accomplished.

His heart raced and his tall body tensed. He took the safety off the pistol and delved into a special pouch on the bottom of his holster for the silencer he always carried. If worst came to worst, he'd drop the man right through the window. If he came into the room, it would be quieter. Either way, he couldn't risk discovery, not when he was this close to bringing down Gruber's evil empire.

Back in the duct, Maggie was making quick decisions. She closed her eyes and worked to remember the map Cord had shown her. Her hands trembled as she fought fear and confusion. Then she remembered. The corridor split, but the kitchen door was to her immediate left. That meant the duct on her left was the correct one!

She slid to it and began carefully to push at one corner of the metal while catching the grate firmly with her free hand to prevent it from falling and alerting someone.

It was new, fortunately, so it gave easily, loosening itself from its hinges obligingly. She caught it with both hands and gingerly drew it up into the duct with her, placing it carefully to the side but with an edge easily reachable from someone below in case it had to be placed back after they were through.

Heart pounding, blood racing, she caught the edges of the opening and slowly, carefully, lowered herself from it. It was about a three-foot drop to the linoleum floor, but she did it as lightly as a cat. She stopped, waiting, listening for sounds. She didn't hear anything, except for a faint noise from the kitchen. Surely that was Cord.

She padded quickly to the kitchen door and worked the bolt quietly, drawing it back until the door was easily opened.

But just as she started to turn the doorknob, she felt something, a flash of intuition, almost as if someone had called her name quickly, in warning. She frowned, wondering if she were being fanciful. But she hesitated.

In the kitchen, Cord had both hands on the butt of the .45 and had tensed to turn and throw a shot out the window the second it became necessary. The guard was standing there, fixed securely in place, talking to someone on a mobile phone. His voice was too muffled to understand, but Cord feared discovery.

Shooting the guard was going to solve nothing if he'd relayed the news of their presence to a third party. He cursed under his breath, furious at the unexpected complication.

And there was now a worse one. He caught a movement out of the corner of his eye and turned his head in time to see, just for an instant, the turning of the doorknob that led out of the kitchen into the rest of the house.

He ground his lips together. If Maggie walked into the room, she would be shot immediately by the guard, who was standing just outside the window. He had to save her, at whatever cost. If only he could warn her to stay where she was, not to proceed...!

At the window, the guard hesitated, spoke into the phone once again, made a short reply, and suddenly the light was gone. Bushes outside made a crackling sound as the man retreated to the pavement with lazy steps and looked around the driveway with the flashlight before continuing on his way.

Cord almost shivered as he relaxed his tense muscles. And at that moment, the doorknob slowly turned again and a pale face peered around it cautiously.

Cord rushed to her, opening and closing the door quickly behind him as he went into the next room with her. He crushed her into his body and kissed her hungrily. They'd had a close call, and she didn't know. He didn't want her to know.

He nodded toward the door ahead of them and deployed her just behind him.

They moved slowly into the hall. From the schematic, Cord knew that Gruber's office was upstairs, and protected by various electronic alarms, including infrared. But he had that angle covered. The wooden doors that locked front and back were only window dressing. It was the two inside steel doors, one blocking the entrance to the hall in front, and the other in the kitchen, in the rear, that were Gruber's real protection. Gruber was certain they were impregnable, and they were—but he'd overlooked the air-conditioning ducts.

Footsteps alerted Cord a second time when they were going up the stairs. He pressed Maggie back against the wall beside him and they waited until the steps died away down the upstairs hall, in the opposite direction from the office.

Cord moved forward again, like lightning this time, and straight down the hall to Gruber's office. He whipped out a small case, had Maggie hold a penlight for him, and set to work. Barely a minute later, they were inside the door and it was closed behind them.

Cord knew that the room was certainly bugged, and booby-trapped. He positioned Maggie by the door and signaled her to stand there and listen for visitors. He took out a small device and watched it reveal a crisscross of laser beams sweeping the floor. He moved cautiously past them, avoiding a last one that swung neck-high, and went to the big safe behind Gruber's sweeping oak desk and went to work.

* * *

Every sound was magnified. Maggie chewed on a fingernail, absently wondering if Cord still had her shoes. Her feet felt good on the bare floor, but it was going to be difficult to explain bare feet in the restaurant. But there were other concerns just now. She checked her watch and groaned. They had barely ten minutes to finish and get back to the restaurant before the food was served, if they didn't want to arouse suspicion. How could they possibly break into a safe and get out without discovery and get back in that short length of time?

Her heartbeat intensified. She watched Cord's quick, deft movements with terror. This was the real thing, she realized. This was what covert operations was all about—stealth and danger. Discovery was behind every heartbeat, death at the trail of every drop of sweat. One wrong move, one accidental sound, and it was all over. She thought of how many times Cord must have done this very thing in his career, first in law enforcement, and then in mercenary work, and she paled.

She wasn't a coward, but the waiting was unbearable. She knew that her muscles were going to start convulsing any second from being held so tight.

Then, all at once, the safe door swung open gently and Cord was inside, with his penlight, going through sections as if he had all the time in the world. She wanted to go and see what he was doing, but she kept her ear to the door and listened. Far down the hall were footsteps. Slowly, she realized that they were coming closer!

She couldn't tell what Cord was doing. He didn't seem to be taking anything out of the safe. He worked quickly and then suddenly closed the safe, just as heavy footsteps came closer down the hall, and sounded as if they were going to make it right to this door! What if it was the guard, and he had a key?

Cord glanced at her, and she motioned furiously toward the door. He nodded, eased cautiously but quickly back through the laser beam pattern to her side, and drew her with him behind the thick drapes that fell to the floor. He held her hand tightly in one of his, while the .45 was now held, with the safety off, against his chest.

There was a loud noise, as if of a key going into a lock. Suddenly the door opened and the light went on. Maggie had steeled herself not to react, not to move, not to breathe. Beside her, she could feel Cord's tall body still and tensed. Neither of them breathed.

Seconds later, the light went off, the door closed, and the key went into the lock again. There was a whine, as if electronic devices were being reset. Then the footsteps died away.

Cord laughed softly at her ear, but he didn't speak. He drew her from behind the curtains, handed her the pistol, with the safety on, and listened at the door. The footsteps had droned away and ended.

He went to work again, and seconds later, they were in the hall. He reset the security switches again, eased down the hall with Maggie at his back, listened, and then worked down the steps with her, avoiding one particular one—the same one he'd avoided on the way up. She'd have to remember to ask why.

He led her back into the room adjoining the steel door of the kitchen, put her up into the air duct, removed the chair and waited until she replaced the grate and was moving toward the kitchen. Then he moved to the steel door, positioned the bolt, went through it and heard it slide satisfyingly into place. He tried the door, relieved to find that the bolt was secure.

Maggie appeared in the kitchen duct. He reached up to help her down before he replaced the duct cover and moved her to the door with him. He checked his watch. The guard was due to make the rounds again in three minutes. It would be close.

He interrupted the electric current, put Maggie out onto the stoop and followed her, reinitiated the current flow and reentered the security codes. Then he grabbed her arm and said, "Run!"

They dashed across the driveway, into the bushes, through them, and sprinted down the street. Behind them, they heard no following footsteps, no alarms.

Breathless, they didn't stop until they reached the courtyard of the hotel. Cord was laughing.

Maggie shook him. "That was terrifying!" she squeaked. "How can you do that day after day...?"

He caught her up in his arms and kissed her so fiercely that he bruised her mouth. She held on for dear life, aroused, hungry for him. The danger had been the catalyst. She wanted him...!

While she was feeling it, she was saying it. He eased them into the little shed where they'd left their clothing and closed the door, shooting the bolt home to shut them in, away from the world. Oblivious to time, danger, threat, he backed her against a cold, stone wall, jerked fabric out of the way and put his mouth hard over hers while he went into her with an economy of motion that left her gasping.

His mouth opened and bit at hers while the rhythm curled her hips up into his with heated abandon.

"Don't cry out," he cautioned, his voice clipped and husky with passion. He pinned her there with the weight of his body, the rasping of silk and the quick rush of their breathing the only sound in the confined little space. His body thrust into hers fiercely, his mouth hard, insistent, on her parted lips as he felt the spiral of pleasure build like gas-ignited flames.

"Harder," she groaned into his mouth, her voice breaking. "Oh...Cord...do it...hard!"

Her body opened to him, incited him. She could hardly believe she was the same inhibited woman of only a month ago. Her nails bit into his shoulders as she lifted into the hard curve of him, her mouth searching feverishly for his as she pushed up to meet the violent thrusts. He was potent, so potent, and she felt him inside her body, filling it, expanding it until she thought she might burst open...!

She groaned piteously into his mouth and clung with her legs as well as her arms as the waves of fulfillment caught her up and convulsed her in his powerful hold. She felt his fingertips biting into her flesh as he crushed her hips under his in one long, exquisite straining together that brought a sound very like a harsh sob from the mouth possessing hers. He shivered with the aching, hot pleasure that riveted his body to hers.

She shivered with him, drowning in the exquisite heat of joy that was so new and so exciting. She felt him deep in her body, throbbing, sated, helpless to withdraw. She laughed secretly and pressed her open mouth to his throat.

He moved against her involuntarily, prolonging the stabs of delight, until he was able to get his breath again.

"No," she protested huskily when he began to withdraw.

He kissed her hungrily, but he didn't obey. "I don't want to stop, either. But we have to get back to the table, or we're going to arouse suspicion," he said unsteadily, kissing her one last time.

"I don't want rice and mutton, I want dessert again," she moaned.

He chuckled weakly. "And I thought you were inhibited," he drawled.

"Not with you. It's the danger, isn't it?" she whispered. "It's an aphrodisiac...have you done this with other women after a mission?" she demanded jealously.

"In a potting shed behind a hotel with armed men all around?" he exclaimed while he did up fastenings again. "With any other woman but you? Are you nuts? Here," he added, handing her a tiny package of antibacterial tissue. "It won't do for an old man and a young woman to come back in smelling suspiciously," he added with a grin that grew even more wicked when she gasped.

She adjusted her own clothing and put her dress back on. But her feet were still bare. "Cord, my shoes…!"

He pulled them out of his pockets and handed them to her. He also produced a small brush, and smiled while she put her hair back into order.

"There," he murmured, studying her. "You'll do." He put his white wig back in place, reacquired his stoop and his cane, and opened the door.

"But, the safe…you didn't take anything out of it," she protested, suddenly remembering his bare hands.

"Didn't I?" he asked, but he smiled and didn't say another word as he escorted her slowly back into the restaurant.

The waiter was just bringing the mutton as "Jorge" seated Maggie at the table.

"Just in time," Cord said in his thready adopted tone. "And I have worked up an enormous appetite in the garden!"

To Maggie's credit, she didn't blush or gasp, but she couldn't quite stop smiling.

13

The return to Ahmed's house was almost anticlimactic, after the exciting evening Cord and Maggie had shared. She looked back on it with wonder. She'd passed her first test of fire, and come through it relatively unscathed. She didn't have to ask if Cord was proud of her. The answer was in his eyes.

She was a little uneasy about their passionate encounter in the shed. It had been a spur-of-the-moment thing, and very satisfying, but it disturbed her that she had so little control over her passions. Was that normal? she wondered. She had no way of knowing. Cord looked at her in a different way now, with possession and pride. It made her heart sing. If only she could stop time, she thought, and keep him from ever knowing about the past that haunted her. If only this tiny space of days could be insulated, packed carefully into a box and held, cherished, forever!

"We must leave in the morning on the ferry," "Jorge" announced when they were inside Ahmed's elegant living room. "I am sorry, but I worry to leave Cord alone, in his condition."

"I quite understand," Ahmed agreed with a sigh. "But it has been a delight to have you here, and to meet Maggie." He lifted her hand and kissed her fingers gently. "You are exceptional, *mademoiselle,*" he added, and with hidden meaning that didn't escape Maggie, or Cord.

"It has been a great pleasure to see something of your city," Maggie said. "I hope to come back again one day."

"You will always be welcome," Ahmed said. "And, of course, so will you, Cousin Jorge."

Cord only grinned.

The ferry was supposed to leave at 8:00 a.m. But, as on the trip over, it left at the whim of the operator. It might be nine, it might be ten, and people lined up in their cars, talking and reading and listening to music while they waited. In this part of the world, Maggie noted, hardly anybody rushed.

Her hands gripped the steering wheel hard.

"You must relax, *niña,*" "Jorge" said, nodding toward the dash and making a sign that it was bugged.

She groaned out loud. Would they never be free of surveillance? She could understand that Gruber would be having them watched. But they'd successfully penetrated his defenses the night before. What they'd accomplished was still a mystery to her, but Cord seemed satisfied. She wondered what he'd learned, and was frustrated that she couldn't talk normally.

"It's so frustrating!" she exclaimed, and she didn't mean the wait for the ferry.

"Jorge" threw up a careless hand and grinned at Rodrigo and Bojo, who were sitting unperturbed in the backseat, listening to a Spanish radio broadcast. "It is so natural," he chuckled in his disguised voice. "Be patient. It will not be so much longer. Then we can tell Cord about our exciting visit with Ahmed. He is a good man. *Simpatico,* no?"

"Sí," she replied without thinking.

"I forget! You speak my language!"

She grinned at him. "Yes, I do, don't I?" she teased.

Suddenly there was movement ahead, and she began to relax.

"Did I not tell you? And here we go!" "Jorge" said contentedly.

They crossed on the ferry to Gibraltar again and then on into Spain with appropriate formalities, such as showing their passports and letting the authorities look in the car to make sure they weren't bringing in anything illegal. It was time-consuming, but Maggie didn't really mind. She felt safer and safer, especially when they were on the road back to Jorge's *finca* and she could drive, relaxed. Well, almost relaxed, she amended, glaring at the dashboard.

When they parked the car, Cord, Bojo and Rodrigo jumped out. Cord immediately motioned to Bojo and pointed to the dash. Bojo nodded, taking a small packet of tools out of his djellaba. Cord said something to Rodrigo in such rapid-fire Spanish that Maggie couldn't easily translate it. Rodrigo went straight to the barn, where the other men were waiting.

Cord and Maggie went into the house, where Jorge was waiting, pacing.

"Did it go well?" Jorge asked, noting that they were suspiciously silent. He laughed. "It is safe to talk. Your men have gone over the house with, how do you say, a fine-tooth comb. There are no surveillance devices here now!"

"Thank God!" Maggie exclaimed huskily. "I'm so tired of spying eyes! I'll never feel comfortable again when I think I'm alone!"

"Now you know how it feels, don't you?" Cord chuckled. He pulled off the white wig and became serious again. "We're flying to Amsterdam this afternoon," he told Jorge. "Rodrigo's going to drive us up to the airport in Málaga, and we're going from there."

"In disguise?" Jorge murmured.

"No. Well, in a way," Cord replied, smiling. "I'll wear my dark glasses and let Maggie lead me. *That* disguise. Thanks for the loan of your identity."

"Did you find the evidence?" Jorge asked.

"Yes," Cord replied. But that was all he said.

Maggie sat up with the men after supper, but only for a little while. She took a leisurely bath in the elaborately tiled sunken tub and enjoyed the luxury of being submerged in water while the jets shot water against her tired muscles. She was sore from the activity of the night before, not having done as much running and climbing in recent months.

The bathroom door opened and closed. She opened her eyes and watched Cord drop the towel around his waist before he climbed into the tub with her.

"Jorge," she began in a thin little protest.

"Is a man, as we discussed once before," he chuckled huskily as he levered down over her and found her mouth hungrily with his.

She moaned and reached up to him, electrified by the contact with his warm, rough skin against every inch of hers. But very soon the water began to splash out of the tub and onto the floor.

With a groan, Cord got out of the sunken tub and reached down to lift Maggie, but the brush of her body against him was too much for his self-control. He dragged towels down onto the wet tile and eased her down on top of them. Seconds later, his body was crushing hers into them.

The rushing of the jets barely touched her ears as they lay on the tiled floor in a tangle of wet towels and urgent movement.

She arched up to the hard, hungry thrust of his body, watching him watch her as they made love. It was more urgent each time, more passionate, more satisfying. She loved his eyes on her while he satisfied her. She loved the muscular thrust of him above her, the ragged sound of his breathing, the fierce darkness in his eyes as he took her.

"I can't...get enough," he whispered roughly.

"Neither can I." She arched her torso to coax his mouth down to her hard-tipped breasts. She watched him suckle them while he moved on her, and she gasped with growing delight.

His hand was at her hip, clenching. "I'm sorry," he bit off. "I can't hold it..."

Her legs curled over his tense thighs. "Don't even try, darling," she whispered into his insistent mouth.

The endearment kindled a climax that stiffened him convulsively. She felt his body jerk rhythmically while his mouth groaned into hers.

It was wonderful to feel him throb, to know that he took such pleasure from her. She lifted to lengthen the tremors and suddenly felt her body explode from the movement. She cried out under his mouth, frightened of the surge of pleasure that exceeded anything she'd felt with him before.

His head lifted. Even in the silvery aftermath of his own climax, he could feel hers. He moved, watching her reactions, measuring his strokes to give her the ultimate pleasure he could offer. She was frightened of it, he could see it in her wild eyes, her trembling body.

He only smiled, because he understood. It was difficult to give up so much control to another human being. But she could learn, as he had, to trust.

"You won't die," he whispered, as he moved even deeper. "But you may think you have..."

The words faded into frantic, desperate movement as she clenched her teeth and strained up toward him with her last whisper of strength...

It was like a dark, sweet convulsion, she thought as fulfillment washed over her like a throbbing, suffocating tidal wave of pleasure. She was blind, deaf, dumb, to everything except the release of tension. Her body was in a painful arch, her eyes on his blurred face as she gave herself to the darkness....

There were tender, breathlessly soft kisses on her closed eyelids, her panting mouth. She felt hard lips moving over every part of her while she lay throbbing, throbbing, throbbing from the hot, drugged pleasure he'd given her.

He chuckled. "You make me feel like the best lover who ever lived," he whispered.

"You are."

He nibbled her ear. "No. You just react to me as if I were. It isn't the physical bond at all, Maggie, it's the emotion that produces the pleasure."

"You mean, because I love you," she whispered back.

There was a faint hesitation in the lips worshiping her relaxed body. "I mean, because I love you, as well."

She was going crazy. She knew it. Her hands, that had been gripping his buttocks so tightly, relaxed.

"Didn't you know, honey?" he asked, lifting his head to look down into her wide, sated eyes. He wasn't smiling.

Her fingers lifted to his beloved face above her. She could still feel him, deep in her body, throbbing, as she was throbbing.

He brushed his mouth lightly over hers. "How many times have I had you," he whispered, "and never bothered with a single precaution?"

"It would be hard for me to get pregnant," she rationalized.

"It's going to be easier than you ever dreamed," he said drowsily. "I love babies."

She was confused. Perhaps the convulsive pleasure had popped a major artery. She said so.

He chuckled again, moving so that the pleasure returned in teasing little spasms. "Probably we both did, but making babies is exciting, and I can't stop trying."

Her hands slid up to frame his face. "It's the excitement of it," she tried to explain, worried. "It's new, and..."

He nibbled her upper lip. "It's new and exciting, and that's why I keep neglecting protection, hmm?"

"Isn't it?"

"New and exciting? Yes." He lifted up from her and looked down their bodies to where they were still tightly joined. "I'm thirty-four," he said huskily. "You're twenty-six." His eyes went back to meet hers. "We're used to each other in all the ways that matter, and now we find an explosive passion that shows no signs of weakening. In fact, if what just happened is any indication," he added, moving again, sensuously, and watching her moan, "we're becoming quite adept at giving each other pleasure."

He started to lift away and she protested, but he sat back from her, kneeling over her prone body, studying every inch of her as if he'd never seen a woman nude before. Probably it should have embarrassed her. It didn't. She liked his eyes on her.

"When we get back to Houston, the minute we get back," he added to emphasize it, "we're having blood tests and getting a marriage license."

That was part of the fantasy. She smiled. She was dreaming, of course. She knew it, now. Cord Romero would never marry again. Hadn't he said so a million times?

"Why are you smiling?" he asked warily.

"I'm dreaming," she said simply.

He moved, an arrogant shift of his knees to push her long legs apart. He was still capable and growing more so by the second. He caught her upper thighs and drew her up to him, positioning her.

"Cord..." she whispered worriedly.

"You can take me," he whispered back. He began to ease inside her in tiny, quick little thrusts of his hips that brought unexpectedly intense spasms of pleasure.

"It's...too...soon," she choked.

He was watching her body absorb him with eyes that contained equal measures of wonder and excitement. "I've never...done it like this," he groaned. His hands tightened on her thighs and his eyes began to dilate. "I've never watched...so intimately..."

"What do you see?" she whispered breathlessly.

"I see you...having me," he bit off, flinching as the pleasure began to throb. "I see you opening...for me!"

She looked down and he lifted her away, letting her see. It was erotic. It was blatant. It was...!

She was moaning, twisting, throbbing. Her eyes were open, but she saw nothing. The pleasure, so intense before, was unbearable now. She caught the wet towels in both hands and gripped them until her knuckles turned white while he invaded her with slow, hard, merciless thrusts that lifted her hips rhythmically at first and then violently quick. Her last sane thought was that they were going to hurt each other. A second later, she became a meteor, flying headlong through space in a throbbing, fiercely hot tunnel of pleasure.

Cord felt her release in the seconds before he was twisted and convulsed by his own. He fell on her, his body heavy and hot and wet with sweat as they lay shivering together on the towels.

She trembled, gasping, as the exhaustion finally worked its way within her and left her too tired to move or speak. Her heartbeat was shaking both of them.

He pulled away before she could protest, if she'd had the breath. She felt him get to his feet and lift her, carrying her to the bed. Her last memory was of the cool sheets above and beneath her, and the darkness all around.

The next morning, she was more sore than ever. She woke

moaning and trying to find a comfortable position, which there wasn't. She got up and dressed, wincing at even the most delicate touch of intimate things against her.

She was brushing her long hair when Cord opened the door and came in. He was wearing slacks and a knit shirt, his dark, slightly wavy hair combed, immaculate. He moved behind the vanity stool, took the brush from her hands, and began to work on her hair.

"You're uncomfortable this morning," he said without preamble. "I'm sorry. I know better, but once I touch you, I can't seem to stop."

She met his eyes in the mirror, surprised by the apology. "I couldn't stop, either," she reminded him, and she smiled.

He bent to kiss her hair tenderly before he renewed his efforts with the brush. "Brought you something." He took a small vial out of his pocket and pressed it into her hand.

"What is it?" she asked.

He looked vaguely uncomfortable. "It's for the discomfort," he murmured.

She was horrified. Had he asked one of the women in the household...?

He smiled helplessly at her expression. "I had to use some myself," he said sheepishly.

Her eyebrows lifted. This was really interesting. Men got sore, too?

He chuckled. "Yes," he said, as if he knew what she was thinking. "Men do, too."

"Wow."

"Now you know," he said complacently. He finished with the brush and put it on the table. "But just for the record, if last night was my last few hours on earth, I wouldn't have one single regret."

"Neither would I." She drew his hand to her mouth and kissed the callused palm. "I love you with all my heart."

"As I love you," he bit off. He bent, tugging her mouth up so that he could kiss it with fierce possession.

A few seconds later, he forced himself to lift his head. His eyes were turbulent, his heartbeat violent. "The more I have you, the more I want you, Maggie," he said huskily. "That isn't going to stop. That's why we have to get married. I'm old-fashioned about kids. Nobody's calling mine bastards."

Her fingers touched his hard mouth. It was contagious. She was beginning to believe she could have his child. Her eyes were wide and soft with wonder, with anticipation. It was all part of the fantasy. It wasn't real. But she was insulated, cocooned, right now. She could believe. She could love. She could accept love and the phantom image of pleasure. She could dream.

"You can have anything you want," he whispered hoarsely, seeing acceptance and joy in her face and misreading the day-dreamy look. "I'll stay home and raise cattle."

And he'd hate it, and her, and the baby, she thought. But it was a dream, and they could share it for now. The risk of someone discovering her past was too formidable to let her look very far ahead, especially with Cord. He was going to be so disgusted if he ever found out. She couldn't let that happen. She had to keep him in the dark, in that one way. She was certain she couldn't get pregnant, after what the doctors had said, and she'd been honest with him. He didn't believe it, but it wouldn't make any difference. She'd grow old alone, but she would have these exquisite, delicious memories of Cord making love to her. Along with the excitement and danger of the present, there was the physical delight of it. She was grateful for every second that he looked at her with desire.

"You're not talking to me," he mused.

"Does it matter?" she asked, letting her eyes trace every inch of him that was visible in her long vanity mirror. "I just want to look at you. You're perfect, Cord. All of you."

He sighed. Something was bothering her, and she didn't want to tell him. He knew it was more than her miscarriage. He spared a mental curse for her ex-husband who'd cost them their child, and for his own maltreatment of her that had kept her from telling him she was pregnant. He cursed the past for the misunderstandings, the torment. He wanted her more than he'd ever wanted anything in his life. He wanted a family and a home and her in it. But she was only giving lip service to his suggestions. Why? What else was she hiding?

He decided that he was going to have to ignore her right to privacy and dig further into her past. She was never going to tell him. He would have to find it out himself.

But he didn't let on. He smiled. "I like looking at you, too, sweetheart," he said softly. "With or without clothes."

She smiled back. And for a few precious seconds, they were almost one person.

The plane trip to Amsterdam didn't take long at all. After a pleasant snack and desultory conversation with Cord about their delightful visit with Jorge, they were landing at Schiphol Airport.

It was big and sprawling and most of the signs were in Dutch and English. A few were in Polish, and she remarked on it.

"They have a large immigrant Polish population," he told her. "But you'll find signs in Japanese, as well. They get tourists from all over."

"Do I have to drive again?" she moaned.

"They drive on the same side of the road we do," he chuckled. "Just like in Spain and Gibraltar and Morocco. But, no, you don't have to drive. We'll get a cab to our hotel."

"Where are we staying?"

"Where the action is," he teased. "Right on the Dam Square. The palace is across the street, a wax museum is next door, there's a sidewalk café, exclusive clothing shop windows to explore, the war memorial, and just down the street a ways, the canals."

"We can see the canals?" she exclaimed.

"We can go on them. There are boat tours. I won't be able

to see anything," he teased, alluding to his dark glasses. "But you will. You can be my eyes."

They both knew it was a joke, but they didn't know if anyone was watching or listening who had ties to Gruber, even in the airport. Stealth was the word of the day.

She took his hand in hers. "I'll be your eyes, your ears, anything you want me to be," she whispered huskily. "Just so you know," she added softly, "the past few days were worth everything that's happened to me in my life. Everything!"

That sounded final. He frowned. What was she trying to say to him?

"We should go," she said, looking around. "How do we get out of the airport?"

"Through passport control and customs, just like Spain," he told her. "Follow the signs."

"They're in Dutch!" she wailed.

"They're in English, too. Just keep looking."

They tugged their carry-on luggage on wheels along behind them, with Maggie leading Cord by the hand as they made their way first to a money-changing booth, and then through passport control and then to the customs desk, where they were passed through. They walked out into bright sunshine and hailed a cab. The cabs, like those Maggie had seen in other countries, were Mercedes-Benzs. She remarked on it.

"They're dependable," he chuckled. "That's why so many people have them." He paused to give the name of the hotel to the driver. The man tried to ask a question in English. Cord, surprising Maggie, switched immediately to Dutch. He and the man laughed together and exchanged pleasantries.

"I told you I spoke Dutch," he said after they were underway, grinning at Maggie's surprise.

"It sounds fascinating," she replied.

"It's an interesting language. And the Dutch are fascinating people, as you'll discover when you've been here a couple of days. They're intelligent, industrious, and they have one of the most efficient land-claiming operations on earth. You did know," he added, "about the system of dykes that holds back the ocean?"

"I read *National Geographic,*" she pointed out. "Yes, indeed, I know how the dykes work and how desperately the Dutch people have to fight to keep their country above water. It's awe-inspiring."

He nodded. He noticed the driver's eyebrows raised and repeated what he and Maggie were saying in Dutch. The driver grinned at Maggie and increased his speed.

It took several minutes to get through the city of narrow streets and trolley cars and bicyclers. There were bicycle lanes next to the trolley tracks. The streets were so filled with natives and tourists that it was a wonder to Maggie that anybody could move at all.

"It's so crowded!" she exclaimed. "Is it because of the summer tourist season?" she asked as they approached a huge hotel and pulled up to the door under an awning, where a uniformed man waited to greet them.

"It's always crowded," he assured her, reaching into his pocket for the fare in Dutch guilders.

"Is this it?" she asked as the doorman helped her from the cab. She wasn't terribly impressed with the outside, and nearby, where a statue sat in the cobblestoned square, dozens of young people lounged around looking bored. Some had guitars with cups sitting nearby, obviously for tips.

"This is it. Wait until you see inside," he added with a grin.

She took his arm and led him to the desk. The whole of the inside was carpeted. The desk was long and busy. Beautifully upholstered furniture was spread around the lobby. There was a photograph of the royal family including Queen Beatrice on a nearby wall, a reminder that the Netherlands had a monarchy.

Past the chairs was a dining room, and elaborate desserts and tea in delicate china cups were being placed on linen-covered tablecloths.

"Isn't it too early for supper?" Maggie asked. "People are eating..."

"That is high tea, Madam Romero," the clerk told her with a smile, lifting his eyebrows at her look of surprise. "When you are taken to your room, you might like to come back down and experience it, if you haven't before. Also, we have an exquisite restaurant with a world-class chef, and our morning room for breakfast is a botanist's dream."

"Yes, it is," Cord replied, pushing the register to one side. "You need to sign us in, Mrs. Romero," he added pointedly.

She could tell that his eyes were smiling behind those dark glasses. She didn't have to ask if they were sharing a room, either.

14

In fact, they were sharing a suite. It had a sitting area, with a fax machine and phone, a safe and a small bar with a refrigerator, and a separate bedroom with a double bed. The bathroom didn't have a whirlpool bath, but Maggie wasn't sorry. Her memories of those were delightful, but temporarily uncomfortable.

Cord tipped the bellboy, and waited to speak until he'd explained where everything was and how it worked to Maggie and closed the door behind him.

Cord put his finger to his chiseled mouth and took out the electronic device, which was now familiar to Maggie. He swept all the rooms twice before he was satisfied that there were no bugs in the room. But afterward, he glanced across the way at the building behind the hotel, and when he closed the blinds, he put another device on the table and activated it.

"In case anyone's listening, all they'll hear is static," he told Maggie.

"But there aren't any bugs, are there?" she asked, confused.

"A man in the building across from us could point a microphone this way and even through glass and concrete, he could hear us whisper," he confided. "He can even see us, through the walls—or, rather, our body heat—with an infrared device that's readily available on the market."

She shook her head. "I never heard of such things."

"You will, if you ever go to work for Lassiter." He took her by the shoulders and bent to kiss her forehead gently. "I've got some work to do on the laptop, but we can go down and sample high tea first, if you'd like to?"

"I would," she confessed. "I've read about it for years, and I don't know what it is, really."

"Let's go find out, then!"

It was delightful. There were cucumber sandwiches, small pastries, any sort of tea you liked, or coffee with real cream, and even fruit and vegetable medleys with dipping sauce. There were also real linen napkins.

"It's so elegant," Maggie exclaimed, fascinated by the people around her as well as the little meal.

He smiled through his dark glasses. "So are you," he said softly. "Elegant, strong, fearless and passionate," he added huskily.

"Adjectives that would also apply to you," she replied.

He reached across for her hand and held it close. “We make an interesting couple.”

“Don’t we, though?” She smiled and reached for her teacup.

There were all sorts of shops on the same level as the lobby, with expensive designer goods as well as souvenirs. Maggie bought watercolors of the canals, along with wooden-shoe key chains and blue delft china pieces that doubled as salt-and-pepper shakers.

“I know, I’m a tourist at heart,” Maggie confided. “But I can’t go home without taking something for my friends. I wonder how Gretchen is doing in my job?”

Cord grinned. “I know, but I’m not saying,” he murmured. “They’ve had their own little disturbances lately. But very soon, you’re going to see your friend Gretchen in a way that will shock you.”

“We’re going to Qawi?” she exclaimed.

“Not yet.”

“Tell me!” she insisted.

But he wouldn’t. When they got back to the hotel room, he suggested that she have a nap. While she slept, he plugged in his laptop and went to work, sneaking inside protected files with an ease that would have sent cold chills up Maggie’s soft arms.

Three hours later, she woke up. Cord was already dressed in a suit. He looked strange, remote, and his eyes were very dark and shadowed.

"Did I oversleep?" she asked worriedly.

He shook his head, a mere jerk. "You need to put on something nice," he said in a neutral tone. "It's a five-star restaurant and it will be full. I made reservations for eight."

"Eight! I'll never get used to the time people eat in Africa and Europe," she murmured as she slid her long legs off the bed and sat up.

"It grows on you," he said. "I'll wait in the sitting room. I've got a few more contacts to make."

"Cord?"

He paused with his hand on the doorknob. He wouldn't look at her.

"Is everything all right?" she asked, concerned. "Has something happened?"

"Something." His voice was oddly choked. "Come out when you're ready." He closed the door.

It was as if all the teasing and delight in each other's company had gone in a puff of smoke. Cord was good company, pleasant and courteous, and as remote as if he were living on another planet. He barely looked straight at Maggie, and he was unusually tense. He ordered whiskey as well—something she'd never known him to do. He didn't drink.

After the second highball, he ordered a seafood dish for himself and a special salad that Maggie wanted. They ate in silence. She finally got up to help herself at the dessert counter mainly to get away from his brooding countenance. She couldn't imagine what had upset him like that. She knew instinctively that he'd had an emotional blow of some sort. She wondered if there was another woman in his life, if he'd had second thoughts about their sudden intimacy, if he had cold feet about committing himself to her. Maybe he'd satisfied his hunger and his curiosity about her body, and he was already tired of it. That thought was depressing, so she picked up a flan and a piece of cake and devoured both with after-dinner coffee. Cord sat nursing a third highball and didn't eat half his seafood. He had no dessert at all.

The worst surprise came when they were back in the room. He took off his dark glasses and suggested quietly that she might want to go to bed, because they had a long day ahead of them. She asked wasn't he coming, and noted that he stiffened as if the question was actually offensive to him.

She swallowed a choking misery of lost confidence, smiled forcibly and went into the bedroom alone.

He didn't come to bed. When she woke the next morning, she found him sprawled on the sofa, still in his suit, with disheveled hair and smelling of whiskey. She noted four empty little bottles of it stacked on the coffee table along with two empty Coke cans and a glass. On top of what he'd had in the restaurant, that was enough to render even a strong man like Cord unconscious. It bothered her that he drank like that. Something had to have gone wrong. She didn't know what.

But what upset her most was something she found in the fax machine, a message that had come from Houston, from

Lassiter's detective agency. It contained only a couple of sentences, but they were enough to make her wish she was dead. The message gave the date of a trial, and she knew whose. There was one other brief sentence. "Hard copy confiscated and destroyed, no negatives. Information available when you return, if you insist on seeing it."

She didn't wake him. She went down alone to breakfast, feeling numb. Lassiter had somehow managed to get the information about her away from Stillwell, but he still had it. Cord knew there was something, and wanted to see it. Lassiter was going to let him, unless she intervened. She could tell Cord herself. Or she could play for time and simply vanish when this was all over and they went back to the States. She had her memories. Perhaps they would be enough.

She knew why Lassiter hadn't included particulars of the case in a fax. It was too explosive, and Gruber would be around. Her face paled as she wondered if Gruber, too, knew what was in those files? He must, because he'd been in the office with Adams and Stillwell when Lassiter said he'd heard about the information on the tape. All three men knew, whether or not they could prove it. If they'd obtained hard copy once, what was to stop them from duplicating it again?

Her life seemed less valuable now. She was going to be prey for the rest of her life if she didn't find a secure hiding place. It would take her away from Cord, because he was going to see the truth for himself when they got back to Houston. Once he knew—damn Lassiter for offering to tell him!—she'd be alone for the rest of her life. Tears of frustrated fury stung her eyes. Lassiter could have found some excuse not to tell him! He sold her out. Every single human being she'd ever known had done that. Why would she never learn that she couldn't trust people?

She sipped hot coffee, infused with warm cream, and stared fixedly at her untouched breakfast. She must make an effort to eat something, she told herself. Starving would solve no problems. She picked up her fork and made small inroads into bacon and eggs and a buttery croissant. Idly her eyes went to the abundant greenery in the huge structure, which was like an indoor greenhouse. Ordinarily she would have delighted in her surroundings. Now she just felt sick.

She was aware of movement, and looked up into Cord's quiet, lifeless eyes.

"Care for company?" he asked with narrowed eyes.

She shrugged, and wouldn't meet his gaze.

He knew then, without a doubt, that she'd seen what was in the fax machine before he took out the sheet of paper and destroyed it.

He put down his own breakfast and coffee and pulled out the chair next to hers.

"Secrets are dangerous, Maggie," he said curtly.

She lifted her eyes to his. She looked like a cornered cat. "If you read that file about me that Lassiter has, when you get back to Houston," she said, her voice trembling as she chose her words carefully, "you'll never see me again in your lifetime."

His hand hesitated on the thick china coffee mug. He studied her, frowning. "Is it really that important?" he asked warily.

She swallowed. Her hands trembled as she picked up her own coffee mug. "Can't you just have somebody burn it?" she asked on a cold laugh.

"Can't you tell me what's in it?" he countered.

She spilled coffee, hot coffee, on her slender hands. She managed to set the cup down without doing further damage. Cord cursed under his breath and got a napkin around her stinging fingers, wiping them gently.

"You don't share anything," he said in a slow, cautious tone. "I had to find out about the miscarriage and your husband's abuse the hard way. Now here's one more secret that you're not going to tell me. You don't trust me at all."

"That's right." She looked straight into his eyes. "You're already suspicious of me," she said, nodding when he reacted to the remark. "Lassiter told you just enough to make you wonder, to question what you think you know about me, about my life. You want to see the file. You want to know everything. But there are secrets that should stay buried, Cord. There are things about me that you should never have to know."

"That's rather an odd wording, isn't it?" he asked curiously.

She lowered her eyes quickly to her stale breakfast. "I hate my life," she said huskily.

"Maggie!"

"I do!" She put down her napkin and pushed back her chair. "I never should have gone back to Houston," she said wildly. "I should have stayed in Tangier, found a job doing something, anything, so that I would never have had to see you again!"

His face hardened. "You haven't been acting as if you felt that way," he said at once, and then could have bitten off his tongue when he saw her reaction. "Certainly not in bed with me!"

She felt the accusing words like a body blow. "No, I haven't acted that way," she said in a thready whisper. "I've been behaving...just as people always expected that I would, when I...grew up!"

She whirled and took off, right out the door of the hotel into the street, with her purse clutched close against her body. Cord couldn't chase her, at least, not without giving up the pretense of blindness, and why would he risk that? She didn't know where she was going, anyway. She had her purse, but not her passport, it was locked up, with her airline tickets and Cord's passport, in the safe in the hotel room. But she could get away from Cord for a while, and she was going to.

She made her way to a shop that sold tickets for the canal boat ride, a two-hour tour of the city by water. She doubted that Cord could find her in the throngs of people, and she didn't care. If Gruber or his people had followed them, if he was watching her, so much the better. Maybe he'd shoot her and put her out of her misery!

That was great thinking for a strong, adult woman, she

thought, chiding herself for her cowardice. But she was losing Cord already and it hurt so much that she wasn't thinking clearly. What he'd said before was exactly what he was going to say when he knew the truth about her. He thought she was a tramp. Maybe she was. Maybe she always had been. With the ticket in hand, she followed the clerk's directions down the long street to where the tour boat was docked.

Cord was furious. He'd already made one serious error of judgment, and at the worst possible time. He had agents here in Amsterdam who were processing the information he'd given them from Gruber's safe, and they were even now questioning his business associates over a thriving child pornography network. In fact, there was a studio within a stone's throw of the hotel where Interpol agents, aided by Dutch police, were serving a warrant at that very moment. Gruber was securely linked to Global Enterprises, where surprise raids in Africa, South America and the United States were taking place this very day. Stillwell was already in custody, along with Adams, and both men were so intimidated by a contact of Lassiter's that they'd sworn never to reveal a word about Maggie to anyone.

Gruber, however, was a different story. He'd blow Maggie's cover if he could, any way he could, to the international press if he could get them on the story. By now, he knew that Cord had unmasked his illegal operation, and he would be out for revenge.

Cord was going to tell Maggie at breakfast that she had to stay close to him, in the hotel, where she'd be safe while Gruber was being taken into custody. But he'd made stupid mistakes, blurting out things he should never have voiced. The fax had been a really stupid one. He could have asked Lassiter to e-mail him the message, but he'd been busy on the Internet at the time and Lassiter needed to reach him at once. It made him furious that he'd been careless enough to let Maggie see that fax. He'd done collateral damage already, and then he'd made that defensive remark about her going to bed with him, which put the knife into her with a vengeance. She'd never forget. He could understand how she felt, too. The information he'd seen had been...traumatic.

He hadn't been wearing his dark glasses, and he'd come into the restaurant alone, without the pretense of being guided, and Maggie had been too preoccupied to notice. He was trailing her now, certain of the one place he was likely to find her. She'd be on a boat somewhere. He knew it. All he had to do was find her, but he had to do it quickly. He whipped out his cell phone, dialed a number, and spoke into it briefly.

He found out that Gruber's studio had been raided, and two employees were now in custody. Several small children were also in custody, protective custody, while agents fanned out in all directions trying to locate Gruber, who had fled the scene.

The man was armed and would be comfortable killing Maggie, if he could find her, and Cord as well, if it were possible. Cord's heart stilled in his chest as he imagined how hurt Maggie had been by his remoteness last night, and his verbal cruelty this morning. She had no idea that he was trying to deal with his own actions in the face of what he'd learned. He was heartsick, heartbroken, at the way he'd treated her for so many years in his ignorance of her real background. He was paying for that in ways she couldn't imagine, and not dealing with it well at all.

Now he'd apparently given her the idea that he felt distaste for her. She, not knowing what he'd already ferreted out, was afraid of their return to Houston and his discovery of the truth. She expected censure, disgust, distaste—and with his reactions of the night before to go by, she was certain of the outcome. But she didn't know. She couldn't know how he felt!

He broke into a fast pace as he neared the canal with its boat docks at its edge. His heart was hammering. Amsterdam was a big city, but Gruber knew it intimately, and he had spies who could find anybody. Cord had his own contacts, but they weren't helping him. He had to find Maggie before Gruber did!

There were plenty of tour boats, and they covered a lot of area on this stretch of the canal. Cord had no idea which one Maggie would have taken without searching them. He had one photograph of her, however, a dog-eared, crumpled one of her at Christmas when she was sixteen, that he'd carried around with him most of his adult life. She didn't look much different even now.

He pulled it out and started showing it to employees of the various tour boats all along the canal.

Just as he reached the last boat in line, which was pulling out into the canal, a woman recognized the face he showed her and pointed to the boat, which would clear the dock in another few seconds.

He handed the employee a large bill and made a flying jump at the boat while she was shouting to him that he had to buy a ticket in one of the shops, that she couldn't sell him one.

It was no use. He was limber and athletic, and used to taking chances. He went flying along the dock and jumped right out over the canal, landing hard and rolling on the deck in the nick of time to avoid diving into the dark brown, smelly waters of the canal.

Maggie was seated at a table with two couples and an elderly woman. One of the couples, newlyweds the old woman said complacently, were passionately immersed in each other while the boat pulled out into the canal.

She felt alone and betrayed and utterly miserable. She didn't have a camera, which was just as well, because there was nobody to take a photo of. She stared blankly out at the water as the boat rocked and turned and started out into the water. There was yelling outside on the pier, but she couldn't see above the level of the poles that held it out of the water. There was a hard thump and raised voices up ahead in the cabin where the pilot was sitting.

She stared at the aisle, barely hearing an offer of refreshments from a young woman going down the other way. Seconds later, a disheveled Cord Romero strode down the aisle toward her, looking furious.

Her heart bounced into her throat. He took a seat beside her, watching all around for signs of danger.

"Go away," she choked.

"The only way back to port is to swim," he muttered under his breath, "and it would take an act of God to get me into *that* water voluntarily."

She wouldn't look at him. She folded her arms across her breasts defensively. She felt eight years old again.

He leaned back, not touching her, and studied her averted face. "Gruber escaped," he said at her ear. "We've got enough evidence to send him up for years, but we have to catch him first. Meanwhile," he added darkly, "he'll be looking for us, and it won't be to wish us a pleasant holiday!"

She swallowed. They were in a very public place. She turned and forced her shamed eyes to look up at Cord, who wasn't even trying to disguise his anger and frustration.

Her lower lip trembled as she tried to find something to say to him. She'd never been so unsettled, so terrified of the future.

His big hand caught in the hair at her nape and pulled her face under his. He kissed her very gently, aware that she trembled. His mouth moved to her eyelids, her cheeks.

"Ah, you are newlyweds, too, *ja?*" the elderly lady asked with a chuckle.

Cord glanced at her. "Not yet. But very soon, we will be," he agreed huskily, and the look he gave Maggie was smoldering.

She didn't even have a protest. She stared at him with her heart in her eyes and wished with all her soul that he meant it. But she was remembering what she'd found in the fax machine.

"Don't look back, Maggie," he said softly. "We've both done too much of that already. We have a future, together. I promise you, we do!"

His eyes were punctuating that promise. She gave in to temptation with a shaky little sigh. Without another peep, she moved close to him and laid her cheek against his broad chest. Odd, she thought, he'd jerked when she did that, as if the action surprised him. But she felt safe close to him. It was the only place she'd ever felt safe.

His arm contracted protectively and his cheek rested against her dark hair. "You haven't been thinking straight for the past couple of weeks, have you?" he asked.

She blinked. "I don't understand."

"I know." He kissed her dark hair and sighed heavily. "We're closer right now than we've ever been." His arm tightened again, and his mouth eased down to her ear. "I want to marry you, Maggie. I want it more than anything in the world."

Her indrawn breath was so audible that the others at the table glanced at her curiously.

She looked up at him, confused, thrilled, afraid. She couldn't agree, she couldn't...

He moved to fish out his wallet. He produced a folded paper and handed it to her. "Here. Have a look."

She noticed an official seal embossed at the bottom even before she unfolded the paper. Her lips parted on a soft explosion of breath as she studied the paper that Cord had obviously carried with him for some time.

She looked up at him with wide, shocked eyes. "It's a marriage license," she said huskily, "with both...with both our names on it!"

He shrugged. "It seemed like a good idea at the time," he murmured, searching her eyes. "In fact, it still does, never more than now."

She bit her lower lip almost in two. "It's a very...bad one," she choked. She handed him back the paper and fought down tears. "You have no idea at all what this could do to you. You don't know what Lassiter has in those files, what Gruber would do with the information if he could get to a reporter!"

He held her close while he refolded the paper with one hand and stuck it in the pocket of his jacket. "I don't care what he does, or with what," he said fiercely. "You belong to me. I'm not giving you up. Not ever!"

She closed her eyes and wanted to believe that he meant it. But he didn't know what Gruber had. Once he did, it would change everything. She wanted to bawl. It wouldn't help, but she didn't know what else she could do. That little piece of paper destroyed her peace of mind, even while it made her glow inside as if from the light of a hundred loving candles...

The sudden shattering of glass was surprising. She lifted her head and looked at Cord blankly in the space of seconds before she was pushed forcibly to the deck and held down.

There were screams and shouts of fear. The boat stopped dead in the current and began to drift.

Cord lifted his head long enough to look toward the cabin. He saw the pilot slumped in his seat and knew everything at once.

"Stay down, baby," he whispered to Maggie. "Don't move! Do you hear me?"

"What's going on?" she asked unsteadily.

"Gruber, unless I miss my guess, and we're sitting ducks here in the middle of the canal!"

"But what are you going to do?" she exclaimed.

"Get us out of here, while there's still time. Stay down. Everybody, keep your heads down and keep calm!" he called to the other passengers. "Keep away from the windows!"

He darted down the aisle to the accompaniment of other bullets that rained down into the boat. Apparently someone was shooting at them either from the nearby bridge or the walk beside the canal. The angle of the bullets, though, indicated a high place.

Maggie peered up over the table and looked through the wide windows. There was a glint of metal on the bridge just ahead of them.

"Cord, he's on the bridge!" she yelled.

He'd already pushed the pilot onto the floor and shouted at the tour guide to take care of him. He worked the controls and suddenly shot the boat ahead, zigzagging it so that he made a difficult target. There was shattered glass in front, but he'd knocked enough of it out so that he could see ahead.

The trick was going to be getting the boat through the narrow opening under that bridge. It was one he remembered from other trips to the city. The boat had to be angled in, and even then, there was only a couple of inches of clearance on either side. Added to that, there were other tour boats on the canals and they often came close on the ride.

He had an idea. If he could get the boat under the bridge and get out, he might be able to get to Gruber. But that would require someone to drive the boat through.

"Maggie!" he yelled. "Get up here, quick!"

She darted down the aisle without hesitation, and went right to him, weaving as he darted the boat along the river to the accompaniment of gunfire.

"What can I do?" she asked at once.

"You can drive the boat, honey, I'm jumping ship."

"What?"

He gunned the engine and set his jaw as he guided the wide boat under the bridge, scraping one side, and put it in neutral. He jerked out his .45 automatic and put Maggie into the driver's seat, hurriedly familiarizing her with the controls. Her hands trembled, but she listened and nodded.

"I don't want to do this," he said huskily. "I don't want to put you at risk, but if I don't stop him, he'll kill somebody. You understand?"

She pulled his head down and kissed him hungrily. "Don't get killed. I love you so!" she choked.

"No less than I love you, Maggie. Nothing in your past will ever change that!" he swore fervently. "Believe it!"

He kissed her hungrily, feeling her instant response even as he pulled back and stood up, cocking the gun and taking off the safety as he headed for the steps that led up to the hull. "Get the boat through the bridge, even if you have to scrape the paint off doing it, and zigzag it when you come out from under that bridge. Don't stop for a second. If he gets a clear shot, he'll take it. The only advantage we'll have is that he'll be shooting from overhead and he won't be able to see inside. Can you do this?"

She nodded. "I can do anything I have to," she replied fearlessly, and looked at that moment as if she could.

"Don't panic, whatever you do," he counseled. "Just concentrate on the job at hand."

"I can do this. You be careful and don't get yourself shot!" she added firmly.

"Who, me?" He grinned. "Be careful yourself, sweetheart."

He savored the look on her face for an instant before he turned and dashed up the steps with deadly efficiency.

Maggie watched him go, but she turned immediately back to the controls and put the boat in gear. It was time to emulate a racing-boat driver and save lives. She wasn't going to let Cord down.

15

Cord leaped from the boat to the filthy underside of the stone bridge and darted to the iron steps that led up to the top of the bridge. He clutched the .45 carefully in one hand while he climbed with the other.

He could hear the boat start. He knew that Maggie would have it in sight of Gruber any second now. Gruber, with any luck, would think that the scraping sound meant that the boat was temporarily stuck underneath and the pilot was having trouble getting it out. He might think the pilot was dead and somebody else was trying to free the boat. Either way, he wouldn't be expecting Cord to attack him. Cord hoped.

The man was desperate, and he would kill. Knowing that, Cord steeled himself for whatever happened next. His only regret was that he hadn't spoken honestly to Maggie first and told her what he really knew.

The noise of the motor boat below camouflaged the last few steps he took. He saw a short, dark-haired man with an automatic weapon huddled against the bridge looking down.

Cord aimed and yelled at the man, in Dutch, to drop his weapon.

Predictably the man turned and fired at him. Cord fired back, even as he felt a hot stinging pain in his left shoulder. The other man crumpled.

Cord didn't take time to go to him. There was a bridge farther up, and he saw the glint of metal there, too. This man wasn't Gruber. Maggie was on the canal, heading toward sudden death, and there was no way to get to her in time. His only hope was to draw Gruber's fire or get to the next bridge before Maggie did.

Or... He had an idea. He grabbed his cell phone from his pocket, noting idly that there was blood on the face of it, and dialed the emergency services number. He gave his name, what was happening, and asked for assistance. Luckily there was a police car nearby. It would be sent at once.

Cord was running even as he stuck the phone back in his pocket. It would take more luck than he believed in to get a police car there in time to save Maggie. He felt sick and his arm was throbbing now, but he wasn't going to let Gruber kill Maggie.

He darted past a throng of tourists, aware that he was frightening people, both with the pistol and the bleeding wound visible against the paleness of his shirt. But he kept going, his heart pounding, as he pictured a bullet finding its way right into the cockpit, right into Maggie, from that bridge ahead.

"Gruber!" he yelled at the top of his lungs.

Even above traffic and mumbled conversation, his voice carried. The man on the bridge stopped, turned, looked.

"I'm here, Gruber!" Cord yelled, his long legs making short work of the distance between them.

Gruber moved to the edge of the bridge and laughed, aiming his weapon down at the boat that was quickly approaching him.

"Maggie, turn the boat, turn the damned boat!" Cord yelled at the canal. Certainly she couldn't hear him, not above the roar of the engines...!

But even as he told himself that, the boat began to turn, slowly, awkwardly, but presenting its back to the angry man on the bridge who was now firing haphazardly in a furious temper.

Cord was within firing range. He wasn't sure of his aim. He felt as if he might pass out soon. He dropped to one knee, yelled at milling pedestrians to get the hell out of the way, aimed as carefully as he ever had, took a breath, and fired.

It seemed to take years for the bullet to get to the bridge. It was as if everything was moving in slow motion. His vision slowly blurred. The pain was monstrous all of a sudden. His shoulder was so heavy that he couldn't hold it up. Nausea rose in his throat. He watched the man on the bridge turn in his direction, slowly, and he knew that he was a sitting duck. But he was going down fighting...

* * *

The police were everywhere in the aftermath of explosive gunfire. They directed Maggie to get the boat to the side of the canal, where a policeman jumped on board and guided it to where another policeman could use the bow rope to tie it to the steps temporarily. Paramedics appeared.

Maggie was helped out of the boat, because she was insisting at the top of her lungs that she had to get to Cord and she wouldn't listen to excuses. She didn't see him anywhere. There was a man down on the bridge, but that couldn't be Cord. Where was he? Was he all right?

She raged at the authorities to hurry. In desperation, one of the policemen led her to an area of sidewalk surrounded by concerned faces.

Cord was propped on an elbow, bleeding from the shoulder, his pistol still gripped in his big hand as he cursed roundly. "Will you get to her...?" he was yelling.

Her sudden appearance electrified him. "Maggie!" he shouted, in a tone she'd never heard him use.

"Cord!" Maggie cried, throwing herself down beside him. She touched his face, his throat, while he gathered her in forcibly with the arm that still worked, holding her as close as he could, mindless of the blood he was smearing over her clothing. She held him, too, sobbing with relief.

"I couldn't see you!" he growled at her throat. "I didn't know if I got him in time!"

"I'm fine! I heard you telling me to turn the boat, even if

it did sound like a whisper in my ear. Oh, thank God, you're alive," she choked. "Thank God!"

"I'm alive," he said huskily. "Even if a little worse for wear."

That reminded her that she'd seen blood on his clothing in the brief seconds before he hauled her down into his arms, and he was sitting on the sidewalk. She pulled back a little and almost lost her composure when she saw the blood pouring from the wound in his shoulder. "You're bleeding!" she exclaimed, horrified. "Please," she begged the policeman above her, "get help!"

"This is all very irregular," the man was muttering, but he spoke into what looked like a cell phone in a language that she didn't understand.

Maggie took Cord's big hand in hers and held on tight. "Don't you die," she choked, terrified by the blood. "Don't you die! I can't live without you. I won't! Do you hear me?"

He chuckled at her vehemence. "Honey, I've had a lot worse than a bullet in my shoulder," he said soothingly. "It hurts and there's a lot of blood, but I'm not going to die. Am I, Bojo?"

"I should think not," Bojo murmured from beside her, with a grim smile. "Cord is a hard man to kill. However," he added with a wry look at the downed man, "if he does, I get to keep his pistol and that nice watch he wears."

Maggie was aghast, but Cord burst out laughing.

The young policeman knelt beside Cord while they waited for the paramedics. He pulled back Cord's shirt and looked beneath at the bleeding wound. "It is not a killing wound," he told Maggie in halting English. "You understand?"

"There's so much...blood!" she sputtered.

"It may hit an artery, I think..."

Bojo interrupted him abruptly, kneeling to put pressure against the wound.

"Kill me and be done with it, why don't you, damn it!" Cord cursed. But the bleeding slowed.

Bojo chuckled. "Ah, no, Maggie would take the gun and shoot me if I did." He turned toward the police officer and spoke to him in Dutch. The man replied in the same language.

"What is he saying?" Maggie asked Bojo. "What are you doing to Cord? And where in the world did you come from?" she added, recovered enough now to be shocked at his sudden appearance.

"Never mind what he's saying. I am putting pressure on the wound to slow the loss of blood. Oh, we've been here since the beginning," he replied easily. "Cord had us around the city, staking out Gruber's business associates. You'll be glad to know that the police have all of them, besides enough evidence to have Stillwell and Adams tried in the world court on various counts of international criminal charges. Gruber, too, if he's still alive," he added with a cold glance toward the bridge, where police were standing over a form on the ground.

"He'll be lucky if he is," Cord said quietly. "I couldn't risk Maggie's life by aiming to wound him," he added flatly, clasping Maggie's cold hand hard in his own while Bojo continued to exert pressure on Cord's shoulder.

The young policeman's phone buzzed. He answered it, frowned, nodded, spoke into it and hung up.

"The man on the bridge," he said to Cord, jerking his head toward Gruber. He hesitated, searching for the English. "Not alive."

Cord's dark eyes narrowed. "No loss," he replied curtly.

The other man understood. He looked down at Maggie. "Ambulance comes now," he said, and seconds later, the sirens became loud in Maggie's ears. She held on to Cord's cold hand and prayed and prayed while he just smiled at her and spoke reassuringly through his pain. Bojo kept right on pushing against the wound until the paramedics came running toward them.

She wasn't listening to Cord's reassurances. It might not be a fatal wound, but she wanted Cord in the hospital, and quick. He was losing blood at a fantastic rate. She didn't even know CPR. She was going to have to take courses, she told herself idiotically, if she was going to live with a mercenary.

It didn't even occur to her then that she'd sworn to run if Cord discovered her past from Lassiter's files. Running was the last thing on her mind. Cord had shown her a marriage license and she wanted to use it. The future could take care of itself. For now, at least.

Weary, worrisome hours later, Maggie was sitting beside Cord in the private room he'd been taken to after surgery to remove the bullet—with only local anesthetic, to her dismay. Two policemen, plus Bojo and Rodrigo, were just outside in the hall. They hadn't volunteered any information on why they were there, but Maggie wasn't stupid. Gruber might have associates who were still loose in the city. Cord was going to be watched. It set Maggie's mind at ease, somewhat.

He was going to be fine, they promised. He'd be out of the hospital the next day with an ample supply of antibiotics and painkillers. They could fly home whenever they liked.

This was welcome news, but frightening to Maggie, who dreaded having temptation put in Cord's path by that file of Lassiter's when they reached Houston. But Cord was alive and improving already. He'd be fine. That was all she needed to know.

She'd hoped to have a few minutes alone with him, but men in suits came and went with alarming regularity, speaking in all sorts of languages. One had a thick burr, another a French accent. Two others looked as if they were cut out of sheet steel and had never smiled in their lives. Cord later identified them as American, but wouldn't tell her from which agency. The others were a mix of foreign agents, some from Interpol.

Sitting with her in the hall while Cord entertained his guests, Bojo studied her curiously. He was surprised at the difference a woman could make in a man. First Philippe Sabon, then Micah Steele, and now Cord Romero. He wanted to tell Maggie that her friend Gretchen had been in as much danger as she had been, and was just now in America—a visit that would end momentarily if he knew Sabon—and that he, himself, was already overdue in Qawi after doing this favor for Cord. He must leave the country, and quickly. The aftermath of a coup attempt in that country had almost cost Gretchen her life, not to mention Philippe Sabon's. That terror had been averted, with help from some powerful ex-mercenaries and a lot of courage from the sheikh himself. But there were details to attend to, and Bojo was needed rather desperately, along with his men.

She glanced up at Bojo, noting that he was still bloodstained from his work on Cord, which had probably saved his life. "I haven't even thanked you for all you've done," she said gently.

He shrugged. "I have done my job," he reminded her with a smile. "Cord is my friend."

She looked toward the closed door of Cord's room. "If he had died," she said quietly, "there would have been no place on earth where I would belong, ever again."

"You will find that he feels the same way," he told her. "If you do not know already," he added with a grin.

She grinned back.

When he left, she closed her weary eyes and sighed. Despite the terror of the future, it was better than the terror of days past. She would get through it. Somehow, she would get through the uncertainty and the fear. It wasn't going to be possible to walk away from Cord, whatever happened. He would have to push her away.

* * *

Two hours passed before he was through talking to his visitors. She went back inside to find him lounging in the bed in the unbecoming hospital garment, waiting for her with a rueful smile.

She went to him at once, sitting down in the chair beside the bed. She reached up to touch his face, his mouth. Tears stung her eyes. She tried to avoid them, but the fear and pain and worry of the past hours had ruined her self-control. Hot tears rolled helplessly down her cheeks.

"Hey," he said softly. "I'm not going to die. Honest."

She managed a watery smile and held his hand tight.

He searched her face slowly. "You look like hell."

"Think so? You should look in a mirror," she added.

He forced a grin. "No, thanks. Hey."

"What?"

His fingers edged between hers. "When we get a minute, I'm going to buy us a ring each. My hand feels naked."

Her heart jumped. She remembered, then, the folded piece of paper he had in his wallet. It had been rescued from his inner pocket—fortunately, the one opposite the side of his chest where the bullet had hit. She had it in her purse now, safe and sound.

"You didn't even hint that you were thinking of getting married," she accused, but she didn't sound angry. "In fact, you swore you never would."

He shrugged. "I had a hard time with Patricia," he said after a minute. "I was never in love with her, Maggie, and she knew it. I married her for a lot of reasons, none of the right ones. You were so young, baby," he added huskily, and the anguish he felt was in his dark eyes as they searched hers. "I didn't want to seduce you, and I was afraid I might. You were...you are...the dearest thing on earth to me. It was nothing more than a halfhearted attempt to protect you from a relationship I didn't think you were ready for." He sighed heavily. "Then Patricia committed suicide and I had to live not only with the guilt of her death, but the guilt of knowing that I never loved her. She knew it, too." He caught her hand tight in his. "Just as, I'm sure, your husband knew you never loved him."

"He wasn't lovable," she said tightly. "And after he cost me the baby, I hated him. But I felt guilty that he died, the way he died. He couldn't help being an alcoholic. He started drinking when he was very young and couldn't stop."

He smoothed over her fingers. "I have a lot of regrets. About the baby, about your marriage. About the way I treated you, all those long years..."

She put her fingers over his hard mouth. "You're the one who keeps saying we have to stop looking back. You really...want to marry me?" she added hesitantly.

His face hardened. "More than I want to go on living." He sounded as if he meant every word.

She sighed worriedly. "There are still things about my past. Things you don't know. Things I...can't tell you."

"Hey."

She looked up.

"Let's take it one day at a time," he said gently. "Suppose we fly to the Bahamas instead of sailing?" he added and grinned. "We can get married there."

"We can?"

"Yes, we can." He carried her palm to his mouth. "I want to marry you right away, Maggie," he added. "I don't want you to have a single chance to run away from me, ever again."

"What about Gruber's men?" she added worriedly.

He cocked an eyebrow and smiled. "All in custody. His whole outfit's facing jail time, in countries all over the world. The case will make international headlines. And you and I," he added, "are finally safe."

"Safe." She studied his big hand. "I've very rarely felt that way in my life, except when I was with you. I'd given up on you, though," she added with a rueful smile. "I decided that you'd never be able to care about me and I might as well try to find a life somewhere else."

"You left the country and tried to put an ocean between us." His eyes darkened. "It unnerved me. I don't have a life without you, Maggie," he added solemnly. "I don't think I have, since I was sixteen."

She sighed worriedly. "Cord, about that file Lassiter wants to show you..."

His fingers curled tight into hers. "He can burn it, with my compliments. If it means that much to you."

Her eyes brightened. "You mean it?"

"Yes. I mean it."

Her heart lightened. She felt as if she could fly. Then she remembered how easily Stillwell and Adams had gotten into her sealed records. "But, Stillwell and Adams..."

"Lassiter has friends," he replied. "I won't tell you who, or what, they are. Suffice it to say that Adams and Stillwell are very small fish and they are in imminent danger of being swallowed whole by a shark—even in prison—if they open their mouths."

"Wow."

"Wow." He looked at her with tender concern. "You need some sleep," he pointed out.

She smiled. "I'll sleep when this is all over. I'm not leaving you. Not for anything. I don't care if they do say it's not a serious wound. I'm here until they let you go."

His eyes narrowed with emotion. He didn't even argue. His fingers bruised hers. "Okay."

It was a concession. He was giving her everything she wanted. And Lassiter hadn't betrayed her. He'd saved her. She wondered if it would be permissible to hug a married man. When they got back to Houston, she was going to find out.

They let Cord out of the hospital the next afternoon. They went back to the hotel, to take up residence in the suite he and Maggie had hardly enjoyed since their arrival. The hotel staff was attentive and they lacked for nothing—except Bojo. He'd taken off the night before with a quick goodbye to Maggie and a promise to let Cord know how things were going.

Rodrigo remained, and proved a valuable ally in the logistics of the move from the hospital to the hotel. The other men had gone as well, and Maggie found out only later why. Gruber's entire operation had been shut down overnight, including his multinational corporation. Government agents from all over the industrial world had converged on the shady businesses Gruber had headed, and children had been rescued and taken home from some of the darkest hellholes on earth. Prostitution rings and child pornography rings had been splintered by enthusiastic agents. Stillwell and Adams were under arrest and, after trial, facing extradition to Amsterdam for trial in the world court. Lassiter's clients, whose children had been kidnapped and killed, had found peace.

Two days later, Rodrigo flew to Qawi to join Bojo, and Cord and Maggie flew to the Bahamas, where they were married by an American minister at a beautiful luxury hotel overlooking Nassau—after the appropriate documents were presented and official requirements were satisfied.

Maggie wore a white cotton skirt and peasant blouse, both with acres of white lace and with a spray of white jasmine in her hair. When Cord looked into her eyes after they made their vows, she thought she'd never seen such an expression of tenderness in her life. It was as if she were reborn. Cord remarked with a husky laugh that he felt just the same. The parallel lines of their lives were now a circle, bonded forever. After three days of sightseeing and feverish petting, they boarded a cruise ship for Miami, from which they would fly home to Houston.

Maggie felt as if she'd lived a fairy tale as she lay in her own narrow bed across from her husband's in the elegant stateroom, feeling safe and secure and loved. Cord hadn't wanted them to share a bed just yet, because of his shoulder, he said. But he kissed her coming and going, and she felt on the verge of something extraordinary. It was just that Cord kept watching her with a haunted, dark look in his eyes that she couldn't puzzle out. It didn't go away, either.

The day before they docked at Miami, Cord was on the Internet with his laptop when she went out for air. He came to find her on deck with exciting news. It was a shock to discover that Gretchen had left Qawi for Texas and was back at her old job. She was also married...to the sheikh himself, Philippe Sabon. There had been a coup attempt and Gretchen had been in the thick of battle alongside her husband. Maggie could hardly believe it.

"And to think, it was my job that I gave up," Maggie murmured, nuzzling against Cord's uninjured shoulder as they watched the sea glimmer like jewels in the sunshine. "Just imagine what could have happened."

"You're married," he pointed out, chuckling.

"I was engaged, and I didn't even know it," she accused mischievously. "How could you get a marriage license to marry a woman and not tell her you'd done it? And I did all that agonizing over sleeping with you...!"

"Which you did beautifully," he added with a wicked smile.

"My conscience beat me to death!"

He grinned shamelessly. "You knew when I did it that I had forever in mind. I don't sleep with innocents."

"I wasn't innocent."

He touched her forehead with his lips. "Don't be ridiculous. Of course you were. I'm the only man you've ever had, even if it wasn't an experience you want to remember, that first time."

"Even that time was magical," she whispered. "And the other times have been earthshaking." She looked at him curiously, noting the way he avoided her gaze. "It is just your shoulder, isn't it?" she added worriedly. "I mean, you still want me...?"

"Of course I still want you," he scoffed. "But my shoulder's very sore," he added without looking at her.

"Okay. Just so long as I know that it's temporary."

He pursed his lips and grinned at her, although it seemed a little forced. "So I'm that good, am I?"

She tweaked the hair at his temple as she reached up to hold him. "What a trial you're going to be."

He smiled at her lovingly. "I'll do my best to reform by the time the kids come along."

"You sound very sure that we'll have them," she said, not as confident.

"I am very sure," he said, and looked as if he meant it. "Meanwhile, we'll get to know each other, all over again."

She didn't argue about having children. But she had serious doubts about her fertility, her ability to cope with the past if it ever cropped up again, and even her sudden status as a married woman. Finally she decided to just let the current take her downriver, figuratively speaking, and stop trying to swim to shore.

Houston looked familiar and foreign at one and the same time. It seemed years instead of scant weeks since they'd left it.

The ranch was warm and welcoming. June met them at the door, having been forewarned of their arrival by a call from Cord on the plane. Her father and Red Davis were waiting in the living room to shake hands and offer congratulations and welcome them back.

It took a whole day for Cord to get caught up on ranch business, and there were phone calls and e-mails and faxes that had to have replies. He brought in his part-time male secretary and fell back into his routine, wounded shoulder and all.

Feeling oddly neglected, Maggie walked the floor and worried. She'd had her own room their first night back, mainly because of his shoulder. He insisted that she wouldn't be able to sleep, because he was restless. It was the same excuse he'd used at the hotel in Amsterdam and even aboard ship, when they married. He'd had his own bed, and she had hers, although they shared a stateroom. She knew there was more to the problem than that.

In desperation, because he was totally uncommunicative, she phoned Tess Lassiter and went to see her at the office, pretending that she was going shopping for some feminine necessities. Cord gave her the keys to his car and told her to be careful. Even with Gruber's men rounded up, she might not be totally safe. He had Davis go with her, to her dismay.

"This is your old office building," Davis protested when she parked on the street.

She glared at him. "Thank you, I didn't know that," she drawled sarcastically.

He sighed. "Maggie, what are you up to?"

"Nothing that you can tell Cord, and I mean it," she added, holding up her left hand with the small gold band that Cord had put on it.

He grimaced. "Husbands and wives shouldn't have secrets."

"Tell him that," she replied. "I'm going inside to see Tess Lassiter and if you breathe one word to Cord, I'll have you barbecued over that coal pit out back. Do you hear me?"

He stared at her. "I'd taste terrible."

"Not if we used enough barbecue sauce, and I'm not kidding. Wait for me. I won't be long."

"Okay. If the police come and arrest me for parking in a No Parking zone and I tell them you made me promise to stay here, and they shoot me..."

She gave an exasperated sigh. "All right! You can drive to the mall and have coffee at that famous little shop you like," she chided. "I've got my cell phone. Got yours?"

He took it out of his pocket and showed it to her.

"Great. I'll phone you when I'm ready to leave!"

She got out and went into the building alone.

* * *

Tess Lassiter was uneasy about what Maggie wanted to know. "It's classified stuff," she began.

"What's classified stuff?" Dane Lassiter asked with a smile as he walked into the office with his briefcase.

Tess exchanged a complicated glance with him.

"Okay, come on in," Dane told Maggie, opening his office door. "Sweetheart," he addressed Tess, "how about getting me a bear claw? I'm starving. They don't feed you at federal offices."

"Poor old thing," Tess said with a tender smile. "I'll see what's left at the bakery. Maggie, can I get you anything?"

Maggie shook her head. She was too nervous to eat. "Thanks, anyway."

"I'll be back soon." Tess closed the door behind her.

Dane leaned forward and stared across his desk at Maggie, his black eyes steady and unblinking. "You want to know what Cord got out of me."

She swallowed and flushed. "Yes. I'm sorry I was trying to find out from Tess."

"It's all right," he said quietly. "It must be easier for you to talk to a woman."

"It is," she said, surprised at his perception.

He drew in a long breath. "Even after all the years I've been in the business, some things get next to me. This case has been an example. Stillwell and Adams are in jail waiting to be arraigned. They're going to turn state's evidence, in exchange for lighter sentences." His face hardened. "They won't be a threat to you, ever again. I promise you they won't."

"Cord told me. Thanks." She hesitated, clasping and unclasping her hands. "There was a fax you sent to Cord in Amsterdam," she began finally.

"I told him nothing," he said at once. "But he knows how to break into encoded files," he added uneasily.

Her heart stopped. She looked at Dane with horror in her eyes. "You mean...he knows? He knows...everything?"

"It looks that way."

She bit her lower lip. She was remembering the way he'd acted that night, the odd remarks, the assurance that he loved her, no matter what had happened in the past. He knew, and he hadn't said, because she'd threatened to run away. She'd spent years running away, from emotions, from attachments, from commitment, from everything, out of fear. She was afraid of what Cord would think of her. But he knew. And he loved her. She studied the small gold band on her finger, the one she'd chosen for its simplicity. Cord had put it on for her, and he'd looked into her eyes...what had he said? That no matter what had ever happened in the past, the ring was a seal on their future, a promise of mutual support through fire and flood and disaster. Surely her past would come under the heading of a disaster.

She looked up at Lassiter. He'd been saying something. She hadn't heard him.

He smiled. "You haven't heard a word, have you? I said, Cord phoned me on a secure line and told me that he was going to come home and make sausage out of Adams and Still-well, and that he'd personally hang Gruber out to dry. I've never known anyone that homicidal, except maybe me when my wife was shot, before we married," he recalled. "He wanted blood. I spent half an hour talking him out of it, while he raged in two languages. I think he'd been drinking, too—and I can tell you that Cord Romero doesn't drink. That was the best indication of how upset he was. He was hurt that you hadn't trusted him enough to tell him, in all those years he'd known you. He said there was nothing in his life that he wouldn't gladly have shared with you."

Her face cleared. Things fell into place. Her life became an open book, a pattern, that she could see for the first time. She hadn't trusted Cord. She'd been afraid that he would think less of her, that he wouldn't want her, that he'd judge her, as so many other people had. But when she turned that scenario around, when she considered how she'd have felt if it had been Cord in her place—she was sick at her stomach.

"I failed him, right down the line," she said unsteadily. "I never thought how I'd feel, if he'd had such a past and hadn't wanted me to know. It all comes down to trust, doesn't it?" she added, meeting his dark eyes. "If you love someone, you have to trust them."

He smiled slowly. "I'm glad you're getting the picture."

"And nothing you do, nothing you have done, will ever make any difference," she continued, as if she'd just found pure truth. "Because when you love, it's unconditional."

"Exactly." He pursed his lips. "Why don't you go home and tell Cord that?"

Her eyes brightened. It was like free fall. She didn't have to be afraid. She never had to be afraid again, even of disclosure. Cord loved her. His was the only opinion that would ever matter. It was so simple, and she'd never considered that one simple fact.

She almost leaped out of the chair. "When the kids get bigger, I want to come and work for you. Can I?"

He chuckled heartily. "That's the spirit. And yes, you can."

She grinned. "I'll hold you to that, Mr. Lassiter. Thank you. For keeping my secret. For making Adams and Stillwell keep it. For...everything! I think you're terrific."

He got to his feet and shook hands with her. "Just for the record," he told her, "so does my wife."

She chuckled. "I'm not the least bit surprised!"

16

The next few minutes were a blur of activity. Maggie almost knocked Tess down getting out of the building. She thanked her, blessed Dane, promised to phone, and dived into the car the minute Davis pulled up at the curb. She inspired him to break speed limits and sighed her relief that they weren't picked up by the state police as they pulled up in front of the house.

She opened the door even as Davis was putting on the brakes. She dived into the house, past a surprised June, right into the office where Cord was speaking on the phone to someone about a bull.

She closed and locked the door behind her, almost shivering with her discoveries. "I'm sorry, but you have to hang up now," she told Cord in a shaky little tone.

"Why?" he asked with the receiver an inch from his ear.

She shrugged, smiled sheepishly, and started to take off her blouse.

He dropped the receiver. It was the first time in their lives that Maggie had ever been forward with him. In fact, he'd been certain that her past would preclude any such delightful opportunities.

"I'll call you back," he told whoever was on the other end of the phone and hung up, quick.

Meanwhile, Maggie had shed blouse and bra and was stepping out of her shoes and working on the zipper of her slacks.

She went toward him, totally nude, enjoying his look of shocked pleasure. She took him by the hand and led him to the sofa, sprawling on it in breathless abandon.

"Well?" she asked huskily. "Are you up to it?"

He actually shivered as his hands went to rip off his knit shirt. "I'll show you what I'm up to," he said in a husky tone.

She watched him undress, stretching sensuously as the fabric came away from that tall, powerful body.

"Did you lock the door?" he asked roughly.

"Oh, yes," she murmured with a smile. "You look very sexy."

"I'd love to tell you how you look," he said, sounding as if he were choking, "but I don't think I have time!"

Neither did she, when she saw him without the last brief covering. He came down beside her, leaning heavily on his uninjured arm, and his mouth went homing to hers. His long legs were insistent, feverishly insistent, as they parted hers and he went down against her with uncontrollable desire.

"I'm sorry," he ground out.

She relaxed, smiling under his mouth as he went into her suddenly, urgently. She gasped a little and arched to greet him, feeling his mouth swallow the husky little noise as he began to move on her with practiced skill.

She wrapped her long legs around his and shivered with the increasing stabs of pleasure that built from his uninhibited possession of her. She reached under him, her fingers sliding down the curve of his long back to his buttocks. She dug her nails in, pulling him closer, while he rocked on her in a fiercely ardent rhythm.

She felt him tense more and more as the heated tension built. Their movements were loud in the locked room, their breathing rasping, desperate, as they clung together. She opened her mouth wide and felt his tongue penetrating it as great sudden waves of delicious heat exploded in pleasure deep inside her body. She convulsed, crying piteously into his hard mouth as he thrust against her violently in the last harsh contractions of fulfillment.

He groaned hoarsely into her mouth, his powerful body arching downward and holding there, pushing, grinding, straining, as if even skin close wasn't quite close enough. He shuddered over her even as her own body pulsed in ardent release.

She felt dampness under her palms as he rested heavily on top of her in the aftermath, his mouth open against her throat as he pulsed inside her.

"I can feel you there," she whispered in his ear. Her legs tightened around him.

"I can feel you, too," he whispered back, moving roughly from side to side to make her gasp with returning spasms of pleasure. "My God, what an explosion! I wasn't sure I could bear it."

"I know. Me, too." She strained up toward him. "I love you so much. I love you more than my life!"

He groaned harshly at her ear and kissed her again, his hips moving helplessly against hers until he felt himself suddenly capable in seconds and gasped with returning desire.

"Yes," she whispered at his ear, almost choking on the delight of his movements. "Can we, again? Can we? Oh, Cord, I want...you...so much!"

His mouth found hers and his movements deepened, lengthened, slowed, until she was shivering with every agonizing brush of his body on hers.

He laughed suddenly and rolled onto his back, still joined to her, still shivering. "My arm's giving out," he whispered. He looked up at her with fierce passion. "Take me."

"Wh...what? How?" she exclaimed.

"Like this, you little puritan," he chided, taking her by the hips and showing her the movement. He grimaced, shifting the wounded shoulder. "It's too much, too soon, but I can't stop. You can't stop. Maggie! You can't...stop!"

He groaned harshly. She sighed and set her lips, moving until she found the pressure and the rhythm that made him gasp. After a while, it became exciting, and pleasurable, and then it was fun. She laughed. He laughed. Until the pleasure bit into them so deeply that thought, and speech, became impossible...

She lay beside him, damp and drained, with one leg thrown over his, so content that she never wanted to move.

"I'm not complaining," he said at once. "But could you tell me what brought that on?"

She kissed his uninjured shoulder lazily. "It's all a matter of trust," she said softly. "I haven't given you any. I thought it was time I did. So I had to show you that I could be a woman, without being ashamed of myself, of my past, of my body." She sighed. "It's glorious, being a woman, Cord." Her hand rubbed slowly over the thick wedge of hair that covered his chest, and he arched toward it with a silvery groan.

"It's glorious for me, too," he managed to say, stilling her hand. "But you're overestimating both of us. I'm wasted." He laughed. "Really wasted!"

She smiled complacently. "I'm good," she murmured.

"Oh, you're better than that."

She kissed his shoulder. "Thanks."

He shifted, so that she was closer at his side. "What did Lassiter tell you, exactly?" he asked.

She stilled. "How did you know I went to see him?"

"Simple logic," he murmured lazily. "You couldn't rest until you knew what he'd told me about you."

"He didn't tell you anything," she said knowledgeably. "See?"

Her fingers curled into his chest. "He didn't tell you. But I have to. Cord, when I was six, my mother died," she began slowly, painfully. "My stepfather was left with me. He had a friend. They liked to drink beer and play cards, and they didn't like to work. Neither one of them could hold down a job. For over a year, I was tolerated and not much more. My stepfather was going to put me in care, and then another man said I was a cute kid and he wondered if they couldn't use me to make money." She swallowed hard. "My stepfather and the other man got in touch with someone who was...into child pornography." She felt him tense under her, but she didn't stop. "They got another little girl and two little boys, and they made...movies of us..."

"Stop it!" he ground out, his hand tight in her long hair. "You don't have to do this to yourself! I don't have to know...!"

"Yes, you do," she said, despite the trembling of her lower lip and threatening tears. "I have to tell you. You have to listen. They made movies of us, pornographic movies. We were forced to do things we didn't understand, and if we didn't, they used doubled-up belts on us. That made bad marks, and they were even madder because they had to stop until we healed. After that, they used...other punishments, ones that didn't show." She closed her eyes, feeling Cord's powerful body tense with rage. Unconsciously her nails curled into him. "I wasn't in school and a truant officer came to find out why. It was while we were in front of the cameras.... He saw, through a window blind, and he went to get the police."

"Thank God," he muttered.

"Yes. We were ashamed and frightened. The police were very kind to us. They had a woman officer come to take charge of me and the other little girl. But as we went out, a neighbor woman laughed and said we'd grow up to be prostitutes, and it served us right, nasty little kids." She shivered. "Nothing ever hurt so much."

His arm tightened around her. "Finish it," he said tightly.

"My stepfather and his friend went to jail. There was a long trial and it was a sensational story. It was in the papers, on television, radio. The videotapes were taken into evidence, but one got out and was locked away by someone—that's the tape Stillwell and Adams had, I guess, because we were told that the others were destroyed eventually."

"That was when you were taken to juvenile hall," he guessed. "After the trial."

"Yes. They...thought I was young enough that it wouldn't damage me emotionally," she whispered. "I spoke to a child psychologist a couple of times, and then I just sort of got lost in the system. There are so many little kids in the system," she said helplessly.

He smoothed her hair and kissed it tenderly. "Yes. Too many!"

"My stepfather was killed in a riot in prison. The other man...I guess he's still there, somewhere," she added.

"He died of cancer two years ago, still serving time in a federal prison," he told her abruptly.

"Oh." She sighed heavily. "So they're both gone..." She held her breath even as she felt him tense. "How did you know that?"

There was a long, ragged sigh. "I broke into the protected files, while we were in Amsterdam."

She lifted up and looked at him. "So Lassiter was right? You knew, all along? And you still married me?" She sounded as if she couldn't believe it.

"Of course I did, you idiot!" he said furiously. "What sort of human being do you think I am, that I could hold a past like that against you? I love you! I'm damned sorry for what you went through, and even sorrier that I never knew about it in the first place, but it doesn't make a bit of difference to me!"

"It doesn't?" she asked, stunned.

"No. It doesn't." He pulled her down and kissed her hungrily. "It won't make any difference to you, either, eventually, Maggie," he said gently. "You belong to me, now. I'll cherish you as long as I live."

She looked into his dark, angry eyes. "You belong to me, too," she whispered. "Don't you?"

"All of me," he agreed huskily. "Heart, body and soul."

She felt odd—relaxed, happy, unbearably and pleasantly surprised. She smiled slowly. "I seduced you."

He chuckled, despite the gravity of the discussion they'd been having. "Masterfully, at that," he murmured. "I'm shocked to discover that I'm so easy."

Her eyebrows lifted. She smiled with delight. Until recent days, it had never occurred to her that intimacy could be so much fun. With Cord, life itself was an ongoing adventure.

"I'm very glad," she teased. "It gives me confidence. I might do it again, in fact."

"Wow! Something to look forward to," he murmured deeply.

She smiled and laid her cheek against his biceps to search his eyes. "You aren't disgusted," she asked hesitantly.

"You were a child, Maggie," he said gently, but with gravity. "How could I be disgusted? I don't understand how any adult could exploit a child like that. It's savage."

"Greedy people don't care how they make money."

"True." He traced around her soft mouth. "Amy should have told me," he said. "You should have told me. Things would have been so different..."

"You'd have felt sorry for me," she said simply. "Anything is better than pity."

He winced. "I didn't have a clue what your past was like. I seduced you, that night..."

She put her hand over his mouth. "And now I've seduced you, and we're even," she told him firmly. She pursed her lips then and looked down the length of his relaxed body, enjoying the pleasure of his firm, muscular physique. "But I did it better than you did, the first time."

He laughed. "No argument there. But then," he added, bending to kiss her, "you were sober."

She kissed him back lazily. "You said you knew, in Amsterdam." It explained his recent behavior, which had been a puzzle until now.

He nodded. "I didn't know how to tell you. I was ashamed, shocked, hurt. You've never shared any of your worst pain with me. Not even about our baby, when you miscarried."

"I didn't trust you enough, and I'm sorry," she replied. "I thought you'd never want me, really, and that it would just be one more rejection." She searched his hard face lovingly. "Then you said that you loved me. I...was sure I was dreaming. I couldn't quite believe it."

"But you do now."

"Yes. I do now, or I could never have told you about what happened. I didn't know that you'd already ferreted it out."

He smiled again. "Which proves how much you trust me," he said softly. He kissed her nose. "Maggie, we're going to have a lot of years together. And I'm going to wear your heart out loving me."

"I won't mind." She traced his mouth. "But I wish we could have another baby, Cord."

He drew her close. "You have to start believing in miracles, my darling," he murmured drowsily. "You've had few enough in your life until now. But, trust me, they're going to start popping out like measles."

"Do you think so, really?" she asked.

"Really. Damn. I'm sleepy..."

★ ★ ★

The insistent knocking on the door woke them hours later.

"Mr. Romero!" Davis was yelling. "Are you okay? I've got a key, and I'm coming in...!"

"Davis, you crack that door, and you're fired!" Cord raged just as the door began to open.

Davis saw a pile of clothing on the floor that led in a trail to the sofa, where a pair of furious dark eyes met him over the back of it.

The door slammed, a key dropped on the floor, and booted feet ran pell-mell down the hall.

Despite the near calamity of the situation, Cord looked down at a drowsy Maggie and burst out laughing. When she realized what had almost happened, and her gaze was directed to the clothing strewn all over the floor, she couldn't help joining him. Life was glorious.

Several months later, Cord was helping herd a small group of purebred young bulls to the waiting trucks when a speeding sports car scattered them all over the yard.

He cursed, but not loudly, because Maggie flew out of the car and ran toward him at breakneck speed.

He kicked one booted foot out of the stirrup and reached down to pull her up in front of him on the saddle when he realized that she wasn't even slowing down.

"Would you mind telling..." he began.

Her ardent mouth stopped him in midsentence. He kissed

her back hungrily, instantly aroused by her headlong passion and wondering dimly if it would be possible to seduce her on horseback in front of the whole damned crew.

"Here, feel," she whispered against his hard mouth, pulling one of his hands to her flat stomach.

"Maggie, there are damned cowboys everywhere," he tried to get out.

"There's a baby in here," she whispered, pushing his hand closer.

He stiffened. He lifted his head and stared at her blankly while the tearful joy in her green eyes and the laughter coming from her throat managed to sink in.

"You're pregnant?" he asked on an explosion of breath. "Pregnant?"

"Very, very pregnant," she murmured against his mouth. She linked her arms around his neck. "Three months. I didn't even have morning sickness and I thought I couldn't get pregnant, and then I realized we hadn't had any monthly problems."

"*We* hadn't had any monthly problems?" he asked with growing delight and amused affection.

She hit him. "It's our baby. We're both having it. Now, listen. Anyway, I went to see the doctor and he did this one little blood test. I drove so fast getting here to tell you...!"

Sirens interrupted her.

"Oh, dear," she said nervously as she looked behind her. Two state highway department vehicles were drawing up a few yards away, lights flashing. Cowboys who had stopped loading to watch the boss get kissed half to death were now watching, with interest, the arrival of a herd of policemen.

Two uniformed officers got out of separate Texas Department of Public Safety highway patrol cars and walked around the sports car toward the man and woman sitting so close together on the horse.

"I'm very sorry," Maggie began hopefully.

"Lady, you were going eighty in a fifty-five!" the older of the two men replied, ticket book in hand.

"*And* you passed both of us on the four-lane like we were backing up!" the younger one added belligerently.

"She's pregnant," Cord told them blatantly, chuckling as Maggie squirmed sheepishly and made the horse jump. He calmed it with a gentle hand on its neck. "We've been married four months, but a doctor told her years ago that he didn't think it would be possible in the first place. So we're having sort of a miracle. And a baby," he added, grinning from ear to ear.

The older man looked at the younger man.

"The law is the law," the older one said doggedly.

"Sure it is, and we can give out warnings to people we don't need to arrest," the younger one said, grinning. "I'd put a newly pregnant woman at the top of the list. So tell her not to do it again and then we can congratulate them and go back to work."

The older officer studied the people on horseback. He scowled. "You look familiar," he told Cord.

"I should," Cord replied with a grimace, having belatedly recognized the other man. "You were just leaving to join the highway department force when I was a rookie on the Houston police force here, years ago." He noted the stripes on the man's sleeves. "You've come up in the world."

The man looked back at him and his stoic expression softened. "So have you, apparently, but that's not where I remember you from, I'm sure of it," he replied, with a long look at Maggie. He pointed a finger at her. "You stop speeding in my county," he admonished. "Babies don't do well at supersonic speeds. Got that?"

"Oh, yes, sir," she promised and grinned. "I'll teach him to obey all the traffic laws."

"Her," Cord corrected. "We're having a girl."

She opened her eyes wide. "God doesn't take orders."

"We can ask nicely," he retorted. "I like little girls. We can teach her to breed bulls."

"We can teach her to catch crooks, too," she pointed out.

"That's where I've seen you!" the older policeman suddenly blurted out, slapping his forehead. "You're the two who broke up the international child slavery ring! Both your pictures were in the paper, along with the front-page story. You actually shot it out with the head guy in Amsterdam! And the Lassiter Detective Agency turned in two local businessmen who were up to their necks in the conspiracy. I used to work with Dane Lassiter before he became a Texas Ranger, years ago."

The younger officer was staring from Maggie to Cord

while the older one was speaking and he grinned. "Son of a gun. It is them!"

Maggie felt like the heroine of a cliff-hanger movie serial. She chuckled, tightening her arms around Cord's neck. "I'll say something nice about you when I write my memoirs, if you won't arrest me," she promised.

"Lady, you should write books, not memoirs, after what I read in the newspapers," the older officer said. "With a story like that to tell, what a bestseller it could be!"

She thought about that and lights flashed in her head. "You know," she began slowly, and with growing enthusiasm, "that's not a bad idea!"

Six months later, Maggie turned in a novel about international espionage to an editor in New York who'd read the earlier draft and contracted to publish it. Simultaneously, Maggie produced a baby boy. It came as a surprise, because neither parent had wanted to know the sex of their child until it was born. They'd chosen names for either sex, but Cord was certain they'd be using Charlene Maria.

When they were home with the baby, sitting on the front porch late in the afternoon, Cord looked down at the child in her arms and sighed lovingly. "Jared Mejias Romero," he murmured proudly. "I am very happy to be your father. But we still need a little sister for Daddy to spoil."

"Daddy can spoil Jared until that happens," Maggie told him with a grin, knowing he was perfectly pleased that they had a healthy baby. "Maybe they're right and lightning can strike twice. But even if it can't, I'm very happy with what we got."

"So am I." He kissed her and then his son as they sat in the swing on the warm, enclosed sunporch and watched the big bull eat hay from the back of a pickup truck in the pasture beside the driveway. It was February now, still very cold, and sunset was just brushing the clouds. The horizon was ablaze with color. "My wife, the writer," he murmured. He glanced at her whimsically. "Still, it beats having you run around in a trench coat packing a gun."

She shot him a wicked grin. "Think so? I do have to have fresh material if I get offered another book contract."

He lifted an eyebrow. "I'm not signing on to bust up any more illegal labor rackets, or defuse any bombs, or help Bojo with any more missions, in case you ever wondered," he informed her. "I raise cattle now. Period."

"Cattle are exciting. Just look at old Hijito there," she mused, studying him. She pursed her lips as a new plot announced itself in her head. "Hmm. Suppose somebody stole him and it came out that he had a microchip hidden in his ear tag that could prove someone guilty of the attempted assassination of...hey, where are you going? Cord! Come back here!"

He kept going, laughing all the way down the hall. Maggie turned her eyes to the sleeping face of her baby in his warm little footy pajamas and thought about all the long, hard, painful years that had led her to this place, this time, this happiness.

By facing her pain and her past, she'd stepped into a new world of joy. If only she'd known long ago that the only way to cope with the darkness was to turn and face into it, instead of running away from it. If only...!

But she had Cord and a baby, and life was sweeter than she'd dreamed it could be. Regrets were like the clouds on the horizon, soon blown away by the lazy summer winds and lost in the splendor of the sunset; just as the endurance of pain was rewarded by unexpected pleasure once the ordeal ended. It was one of the shimmery curiosities of life that God kissed the emotional cuts, just as mothers and fathers kissed the real ones. A physicist would quote Newton's Third Law—every action produced an equal reaction. But Maggie liked her poetic version better.

She kissed the tiny forehead softly, so as not to wake the baby, and her heart lifted like a rocket with joy. Down the hall, she heard familiar footsteps coming back to her, beating a firm, steady tattoo that echoed in her heart.

"I thought it was clouding up to snow," Cord remarked as he reached down to take his son in his arms and relieve her tired arms. "But look at that sunset!"

She smiled up at him. "The clouds are all gone, my darling, they've drifted away on the wind," she said softly. "Remember the old saying, 'red skies at night, sailor's delight'? Just look at that sky!"

He drew her up with him. "I'm no sailor, and you're getting fanciful," he teased. "Come and let's have supper. I'm starving!"

She reached up and kissed him. "You're always starving." She grinned wickedly and wiggled her eyebrows. "Lucky me!"

"No," he whispered lovingly, and kissed her back. "Lucky me!"

She clung to his arm as they walked down the hall with their son, watching his father look at him with the most beautiful, loving expression she'd ever seen in those dark eyes, for anyone other than herself.

"You know," she said, thinking aloud, "I think babies are more exciting than international intrigue."

He chuckled. "We're in a perfect position to find out."

"Yes, we are." She sighed contentedly. "We are, indeed." She looked up at him. "For a desperado," she murmured, "you make a pretty good family man."

"Thank you. I'll recommend you for promotion when we're recruited by the French Foreign Legion."

"All right! Do they take women now, and can the baby come, too?" she asked excitedly. "How do we join?"

He aimed a swat at her backside that she dodged skillfully and with a laugh, reminding her that some desperadoes never really lose the habit. And she wouldn't have had him any other way.

★ ★ ★ ★ ★

Danger abounds in a passionate tale from
New York Times and *USA TODAY* bestselling author

DIANA PALMER

As a teenager, Gracie worshipped Jason, a strong, silent young cowboy who left home to seek his fortune. When danger comes her way, she can only hope that her long, tall Texan will come blazing home to save her, despite her secrets—and take control of Comanche Wells Ranch and claim her heart, once and for all.

HEARTLESS

Coming soon for the first time in mass-market paperback!

HQN™

We *are* romance™

www.HQNBooks.com

PHDP450TRR

FROM BESTSELLING AUTHORS

DIANA PALMER

KASEY MICHAELS
CATHERINE MANN

More Than Words:
STORIES OF HOPE

Everyday women from all walks of life are making their communities, and this world, a better place through their caring hearts and unshakable commitment. Three such women have been selected as recipients of Harlequin's More Than Words™ award for their exceptional work. And three bestselling authors have kindly offered their creativity to write original short stories inspired by these real-life heroines.

Visit

www.HarlequinMoreThanWords.com

to find out more or to nominate a real-life heroine in your life.

Proceeds from the sale of this book will be reinvested in Harlequin's charitable initiatives.

Coming soon wherever books are sold!

PHMTWSH670RTR

Mystery unfolds in the heartlands of Texas
in a stunning new novel from
New York Times and *USA TODAY* bestselling author

DIANA PALMER

Darkly handsome and headstrong FBI Agent Kilraven is a man with a haunted past—one he knows shy, innocent Winnie Sinclair couldn't handle, despite the temptation. But Winnie's had her own share of sorrow. And when a discovery about her family makes them join forces in a dangerous investigation that puts her life on the line, will her ruthless Texan confront his past and risk it all for their love?

DANGEROUS

Don't miss this brand-new Jacobsville tale, coming soon wherever books are sold!

HQN™

We *are* romance™

www.HQNBooks.com

PHDP459RTR